Praise for Dear Hero (The Dear Series, #1)

"Put on the AC/DC soundtrack and grab your superhero cape! Hope Bolinger and Alyssa Roat deliver a hilarious, punchy, one-of-a-kind smash—the perfect read for Marvel and DC Comic fans.

DEAR HERO dazzles with its brilliant wit, irony, and loveable characters. Few other books have tugged at my heartstrings and made me laugh out loud, ranking DEAR HERO as one of my favorite reads of 2020."

— Caroline George, author of *Dearest Josephine* (TNZ Fiction, HarperCollins)

"A witty and compelling story, packaged in a delightfully unique form."

— Kerry Nietz, award-winning author of *Amish Vampires in Space*

I0637104

"DEAR HERO begins with a hilarious concept—a dating-style website but with the goal of pairing up heroes with their perfect nemeses—and delivers in a big way! With a cleverly constructed narrative via text messages, Bolinger and Roat carry out a funny, fast-paced plot with authentically flawed and likeable characters. V and Cortex may struggle with what it means to be a hero, but their reader fans are sure to champion their story with superhero-level enthusiasm!"

— KRISTIANA SFIRLEA, AUTHOR OF *THE STORMATCH DIARIES: LEGEND OF THE STORM SNEEZER*

"*Dear Hero* is a unique take on the superhero genre. Instead of explosions and fist fights, get to the behind-the-scenes of a hero and villain trying to match in an online service. Through their messages and texts, read about the up-and-coming Cortex and villainous Vortex. Will these two find a true nemesis in each other, or will their pairing be doomed? Enjoy a funny and romantic romp that turns superhero tropes on their heads."

— JASON C. JOYNER, AUTHOR OF *LAUNCH*

"DEAR HERO is a witty, page-turning send-up of super-heroes and social media and rom-coms. That last sentence was a fancy way of saying it's funny. And charming. And action-packed. If Rainbow Rowell wrote an Avengers screenplay, it might look an awful lot like this book."

— PATRICK HUELLER, AUTHOR OF *KIRSTEN HOWARD'S BIGGEST FAN*

"That was a delightful read. I laughed aloud so many times! Punchy, witty, fast paced, and unputdownable—*Dear Hero* is one of the best books I've read this year. Nicely done."

"A clever, fantastic peek at what goes on behind the scenes between hero and villain, *Dear Hero* tells a great story while putting a unique spin on a number of tropes that ultimately keeps readers telling themselves, "okay, just one more text.""

"Playfully epic, adorably dark—a fun and witty ride."

"From the moment I opened DEAR HERO I just knew I was in for a thrill-ride. It's laugh-out-loud funny, but criminally genius one-liners aside, this book had all the ingredients of a true hero story, with colourful characters that packed a punch - literally - and enough heart, soul, and delicious moral conflict to give me all the feels I crave. Seriously, a total must for any superhero-obsessed-fan who ever looked at their favourite and thought ... what is going on inside their head?"

THE DEAR SERIES

Dear Hero (#1)
Dear Henchman (#2)
Dear Hades (a Spinoff)

DEAR HADES

DEAR HADES

THE DEAR SERIES (A SPINOFF)

HOPE BOLINGER

ALYSSA ROAT

Torchflame Books

ISBN: 978-1-61153-589-1 (paperback)

ISBN: 978-1-61153-590-7 (ebook)

Library of Congress Control Number: 2024910024

Dear Hades is published by: Torchflame Books, an imprint of Top Reads Publishing, LLC, USA

Previously published in 2023, by Love2ReadLove2Write Publishing, LLC, Indianapolis, Indiana

For information about special discounts for bulk purchases, please direct emails to: publisher@torchflamebooks.com

Cover Illustration: Bailey Steffen

Cover Layout: Jori Hanna

Book Interior Layout: Jori Hanna

Printed in the United States of America

Hope's Dedication:

To Carlee who said, and I quote, "I would've been a bombshell in Ancient Greece." Considering you are a runway model with me in modern America, I say that you are beautiful throughout the ages.

Alyssa's Dedication:

To my sweet baby chaos gremlin cats, Greek monsters in their own right, who take turns sitting on my head while I write. And to Juli, who does not sit on my head, but encourages me in more normal but equally as appreciated ways.

Content Warning

This book contains mentions of sexual assault and mentions/brief depictions of murder. Both of these were frequent themes in Greek mythology, as many innocent characters fell under the unjust wrath of merciless and petty gods.

As some of these themes hit home for us, we hope to handle them with as much sensitivity as possible.

But with that said, if you need to shut the book now and not read on, we totally understand.

Another (Not Content) Warning

There are quite a few characters in Greek Mythology, so if you ever are overwhelmed by the size of the cast in this book, we have a Glossary available in the back. It does contain minor spoilers, depending on which character you're reading about. So we don't recommend reading the Glossary straight through until you're done with the book. But if a character name is mentioned, their entry in the Glossary should be spoiler-free.

Private Message

Persephone changed group name to "Wanna Commit Murder with Me, Babe?"

7:30 PM
Persephone: You ever wanna murder a deity?

    7:34 PM
    Hades: ... Let me guess, your mom?

Persephone: Wow, babe. You're great at this game. Just get off work?

    Hades: Had to deal with some paperwork. More shades are getting loose from the Underworld. But we can get back to the undead coming back to life later.

    7:35 PM
    Hades: What's up?

Persephone: Sorry, had to go to a coffee shop on our street to get out of the house and avoid Mom.

Persephone: "What's UP?" Well, I'll tell you what's bringing me DOWN. Demeter has been telling more peeps on Olympus about how you "kidnapped me."

7:36 PM
Hades: Which I didn't.

Persephone: Obviously. But it's still her favorite story to tell at Harvest Festivals and all that. Speaking of, have you heard of American Thanksgivings? Is Thanksgiving mac and cheese any good? I hear people get up in arms about the stuff for that holiday. I mean, I personally like the Kraft spiral kind. But you could convince me the character mac shaped like SpongeBob could be a worthy appointment for Thanksgiving tables alike.

Hades: Sweetheart, focus.

7:37 PM
Persephone: Right. So.

Persephone: It's gotten bad. Not the mac and cheese, I mean. That could never be bad.

Persephone: But Demeter.

Persephone: She's almost convinced Zeus to shorten the amount of time I can spend in the Underworld. Zeus has some magical substance that can undo the effects of the pomegranate seeds that got me a three-month ticket down there in the first place.

7:38 PM
Hades: You don't mean.

Persephone: *shudder* Yes, kale.

Hades: I'm gonna kill him.

7:39 PM
Persephone: Mind murdering my mom first? Not that I'd be opposed to offing Zeus, but ...

Hades: How long would the kale allow you to stay with me every year? I only get you from late December through early March. And that was after your mother forced me to let you out of the Underworld nine months a year.

Persephone: ...

Hades: Babe, how long would the kale let you stay with me?

7:40 PM
Persephone: One week.

Hades: You're kidding.

7:41 PM
Persephone: Ninety percent of the time, yes. Now? No.

Hades: Cool, I'll go get a sword.

Persephone: Obviously we can't actually KILL a god, but I blame myself for this.

Hades: Why?

7:42 PM
Persephone: Well, the whole "Kale Debacle" wouldn't be a thing had I not pushed my mother to take up a bet with me.

4

Hades: What bet?

Persephone: Of course, I really should've remembered her days of playing Blackjack in Vegas. She's a killer.

Hades: Seph, what bet?

Persephone: Those kids in the Stanton Elementary School in Las Vegas didn't stand a chance when she bet them cheesy fish crackers at snack time.

7:43 PM
Hades: Seph.

Persephone: Right, well.

Persephone: I bet her that if I could prove to her our love story wasn't a fluke—or created from a kidnapping—she would let me stay with you in the Underworld year-round.

7:44 PM
Hades: Sounds easy. So why's there a growing pit in my stomach?

Persephone: She took me up on it, and gave me A YEAR to do it ... but she doesn't want us to prove OUR love story isn't fake.

Persephone: Something tells me she knows it wasn't a kidnapping, but her perpetuating that story is the only way to convince the gods to keep me away from you nine months out of the year.

7:45 PM
Hades: I'm confused.

Hades: If she doesn't want to prove our story is legitimate, what does she want?

Persephone: Demeter wants us to prove it's REPLICABLE.

Hades: That it's what?

7:50 PM
Persephone: Darling, don't be daft. And sorry, had to order something. Line was out the door. These scones are dry.

Persephone: My mom's of the opinion that our love story is unnatural. That we should leave the matchmaking to people like Eros and Aphrodite.

7:55 PM
Hades: Sorry, more paperwork. I swear a quarter of the Underworld has emptied. I don't know what's happening.

Hades: And ugh, yes, if I see Aphrodite's name one more time after she created that gods-awful app StupidCupid.

Persephone: Dude, don't remind me. That app is for flings, not meaningful relationships.

7:56 PM
Persephone: According to my mother, you and I are unnatural because we forged our relationship on our own and didn't let the Goddess of Swipe-Right Apps determine our fates.

7:57 PM
Persephone: Oh, ordering a lavender latte was a mistake. Who thought lavender goes well with coffee?

Persephone: So unless we can prove it's replicable ...

7:58 PM
Hades: How would we even do that? Most Greek heroes and gods are scattered throughout the world. How would we monitor that?

Persephone: Wait a second.

Persephone: You said a quarter of the shades have escaped the Underworld?

7:59 PM
Hades: Yes, darling. Hence the paperwork. It looks like they're all popping up as eighteen-year-olds in the twenty-first century.

Persephone: Weird that they're all eighteen. Like a YA novel or something. Guess that's just how it works when you come back from the dead. Any leads on what's causing it?

Hades: Well, that's an interesting point you make.

Persephone: About YA novels?

8:00 PM
Hades: About aging. At first, I thought furies or Titans or other malevolent powers might be trying to cause a little chaos. But gorgon blood tends to have anti-aging and healing powers—including bringing people back to life. Of course, to my knowledge, only one gorgon has been brought back to life.

8:01 PM
Persephone: So maybe some god stored a jar somewhere of one of her sisters' blood? Ew, gross. Don't want to think about that.

Hades: But why? I can't figure it out. Humans, monsters, demigods ... what's the pattern?

8:02 PM
Persephone: Ack, why do I keep drinking this latte? It's so gross. You put a drink in front of me and I swear it's just force of habit.

Hades: Are we ... still talking about gorgon blood?

Persephone: Oh yeah, that reminds me, I ran into a hero the other day who was missing his lover who hadn't returned. Seemed like he would kill to get her back.

8:03 PM
Hades: Kill?

Persephone: I'm just glad I taught all those English classes to the shades in the Underworld so they can adjust to their modern lives. I knew it was important they be well-rounded members of the undead—since it's the lingua franca until Tolkien elvish finally reigns supreme—but I didn't anticipate this.

Hades: Killing ...

8:04 PM
Persephone: Yes, darling? Are you in the mood for some stabbing?

Hades: No, but I think someone might be. Monsters, mortals, and demigods, groups who hate each other, all brought back to life? All upset over who has and hasn't been brought back?

8:05 PM
Persephone: Oh! I'm buzzing in with an answer. Let me guess: Someone wants a big juicy war?

Hades: Bingo, as the mortals say.

Persephone: Wrong game, dear.

8:06 PM
Persephone: Well it's a good thing you're keeping an eye on the situation, babe. I know you won't let any shades get too out of hand.

Hades: Er, yes. I'm keeping the shades in line, at least ... even if there are fewer and fewer of them ...

Persephone: All this chaos makes Mom's demand even harder. She wants us to prove we can bring together two people in those camps who would be rather opposed to each other by Aphrodite's definition of the word "love." Humans and demigods. Monsters and mortals.

8:07 PM
Persephone: To prove our union isn't unnatural.

Hades: All right, so how do we do that?

Persephone: That's where I'm stumped.

8:08 PM
Hades: Wait a moment, I had a bizarre exchange with a mortal today.

Persephone: Did they put lavender in your coffee?

Hades: No, but he gave me an idea.

Hades sent a screenshot

8:09 PM
Hades: In this chat with a mortal named Liam, he talked about an app that matches villains and heroes. You know those people who fly around in capes all the time? It was called MetaMatch, or something.

8:10 PM
Persephone: Yes, I know who they are. It's hard to ignore people flying around in spandex outside your apartment window.

Hades: Liam talked about how a hero and a villain—two foes—got together. They matched and fell in love. Maybe we can replicate that. Match two beings who would typically be enemies.

8:11 PM
Persephone: You mean in an app?

Persephone: Like StupidCupid.

Hades: Don't defile this chat with the name of Aphrodite's dating app.

8:12 PM
Persephone: Whoops, sorry. Forgot our rule never to mention the stupid name of StupidCupid. I think one of us mentioned it earlier and should've been dutifully chastised. Anyway, that's what you're getting at, right? Creating an app?

Hades: Yes. But ours would be for lasting relationships.

Persephone: Give me a second to think it over and tip this coffee into this plant on my table.

8:13 PM
Persephone: Update, the plant is plastic.

8:55 PM
Persephone: Okay, it's doable, but I created a list of steps needed to make this app a reality.

Persephone sent a screenshot

———

How to Make Hades's Dating App a "Thang"

App Developer—Sad to say it, babe, but we're probably going to need to go into the belly of the beast itself. You heard me right. Aphrodite's husband, Hephaestus.

—He has recently spent time developing apps. As you know, many gods have translated their original roles into more modern ones.

—But he's pretty peeved about her app StupidCupid because she's known to use it from time to time.

—He'd probably be on board just to stick it to her. Gotta love gods.

Messenger Developer—To offload some of Hephaestus's work, let's have Iris and Hermes collaborate on messaging capabilities for the app. Since—as messenger gods—they like envelopes and Amazon packages and stuff. They're also great at advertising, so they can get the word out for the next few months. Hopefully, we should see huge participation during launch week.

Name—Something all one word, like StupidCupid, but with our own spin. Like DearHades ... remember? How I used to start your letters that way because I got so excited and forgot to add a space? ... OOOOOH I LOVE THAT. THAT'S IT. THAT'S THE NAME WE USE.

Way to Moderate Content—Why don't we use the shades who haven't, you know, resurrected, to serve as admins and moderators, in case we need to boot out any unsavory characters? Dating apps can draw in some weirdos.

Timeframe—I messaged Hephaestus, and he got back to me. They would probably have it finished around Christmas. Just in time for me to go down to the Underworld to see you. (And enough time for people to start adjusting to twenty-first century life).

————

9:00 PM
Persephone: That's it. Those are all the notes I've got.

Persephone: But we also only have twelve months to get two people together, and I'm assuming get them hitched. Demeter has a pretty strict idea of what a successful relationship looks like, and that means, at the very least, an engagement.

Persephone: So by the time the app is up, there's only nine months for one couple to pull that off.

Persephone: Let's hope tons of people sign up, eh?

9:01 PM
Hades: Sounds like a plan. We'll probably think of more items for that list later, but for now, it's a good jumping-off point.

9:03 PM
Persephone: Good. And once I get a Pinterest mood board and Spotify playlist going for this ... Aphrodite, Eros, Mom, be prepared to eat your hearts out.

Wanna Commit Murder with Me, Babe?

December 21

12:01 AM
Hades: Happy First Day of Winter, Sweetheart.

Persephone: Hey, at the gates to the Underworld. Definitely did NOT just give Cerberus a belly rub or anything.

Persephone: But before I enter for what I *hope* will not be my last three months with you, check your message notifications.

12:02 AM
Hades: The app went live this morning?

Persephone: You betcha.

Persephone: Now which of these beings is gonna become an engaged couple and save us?

Hades: Because they have less than nine months to do it.

12:03 AM
Persephone: Yeah, because of that.

DearHades's Mission

Finding love after coming back from the dead can be hard. We know you've probably spent the past few months adjusting to your new life in the mortal realm. Gone are the days of eating stingrays and ambrosia—now we have taco bars and plant-based meat.

But one thing stays constant, whether in 300 BCE or 2000 something-or-other CE. (Can't be too specific here or we'll date the app. Get it? DATE THE APP. Okay, okay, Hades. Yeesh. I'll delete this. It won't make it into the final copy ... or will it?)

Anyway, the one constant: the search for love, for finding our other whole. Not half. Because, after all, you already are whole. But when you bring two wholes together ... woo Gaia, sparks fly.

Our mission is to help you find that special someone.

After all, those who we married in our past lives may not have crossed the threshold back into the land of the living. And many of you have told us you're starting anew in your search for love.

If you're looking for your forever with a monster, mortal, or whoever, Hades and I have got your back.

Our Story

You know it ... or some version of it.

Goddess meets the god of the Underworld.

Goddess eats some pomegranates on a date night. Because, come on, pomegranates are delicious and totally worth spending the rest of your life in the world of the undead.

Goddess's mother flips out. As Goddess's mother tends to do, because she doesn't understand the meaning of "chill."

I HOPE YOU DOWNLOADED THE APP AND ARE READING THIS, MOM.

Goddess's mother insists Goddess only stays in Pomegranate Land for three months.

Ohioans curse Goddess because of winter, and the fact their government never salts the roads and creates potholes large enough to swallow a minotaur.

And boom, there you have it. I'd love to stay longer with Hades, WITHOUT MOM THROWING A BLIZZARD TANTRUM, but this app serves as a proof of concept to her. It fails, I only get to hang with Hades for legit a week. My Ohioan audience informed me they won't be downloading the app in this case.

It succeeds ... well, I can head down to Hades whenever the heck I want. And Mom will only throw winter for three months—because, you know, "tradition" or whatever. But she does vow to keep Ohio winters for six months, like usual. Because, everyone hates Ohio.

So no pressure.

But we really want this app to succeed.

So convince all your not-dead friends to download it?

How to Use DearHades

Right, so, thanks to a certain god who may or may not be known for technological innovations, we tried to make this app as user-friendly as possible. So let's break it down for you.

DMs

Like any mortal dating app, you swipe right, you start talking. If you feel like murdering them, it's probably time to **unswipe**— unless you're really into that.

But if you don't feel a bloodlust for them, and conversation's going well, go ahead and set up that first date. ;)

Groups

We know we have a lot of different beings on here. Monsters, mortals, demigods, etc. So we have support groups for each of you. You can find them in our **forums.**

Profiles

This is where you get to show off your personality—but please don't show off too much in your pictures, gentlemen. That will earn you a ban for life.

As any good editor will tell you, show, don't tell. So I'll give you a peek of the ADORABLE sample profile I created for my boo.

Name: Hades (Greek, preferred), Pluto (Roman)

Interested In: Deities

Bio: I am the lord of the dead. And I have a cute puppy with three heads who loves belly rubs. And I have the cutest tushie in the world. Yes, my wife wrote my bio, how can you tell?

See? Pretty simple. If you're into more than one type of being, you can add that to the **Interested In** section. We have an easy interface for you to select who you're interested in.

Is There an Issue?

We want you to be safe. Although there seem to be fewer wars fought over women who launch ships with their faces, we aim to prioritize your well-being.

If you run into a user who seems to give you all the bad vibes, unswipe or **block** them.

And make sure to **report** them. We have a number of people from the Fields of Asphodel working as admins—and since they literally have nothing better to do, they can review your complaints and work on banning unsavory characters ASAP.

Have Fun!

My future with Hades depends on it, so yeah. Make me proud.

—Love, Seph (and Hades, who didn't proofread this and probably regrets it now)

You Matched!

Name: Tiresias (Greek), Ty (American, because baristas have a hard time spelling the other one). No preference which you use.

Interested In: All Beings

Bio: I'm a prophet, so I can foresee many future conversations about art and dogs. Joined the app on the first day it was out, but apparently, it's important to include I'm also blind. Some people DMing me said so. So I'm blind. There. Anyway, let's talk about my dog. :D

———

Name: Medousa (Greek), Medusa (Roman, preferred because everyone always refers to me that way)

Interested In: Mortals and Monsters

Bio: Yes, I have snake hair. No, the tusks and wings, though cool, are just rumors. Looking for online pals because I will turn you to stone in person, unfortunately.

PRIVATE MESSAGE

DECEMBER 29

11:02 AM
Tiresias: Oh my goodness, I'm so sorry. I accidentally swiped right.

> **Medusa:** Oh, that's okay. My friend Echo was on my profile trying to set me up ... and swiped on EVERYONE she came across.

Tiresias: Nice! I can't really say I have all that many friends. The transition, I think, has been hard on us. Been giving local theater a go.

11:03 AM
Tiresias: It is interesting, though. I did see in one of the forums that someone named Hector went on a date with you? Did that not go all that well?

> **Medusa:** Ah ... Hector. Echo is REALLY gunning for me to make some in-person connections. So I went. And unfortunately, he drew a knife, I freaked out, my veil fell off, and ... that was that. I didn't mean to turn him to stone. :(

11:04 AM
Tiresias: Happens to the best of us, I suppose.

Tiresias: So what have you been up to in the few months back from the Underworld? Weren't Persephone's English lessons wild? At least, from what I can remember of them. My memories from the Underworld are pretty fuzzy.

> **Medusa:** I don't know why she had so many lessons about dogs and what cute names we can call them. But I am well prepared to meet canines now.

11:05 AM
Tiresias: Well, I know you're not all for meeting canines in person, but I can try to snap a picture of Artemis, my golden retriever. Can't really guarantee if the picture is going to be blurry or not.

Tiresias sent a photo

11:06 AM
Medusa: Oh my gods, she is SO CUTE.

Unknown Source: *woof*

11:07 AM
Tiresias: Ah, that's the speech-to-text function on this app. It's crazy the amount of technology they have for blind people now. We could've really used this thousands of years ago.

Medusa: It's incredible. I've been working with a lot of animals at an animal shelter, since, you know, I can't turn them to stone. I'm learning how to train seeing eye dogs. I kind of love the twenty-first century.

11:08 AM
Tiresias: That's really incredible.

Tiresias: You know, I think this whole rebirth into the twenty-first century is a great chance for us to be seen as more than monsters or prophets or whatever, you know?

Tiresias: Anyway, I'm so sorry for wasting your time. You do seem really nice. I'm just wary on this app. I think when we've all lost someone, it can take time to recover.

11:09 AM
Medusa: I understand being wary. In my last life, I had an ... interesting encounter with a very demanding god who may or may not be named Poseidon, followed by my, uh, demise at the hands of that hero Perseus. Oh yeah, and the cursing by Athena in between. It was a short life and a wild one, I guess. Trust issues abound.

11:10 AM
Tiresias: Yooooo, you were cursed by Athena too? Can I tell you my story? It was wild.

Tiresias: Also, I'm sorry to hear about Poseidon. He's one of the worst, next to Zeus.

Medusa: Ooooh, you have an Athena story? Spill. The. Tea. (I have a lot of monster friends who like to spill tea about her together, haha. Please don't strike me down if you're watching, gods.)

Medusa: And yes, Poseidon is ... well, I think we're supposed to keep our language PG on here.

11:11 AM
Tiresias: Ooooh, monster tea. I wonder what flavor that tea would be.

Tiresias: Okay, so picture this. I'm walking around. Doing my thing. Just going for a hike in the Greek mountainside.

Tiresias: And then there was this random bathtub on the Greek mountainside.

Tiresias: And I thought, that's weird. Bathtubs don't belong in the Greek countryside.

11:12 AM
Tiresias: So it turns out Athena was bathing in that tub, and long story short, I cannot see now.

Medusa: Wow. She REALLY loves cursing people for things they had no control over, doesn't she?

Tiresias: Oh, well if you think she's bad, Hera's even worse.

Tiresias: Got more tea for ya, sis. Prophet tea probably doesn't taste as good.

11:13 AM
Tiresias: So I was ONCE AGAIN walking in the Greek countryside. This time using a staff to guide me.

Medusa: I get the impression you like hiking.

Tiresias: And apparently, these two snakes were, um, getting it on.

11:14 AM
Tiresias: And my staff accidentally hit the snakes.

Tiresias: And Hera was all like, "Wow, you hate love. Now you're going to be a woman for several years."

Tiresias: Ancient Greece was wild, yo.

Tiresias: Anyway, I must be talking your ear off.

11:15 AM
Medusa: WOW. My snake hair even thinks that's ridiculous. They think you're very fun to talk to, by the way.

Tiresias: You know, no one tends to laugh about what I have to say. Mostly because I'm predicting their deaths. So I'll take it!

Tiresias: What are their names? The snakes, I mean. Please tell me you didn't name any of them Hera.

11:16 AM
Medusa: I'm so glad you asked! When I was a mortal instead of a monster, apparently I had REALLY nice hair, but I can't imagine living without my snakeys now. There are a lot of them, but the most outgoing are ... well, I renamed them upon entering the twenty-first century, upon their request.

Medusa: They can be very demanding. They wanted to be "hip with the kids."

11:17 AM
Medusa: So there's George, Lily, Bobart, Gertrude, Jack Black, and Winston. They chose the names themselves.

Tiresias: Wow, very chic.

Medusa: I would send a picture of them, but I learned even pictures of me can turn people to stone. My profile pic is an artistic tapestry rendering from my friend Arachne. She likes doing woven portraits.

11:18 AM
Tiresias: Well, I don't know about that. If I can't really
see the picture, would it count?

Medusa: Oh my gods, I forgot about that, so sorry. I guess a picture
wouldn't help you meet them anyway.

Tiresias: Oh, really, it's fine. Honestly, some people are
really wary about what language they use around me. Sometimes I'll say I "see" something, and I don't mean see in the
same way. I'm honored you would want me to take a look at
your "snakeys."

11:19 AM
Medusa: Of course! It's been fun chatting ... oh, I'm being called
away by my monster friends. Catch you later?

Tiresias: Now that you mention it, I was just added to
some hero chat.

Tiresias: Probably a mistake. I'll go clear it up.

Heroes before Monster-os

December 29

Group Information

Group Name: Heroes before Monster-os

Description: No monsters allowed, obviously. A group of notorious Greek heroes who have a bone to pick with this app for allowing any being to just waltz in. We've had many applications for this group, so be forewarned we're only allowing a limited number of people in. But we are open to trials to prove yourself worthy of joining.

————

Odysseus added Tiresias to the group

11:22 AM

Tiresias: What? Guys, I think you added me to the wrong place.

Tiresias: Also, what's with the group name?

11:23 AM
Odysseus: That's what happens when you leave Perseus in charge of the group name.

Perseus: MONSTER-OS.

Odysseus: And Perseus should be reminded that we are not a political aunt on social media. We do not need to post comments in the chat using all capital letters.

11:24 AM
Perseus: Sorry.

11:25 AM
Tiresias: So again, incredibly confused why I've been added to this group. During my lifetime, I had a tendency to prophesy how heroes would die. Since heroes tended not to make the wisest of decisions—no offense. I was never the "swinging a sword on the battlefield of Thermopylae" type of guy.

11:26 AM
Tiresias: Especially since your group description seems to imply it's exclusive.

Odysseus: Oh, it is. But how rude of us not to introduce ourselves. Not that we need much of an introduction. But it has been a few thousand years, so maybe a refresher?

Tiresias: Sure.

11:27 AM
Odysseus: Name's Odysseus. War hero. Took quite a while to get back to my beloved wife Penelope.

Tiresias: Yes, I'm sure you were devastated when you made some pit stops with Calypso and Circe.

Odysseus: What?

Tiresias: You're just not exactly known for your faithfulness to your wife.

11:28 AM
Odysseus: Listen, Circe and Calypso came on to me. What's a man to do when a sorceress turns his fellow sailors into pigs?

Tiresias: Maybe NOT cheat on his wife with her? Invest in a pig herding business instead?

Odysseus: Oh, look who's a wise guy.

11:29 AM
Tiresias: Speaking of wisdom, you're known for your cunning and trickery, so why have I been added to this group?

Odysseus: Wow, perceptive. Let me finish introductions, and then we'll get to that. Sound good?

Tiresias: Fine.

Odysseus: Anyway, as I was saying before I was so rudely interrupted, I returned to Penelope and laid waste to any man who tried to flirt with her.

11:30 AM
Odysseus: There are three others in this group, aside from myself. You've already met Perseus.

Perseus: HI.

> **Odysseus:** Who will be removing his caps lock button shortly.

Perseus: Sorry.

> 11:31 AM
> **Odysseus:** You may know him as the person who slayed Medusa the first time around.

Perseus: Heeheeheehee.

> 11:34 AM
> **Odysseus:** You've gone oddly quiet, Tiresias. Does something about the name Medusa strike a nerve?

Tiresias: You said you didn't want to be interrupted.

> **Odysseus:** Good boy. Then we have Achilles. Say hi, Achilles.

> 11:37 AM
> **Odysseus:** Achilles, I can see you're live in the chat. Say hello to our guest.

> **Odysseus:** He tends to mope, Tiresias, so you may only spot him in here sporadically.

11:40 AM
Achilles: I do NOT mope.

Achilles: I mourn.

11:41 AM
Odysseus: Yes, and he does so by putting on eyeliner, wearing dark clothing, and consuming a dangerous amount of Ben and Jerry's. Yes, Achilles, I live across the hall from you. I've seen you on the way to our apartment's laundry room.

Achilles: Mourning.

11:42 AM
Odysseus: Okay, whatever you want to call it. He has a tendency to be a drama king. But you can't exactly blame him. We're all mourning in our own ways.

Tiresias: What do you mean?

Odysseus: The transition into the modern world has been a headache in itself. But it's far more difficult without that special someone from the House of Hades.

11:43 AM
Odysseus: I'm getting ahead of myself. I haven't even let you in on why we added you to this group in the first place.

Tiresias: Wait, you said there were four people total in this group. Am I the fourth?

Odysseus: Oh no, you're only *temporarily* here so you can do us a favor.

Odysseus: The fourth person is Hercules.

11:44 AM
Tiresias: So he kept his Roman name, did he? Instead of the Greek Heracles?

Odysseus: Yes, he got obsessed with a certain Disney movie about his origin story and decided to keep the Roman version of his name.

Tiresias: No judgment here. We're all figuring out our way in this new world. Where is he off to?

Odysseus: Doing a job.

11:45 AM
Tiresias: Oh, he's already got one? Was it because of that grant thingy? Who did that ... Hestia?

Odysseus: Grant?

Tiresias: That's the one where she provides job opportunities and homes for displaced mortals, right? Hestia does so many grants, it's hard to keep up.

11:46 AM
Odysseus: Ah yes, the Ancient-to-Modern Transition Grants. Hestia takes her goddess-of-the-hearth job seriously. Of course, considering she placed most of us in apartments in Grove City, Pennsylvania, I think cheap rent was high on her list of priorities.

11:47 AM
Tiresias: So anyway, where is he working? As a personal trainer at a gym? As a veterinarian—since he managed to kidnap Cerberus last time?

Odysseus: Oh, semantics, how hilarious words can be. I meant he's doing a job for us.

Tiresias: For you?

11:48 AM
Odysseus: Hercules hasn't quite earned his place in this chat. We let him stay, but he hasn't been granted full hero status. We've given him a number of tasks—what's the task we just gave him, Achilles?

11:54 AM
Odysseus: Achilles?

11:56 AM
Achilles: He's out getting me more ice cream.

Odysseus: Ah yes, very heroic.

11:57 AM
Tiresias: That's awful. That first of all, you won't let him be a full member of the group chat. He performed plenty of heroic tasks all those years ago ...

Odysseus: But that's the thing about Hercules. He LOVES tasks. Or at least, he doesn't say no when we send him on errands. He's useful.

Odysseus: And I like useful people.

Odysseus: Which brings me to you.

11:58 AM
Odysseus: You see, Tiresias, although we made it out of the Underworld, not everyone we loved did. I'm dearly missing my beloved Penelope.

Achilles: How about your son, Telemachus? Do you miss him too?

Odysseus: Eh. I'm sure he's happy where he is.

Achilles: His son was wimpy.

> **Odysseus:** Oh, fie on you. Go back to eating your Chubby Hubby ice cream.

11:59 AM
Odysseus: Anyway, I'm dearly missing Penelope. Perseus is missing ...

Perseus: Andromeda.

> **Odysseus:** His wife. And Achilles is missing ...

Achilles: Patroclus. :'(

> **Odysseus:** I was going to say the woman you loved, Briseis.

Achilles: Oh, I suppose her too.

12:00 PM
Achilles: Patroclus is a ... very good friend.

Achilles: Just a friend.

12:01 PM
Achilles: Boy, this ice cream is good.

> **Odysseus:** We're all missing someone.

12:02 PM
Tiresias: Sure, I miss my daughter Manto. She had a prophesying gift like me.

Tiresias: I miss her a lot, actually.

Tiresias: I hope she's doing well.

12:03 PM
Odysseus: And the problem is, we've dedicated our time to swiping on as many profiles as we can on here, and we haven't run into them yet. Even checked social media sites, since many displaced mortals have profiles on there.

Odysseus: Nothing.

12:04 PM
Odysseus: Which leads us to believe they're still in the House of Hades.

Odysseus: So we have no guarantee that whatever brought us here is going to bring them back too.

Tiresias: Unfortunately, we have no control over that.

12:05 PM
Odysseus: But here's the thing, Ty, my boy. We DO have control over that. Because I've been thinking about what resurrected us. And after speaking with Perseus about his monster-slaying escapades, I think I've finally drawn my conclusion.

Odysseus: The item that brought us back …

Odysseus: Is gorgon blood.

12:06 PM
Odysseus: It makes sense. Not only has the blood been known to have resurrecting qualities, but anti-aging ones as well.

Odysseus: I don't know about you, but I didn't leave this world looking like I was eighteen.

Odysseus: You've gone quiet again, Tiresias.

12:08 PM
Odysseus: This gorgon talk scaring you?

12:10 PM
Tiresias: I'm working an actual job—not like the ones you're giving poor Hercules. I intern at a local theater. They're planning to give me a full-time position as an associate director by the end of the year.

12:11 PM
Tiresias: You all were lucky enough to catch me on my lunch break. Sorry for not messaging for a few minutes. The director needed to talk with me.

12:12 PM
Odysseus: Well, bully for you.

Odysseus: I'd begun to worry you didn't have the guts to do what we need you to do.

Tiresias: And what is that exactly?

Odysseus: One of the tasks we gave Hercules, since day one the app opened, is to monitor all activity for the only living gorgon, Medusa.

12:13 PM
Odysseus: Mind you, it took forever to walk him through it. The only person denser than Hercules is Perseus.

Perseus: Hey!

Odysseus: Anyway, I'd had my suspicions from the beginning about gorgon blood. Perseus's stories only bolstered them.

12:14 PM
Odysseus: But we believe in order to bring back our loved ones from the dead, we have to un-alive a certain gorgon.

Tiresias: Un-alive?

Odysseus: I imagine if we used a synonym, it would alert the admins. They've been monitoring chats a lot lately.

Odysseus: And this certain gorgon is very picky about who she goes on dates with.

12:15 PM
Odysseus: She seldom matches with someone. So to complete a certain, ah, deed during a date with her—an unaliving deed—we'd need to have an "in" man. Since she seems not to be swiping on heroes anymore.

12:16 PM
Odysseus: She's probably caught on to the fact that we've been sending heroes her way to, um, end her stay in the mortal world.

Odysseus: Do you catch my drift?

Tiresias: I do.

Tiresias: I'm really not the right person for this task.

12:17 PM
Tiresias: In my past life, I was about saving lives. Not ending them.

Odysseus: Ah, the value of life. What an interesting discussion.

Odysseus: See, Tiresias, you never dealt with monsters quite like me and these fellows did in the chat. Right, boys?

Perseus: Monsters. Die. Dead.

12:18 PM
Achilles: Actually, I never went toe-to-toe with one.

Odysseus: Like I said, all of us have dealt with monsters. And let me tell you, they do not value human life.

Odysseus: They swallowed my men whole right off my ship. Crushed them under rocks. Tore them to pieces right before me.

12:19 PM
Odysseus: My philosophy, thousands of years ago, was to strike first, before they strike. And we've adopted a similar mindset today. Me and the boys here have been swiping right on all the monsters we can to, ah, set up some dates with them.

Tiresias: That's barbaric.

12:20 PM
Odysseus: It's strategy.

Odysseus: But we need you to make a certain move on a gorgon when you set up a first date with her.

Tiresias: I told you, you have the wrong guy.

12:21 PM
Odysseus: You don't think she'll strike first? She's taken out two other members in the group chat. Turned them into statues.

Achilles: May Hector and Paris rest in peace.

Achilles: Except for Hector.

Achilles: Man, I hate that guy.

12:22 PM
Achilles: May he rest in conflict.

Odysseus: What's to stop her from trying to un-alive you, Tiresias?

Odysseus: And you see, you have a distinct advantage, my boy. Because she can only turn into stone the men who lay eyes on her.

12:23 PM
Odysseus: Something a blind prophet cannot do.

Tiresias: I don't kill people.

Odysseus: No? Even if it was to bring your daughter, Manto, back?

12:24 PM
Tiresias: Don't.

Odysseus: Surely you miss her. Your own flesh and blood. Do you remember the first time you heard her cry as a newborn?

Tiresias: Odysseus.

12:25 PM
Odysseus: The wife got out of the picture quickly, didn't she? So

Manto was all you had. Too bad you didn't get too much time with her.

   Tiresias: Odysseus.

Odysseus: Considering that when she was the age you are now, she was taken as a war prize to Delphi.

Odysseus: Wouldn't it be great to pick up where you left off?

12:26 PM
Odysseus: And have more than just a meager eighteen years with your daughter?

Odysseus: Does she deserve to be in the House of Hades while you pull curtains for a community theater?

Odysseus: An innocent girl who deserved a far better life, a far better death, than the one she got?

12:27 PM
Odysseus: And the only thing standing in your way from reuniting with her is a monster who wouldn't hesitate to take you out if given the chance.

Odysseus: Or would you prefer to be a statue in her garden while your daughter languishes in the afterlife?

12:30 PM
Odysseus: You've gone quite quiet, Tiresias.

   12:32 PM
   Tiresias: Even if I did agree to this ... I wouldn't know how to ... how to ...

Odysseus: Not to worry, we'll make sure to have Hercules nearby on the date. He has plenty of experience in this, ah, area. And can provide lots of advice and personal help if needed. He'll also be on a DM with you.

12:33 PM
Odysseus: So you don't have to spend much time littering this group chat with messages.

Odysseus: We like to keep it to hero-personnel matters only.

Odysseus: Make sure to have your preferences open to men and women so he can private message you.

12:34 PM
Tiresias: But after I do the … you know, the deed … how would I even get Manto back?

Odysseus: Leave that to us, my boy. It's not like we don't have group members who have stormed the House of Hades before.

Perseus: Breaking and entering. Ohhh yeah.

12:35 PM
Odysseus: Thank you, Mr. Kool-Aid Man.

Odysseus: Any questions before we set up that DM with Hercules? He should be back with the ice cream any moment now.

12:36 PM
Tiresias: No—I—I—

Tiresias: HEROES OF THE DAYS OF OLD, I ADDRESS YOU.

Odysseus: What in the world?

Perseus: Weird font!

12:37 PM
Tiresias: ODYSSEUS OF ITHACA, PERSEUS OF ARGOS—

Perseus: Hey, that's me!

Tiresias: ACHILLES OF PYTHIA, HERCULES OF THEBES—

Odysseus: Yes, yes, we get it. People in this group chat came from a variety of places.

12:38 PM
Tiresias: YOU HAVE GIVEN BIRTH TO A SCHEME THAT WILL END IN THE DESTRUCTION AND DEATH OF MANY.

Odysseus: Typical prophecy fare.

Perseus: Prophecy?

Tiresias: TURN FROM YOUR PLOTS NOW—

12:39 PM
Tiresias: OR FACE THE WRATH OF HADES AND THE GODS AND THE END OF YOUR MORTAL LIVES.

Odysseus: Is that it?

12:40 PM
Achilles: Wow, I go watch one episode of Bridgerton and come back to a bazillion messages and a prophecy about my destruction. Gee thanks, guys.

12:42 PM
Tiresias: Whew, sorry, what happened?

Tiresias: I have the world's worst headache.

12:45 PM
Tiresias: Ah, hearing the messages read back to me, I see I prophesied. I've never done that over chat before.

12:47 PM
Tiresias: Aaand I'm not too keen on facing the wrath of the gods. Any way you can find another guy for the job?

> **Odysseus:** I believe it was talking about the deaths of many monsters, not just the one. I say we sally forth with the plan.
>
> 12:48 PM
> **Odysseus:** And we'll make sure not to go on any more un-aliving sprees with the monsters, right boys? ;)

Tiresias: You DO realize speech-to-text can also read emojis, right?

> 12:49 PM
> **Odysseus:** Fine, we won't un-alive any more monsters if you promise to go through with your end of the deal. Agreed?

Tiresias: Very well.

Tiresias: But if gods start showing up, I'm peacing out.

Tiresias: Are we understood?

> 12:50 PM
> **Odysseus:** Like a Delphic prophecy.

Tiresias: Great. I need to go back to work. I've long overstayed my break.

12:52 PM
Hercules: Hey, everybody!

Hercules: What did I miss?

Monstrously Magnificent Maidens

December 29

Group Information

Group Name: Monstrously Magnificent Maidens

Description: We're a bunch of monster ladies who gather to cheer each other on, spill tea, and keep each other safe. It's a rough world out there for monsters.

———

11:18 AM
Arachne: Medusa, get your booty in here.

11:20 AM
Medusa: What's going on, ladies? Is this about missing the knitting circle last night? You know we had a puppy at the shelter who was under the weather.

Arachne: Something way more sinister than missing knitting circle, as much as I can't believe I'm saying it.

Echo: Way more sinister.

11:21 AM
Echidna: It's bad, snakelets. We have reason to believe heroes are coordinating an organized strike against monsters. We lost two sirens just this week.

> **Aglaope:** *sniff* My poor, poor sisters. I'm composing a song in their honor.

Echo: Poor, poor sisters.

> **Arachne:** Medusa, why is Echo in this chat? I know you two are next-door neighbors, but she's not a monster.

11:22 AM
Medusa: I like to leave the gatekeeping to the heroes and demigods. Echo is a friend, and she needs allies in this crazy world too.

> **Echo:** Echo is a friend.

Echidna: Ladies, focus. I've been keeping an eye on the forums. Check out this group some heroes created.

Echidna sent a screenshot

> **11:23 AM**
> **Medusa:** Heroes before Monster-os? Wow, really twenty-first century of them. Don't you think we've progressed enough as a planet that we're a little too old for this crap?

Scylla: No, men are still pigs, modern or recently brought back to life. Circe, may she suffer in Tartarus, was right about that part.

> **Medusa:** Remember, Scyll, we're working on forgiving the beings that turned us into monsters. We talked about that in group therapy last week.

43

11:24 AM
Echo: Still pigs.

Medusa: *sigh* I'm going to start bringing you to therapy too, Echo. And not just because of this unhealthy obsession with Narcissus.

Echo: Narcissus. Narcissus. Narcissus.

11:25 AM
Arachne: Whoa, girls, big update. You know how the heroes have their group members public? Presumably to show off who's cool enough to be in the group? *rolls eyes*

Echo: Narcissus. Cool. Cool.

Medusa: You're getting a lot better at choosing which words to repeat, Echo. What about those group members, Arachne?

11:26 AM
Charybdis: *blurbleWHOOSHblurb* Yeah please send them to the chat, Arachne. I'm busy sinking some ship, so I've got the chat on voice-to-text. Otherwise, I'd go look it up myself.

Scylla: Chary! Without me?

11:27 AM
Aglaope: I used to lure men to their deaths with my sisters. *sniff sniff*

Echidna: They called me the mother of monsters, but this feels like herding cats.

11:28 AM

Arachne: Okay, okay. Here's the member list.

Arachne sent a screenshot

11:29 AM
Scylla: Oooh, Odysseus. I ate some of his intolerable men.

Echidna: And Hercules harassed my son as one of his heroic tasks.

Charybdis: Ew! *blurglewhooshgurgle* Odysseus is the worst.

11:30 AM
Lamia: Ah, Achilles was a looker. I thought about trying to seduce him, but no one held a candle to Patroclus in his eyes.

Aglaope: His best friend?

Lamia: ... Yes. His very special friend.

11:31 AM
Arachne: Oh hey, Lamia. Glad you're here. We have important stuff going on.

Lamia: I just discovered a place called Hollywood. I'm having all sorts of fun.

Echidna: Be careful, snakelet. Wouldn't want any of my favorite actors to meet their demise.

11:32 AM
Lamia: Fine, fine, I'll stick to the aspiring actors. They're a dime a dozen. And they seem to think I'm so beautiful I must be important in the industry, so they're willing to do ... anything. ;)

Arachne: We're getting distracted here, ladies. Hey, Medusa, you good? Where did you go?

11:33 AM
Medusa: I'm fine. I just ... I see that Perseus is in that group. Which means ... he came back.

Aglaope: Oh yeah, he cut off your head, right?

Arachne: Aglaope!

11:34 AM
Medusa: It's fine. I'm fine. This is a new start for all of us, right? Maybe he's different.

Echidna: Sorry, dear, but I doubt it. Looks like these heroes are up to something.

Arachne: Yeah, sorry, queen, but I have bad news for you. That update I was talking about? Look at the last name in the group.

11:35 AM
Medusa: Tiresias?

Arachne: Yup. Your new mortal friend.

Medusa: Arachne, how do you know that? I haven't seen you for two days, and I first talked to him this morning.

11:36 AM
Arachne: Webs are my thing, chica, including the World Wide Web.

Arachne: And … I saw you put in your password, so I monitor your profile too.

Medusa: Arachne!

11:37 AM
Echo: Monitor.

Medusa: I should have known you were behind it too, Echo. You two are desperate to help me make connections. I'll have you all know Echo stole my phone earlier and swiped right on EVERY being she came across.

Lamia: I approve.

11:38 AM
Medusa: But why is he in the hero chat? He was a prophet, not a hero.

Echidna: Oh, I bet I know. He's blind, right?

Medusa: Yes?

11:29 AM
Arachne: Oh my gods, I see where you're going with this.

Aglaope: I don't.

Lamia: You never do, hon.

11:30 AM
Echidna: You petrified Hector recently, Medusa.

Medusa: Which was completely an accident. I feel awful. I don't want to turn people to stone anymore.

Lamia: Some people deserve it.

Echidna: So they probably see you as a threat to heroes. And what sort of person would be immune to you?

11:31 AM
Medusa: ...

Medusa: Yeah. That ... that sounds like something Odysseus would come up with. Perseus got lucky last time. A bunch of people—gods—gave him special tools. Odysseus would know I'd be more watchful this time around.

11:32 AM
Aglaope: I still don't get it.

Charybdis: *MONCH MONCH MONCH* Yeah. *URP* Sorry, I think I missed something.

Scylla: Maybe you should've been paying attention instead of terrorizing ships without me.

11:33 AM
Lamia: Ladies. Clearly, Echidna is insinuating the heroes have recruited Tiresias to un-alive Medusa.

Echo: UN-ALIVE MEDUSA!

11:34 AM
Medusa: It's okay, Echo. I'm pretty sure I can avoid a blind assassin. I just won't go on any dates with him, problem solved.

Echidna: Yes. Or ...

Medusa: Or?

11:35 AM
Arachne: Or you strike first!

Medusa: Arachne, I REALLY don't want to un-alive people anymore. I hated it enough in Greek times when heroes kept coming to un-alive me or my fellow gorgons. They thought un-aliving heroes was fun, but I ... I never really meant to.

11:36 AM
Aglaope: Ah yes, your sisters, who I'm sure you mourn. We can mourn together. *sniff sniff*

Medusa: Aglaope, I had human sisters. I went to live with Stheno and Euryale *after* I'd been cursed.

Aglaope: ... Oh. Well, I'll mourn by myself then.

11:37 AM
Arachne: But Medusa, if you don't strike first, you'll always be looking over your shoulder. You have to send a message to the heroes. You're not someone to be messed with.

Echo: Send a message to the heroes.

Medusa: I don't know ...

11:38 AM
Echidna: If there's anything I've learned, it's that heroes will do whatever it takes to un-alive monsters. If we want to survive, we need to show them we mean business. That we're one step ahead of them.

Echo: Show them we mean business.

Lamia: I have to agree, love.

11:39 AM
Medusa: So, what, I should ask him on a date just to kill him?

Arachne: That's exactly what we're saying, girl.

Scylla: And if you get a chance to kill Odysseus too ...

Echidna: One thing at a time, Scylla.

Charybdis: *BURP*

11:40 AM
Medusa: Well. Okay. I guess I'll do it.

Medusa: Time to un-alive a blind prophet.

Private Message

December 29

11:59 AM
Medusa: Hey, Ty. I know we just started messaging, but I thought it might be fun to meet in person.

1:34 PM
Tiresias: So sorry, just finished painting a set piece.

Tiresias: Are you sure?

Medusa: To be honest, I'm kind of excited about the prospect of someone I can't turn to stone.

1:35 PM
Tiresias: Cool, well if you're dying to meet me, I guess I can't say no, can I? That's how the Fates work, right?

Medusa: Uh, yes, the Fates. I can't miss knitting circle again tomorrow, so how does the 31st sound?

1:36 PM
Tiresias: That works! Although I will say many places will

be closed for the American holiday. So why don't we meet somewhere nice and quiet and without people? Like a grave-yard or something?

1:37 PM
Medusa: I like the way you think. I always thought graveyards were peaceful. I like reading all the headstones and imagining what their lives might have been like.

1:38 PM
Tiresias: Quirky.

Tiresias: Sounds like a date.

GROUP MESSAGE

DECEMBER 30

Hermes changed group name to "DearHades Force"

3:03 PM
Persephone: What's up, Hermes?

Persephone changed group name to "DearHades Squad"

Hermes: Oh dear. I hope I'm not interrupting anything.

Persephone: Nah, just a game of Battleship between me and Hades.

3:04 PM
Persephone: Hades is losing, by the way.

Persephone: Badly.

3:05 PM
Hades: Yes, I'm sure it has nothing to do with the fact that every time you ask me to go get you "snacks," when I

return, you just so happen to know where my battleships are.

3:06 PM
Persephone: Hades, it's rude to interrupt Hermes when he has important news for us.

Persephone: You DO have important news for us, right, Hermes?

3:07 PM
Hermes: I do. Now, do you want to hear the bad news or the good news first?

Hades: Good, please.

Hades: Persephone makes plants when she gets nervous. Cacti. And with this our-love-life-riding-on-an-app bet with Demeter, she's been very nervous.

3:08 PM
Hades: One cactus is poking me in the—

Hermes: So the good news is that DearHades had a wonderful first week. You lot are on a trajectory to surpass StupidCupid downloads.

3:09 PM
Hades: Well, that is good news.

Persephone: "You lot." Hermes, you've only lived in London for a month. And yes, I heard your terrible impression of a British accent when you were here last, going over app particulars.

3:10 PM
Hades: What was that about being rude and interrupting?

> **Persephone:** A ruse so you would stop figuring out my foolproof Battleship strategy. All righty, Hermes, what's the bad news?

Hermes: It also has to do with Ms. Aphrodite's app.

3:11 PM
Hermes: Perhaps it would be best if I were to show you.

Hermes sent screenshots

———

HERMES'S SCREENSHOT ONE

PRIVATE MESSAGE
DECEMBER 30

11:02 AM
Aphrodite: This is absolutely ridiculous. You must take down their app this instant.

Aphrodite: Anything having to do with someone's love life falls under my jurisdiction.

Aphrodite: Just imagine what you would do if someone started flinging lightning bolts around, willy-nilly. Wouldn't that make you mad? Someone taking over what you do?

> 11:03 AM
> **Zeus:** Well, it depends.

Zeus: In this scenario, is someone doing this to woo a fair maiden for me?

11:04 AM
Zeus: Because, let me tell you, the ol' fling-lightning-at-the-ground-willy-nilly trick works wonders when it comes to the love department.

Aphrodite: Dad.

11:05 AM
Zeus: Well, go on. Is it?

Aphrodite: *sigh* No, in this scenario, the person would not be flinging lightning bolts to get some lady to fall in love with you.

Zeus: A shame, really.

Zeus: What a waste of lightning bolts.

11:06 AM
Aphrodite: Can we focus?

11:07 AM
Aphrodite: If you allow this app to continue, you're allowing your creepy brother—who kidnapped his wife, by the way—to decide the fates of the love lives of every being who came back from the dead.

Aphrodite: Including pairing monsters with mortals. There's no way that can be natural.

Zeus: I don't know, sweetie. I don't really like to get involved in these sorts of things.

11:08 AM

Aphrodite: How do you mean?

Zeus: The last time you tried to get me involved, a whole war ensued over deciding who was more beautiful: you, Hera, or Athena.

Aphrodite: If I recall correctly, we had to ask a mortal because you refused to give us an answer. And that's how the whole Trojan War happened. Because you wouldn't pick.

Zeus: And anger Hera? No, thank you.

11:09 AM
Zeus: And as much as I love wars ...

Zeus: That one gave the Trojans quite a beating. Who gave me a lot of offerings, I'll have you know.

11:10 AM
Zeus: It's very sad when you have to wipe out people who regularly give you animal sacrifices.

Zeus: :(

Zeus: Take a look at my pouty face and have pity on your old man.

11:11 AM
Aphrodite: Okay, two things.

Aphrodite: One, we're in the twenty-first century. So I'm rather sure animal sacrifices are no longer in vogue.

11:12 AM

Aphrodite: Two, you're king of the gods. I'm asking you to be one and get rid of this app.

Zeus: IS THAT ANY WAY TO TALK TO THE KING OF THE GODS? If you think Hera's temper is bad ...

Aphrodite: Please?

11:13 AM
Zeus: Now that you've added the "please," my anger has abated.

11:14 AM
Zeus: Tell you what.

Zeus: Since this is, as you say, "out of my jurisdiction," I can't interfere with the app unless I see something particularly egregious.

11:15 AM
Aphrodite: Like monsters getting together with humans?

Zeus: Well, I once disguised myself as an ant, a bull, and a swan to woo women. So I'm not sure I'm the best to say who can and can't be a pair.

11:16 AM
Zeus: But I'll keep an eye out for anything sinister. The moment I spot something, I'll shut it down. Okay, sweetie?

11:17 AM
Aphrodite: *huffs* Fine.

HERMES'S SCREENSHOT TWO

PRIVATE MESSAGE
  DECEMBER 30

11:20 AM
Zeus: Hermes, do you know anything about this app they call DearHades?

  Hermes: What app, sir?

Zeus: DearHades.

  11:21 AM
  Hermes: No, I don't, sir.

Zeus: It says here on the listing in the app store that you're one of the developers.

  11:22 AM
  Hermes: So it does, sir.

11:23 AM
Zeus: Aphrodite is a little wary of the app.

Zeus sent screenshots

Zeus: Whoops, those are not for you.

  11:24 AM
  Hermes: I will avert my gaze, sir.

Zeus: Oh no, not *those* kinds of pictures. It's something called a meme. Hera sent me those this morning. Funny, aren't they?

Hermes: Ha ha, very good, sir.

11:25 AM
Zeus: Anyway, here are the photographs of my conversation with Aphrodite.

Zeus sent screenshots

Zeus: Women and jealousy, am I right?

11:26 AM
Hermes: Now, I don't know about that. All the women I've been with have been upstanding and sure of themselves, never envious.

11:27 AM
Zeus: Ah yes, women and envy. Hand in hand, like lightning bolts and thunder.

Zeus: As for this DearHades app, I think the best approach is for me to make a profile.

Zeus: Under a pseudonym, of course.

Zeus: Don't want all those ladies falling all over the king of the gods. You know how Hera gets about those, ah, escapades.

11:28 AM
Hermes: A pseudonym?

Zeus: Yes, I ought to sample the app, make sure there's nothing dubious about it.

11:29 AM
Zeus: Perhaps go on a few dates.

Zeus: To be sure they're screening people well.

Zeus: For research purposes.

11:30 AM
Hermes: Oh dear, I don't know about that, sir.

11:31 AM
Zeus: Anyway, I must be off. My afternoon will apparently be booked with this new app.

Zeus: Thanks for the pep talk, Hermes.

11:32 AM
Zeus: I so enjoy our conversations.

———

3:21 PM
Persephone: So I'm trying to decide what's worse.

Persephone: The fact that Aphrodite is trying to take down our app.

Persephone: Or that Zeus wants to take it for a test ride.

3:22 PM
Hades: Definitely the second one. Because if Hera gets wind of this ... she'll shut it down in a heartbeat.

Hades: Or exercise her wrath on us.

3:23 PM
Hermes: Indeed, neither option is ideal.

Persephone: Thanks for the heads-up. We'll have to train the shades who are working as admins on spotting fake profiles.

3:24 PM
Persephone: Maybe they'll pinpoint Zeus and boot him out of here.

3:25 PM
Hades: He's going to create more fake profiles, love.

Persephone: Then we'll have to deal with and boot off each one.

Hades: Yikes, there are fifty more cacti in this room since this conversation started.

3:26 PM
Persephone: Let's hope there's nothing else shady going down in the app.

You Matched!

Name: Hercules (Roman, Preferred), Heracles (Greek, if you want to make me sad, say this one)

Interested In: Mortals and Demigods

Bio: Son of Zeus, hit the gym every day. No excuses. Unless your excuse is you want to go get donuts. I have a weakness for those. And mind control apparently. Since Hera made me go mad and murder my wife and five children and now I will never know love again ... so anyway, Krispy Kreme or Dunkin Donuts?

Name: Tiresias (Greek), Ty (American, because baristas have a hard time spelling the other one). No preference which you use.

Interested In: All Beings

Bio: I'm a prophet, so I can foresee many future conversations about art and dogs. Joined the app on the first day it was out, but apparently, it's important to include I'm also blind. Some people DMing me said so. So I'm blind. There. Anyway, let's talk about my dog. :D

Private Message

December 31

10:34 AM
Hercules: So what do you know about killing people?

> **Tiresias:** That people tend to die very quickly when they ignore the prophecies I tell them.

> **Tiresias:** Remind me again why you have a microphone clipped to the inside of my shirt? And I'm assuming recording this entire conversation for posterity?

> **Tiresias:** And why did you barge into my apartment without warning?

Hercules: I brought donuts.

10:35 AM
Hercules: They're the special kind. Creme filled. But not Bavarian cream.

Hercules: Bavarian cream is like stuffing a donut full of pudding or yogurt. Only monsters could love Bavarian cream.

Tiresias: Right.

Tiresias: So back to my non-pastry-related questions.

10:36 AM
Hercules: Silly, remember? I told you when I broke down your door.

Hercules: I'm here to teach you how to kill monsters.

Hercules: Hey, uh, DearHades app. Change message name to Killer Bros.

Hercules changed group name to "Killer Bros"

Hercules: Heeheehee. Thank you, little app.

10:37 AM
Tiresias: Yeah, so speaking of the app, aren't we not supposed to use words like "kill" and "murder"? Won't it alert the admins?

Hercules: Yeah—huh—so my dad—huh—Zeus—huh—joined the app so—huh—I guess the admins have their hands full—huh—so Odysseus says we're free to talk freely—huh.

Tiresias: What are you doing, are you—?

Tiresias: Are you bench pressing my couch?

Hercules: Yeah—huh—I hope it's okay that your dog—huh—is still on it.

10:38 AM
Tiresias: Oh my gods. Artemis, get off the couch, sweetie.

Come here. That's a good girl. You want some ear scratches? Oh yes. You love the ear scratches.

Hercules: Huh—huh—he-uh.

Tiresias: Hercules, put down my couch.

Hercules: Yessir.

Unknown Source: *WHOMP*

10:39 AM
Tiresias: Let me rephrase, Hercules. Put down my couch gently. Not throwing it down and threatening to cave in my apartment floor.

Hercules: Yessir. Huh-uh.

Unknown Source: *WHOMP*

Tiresias: Did you just ... pick up the couch again and put it down gently? Unnecessarily?

Hercules: Uh, yessir?

Tiresias: Call me Ty, Hercules.

10:40 AM
Hercules: Yes, Ty-Hercules.

Tiresias: I—okay, you know what. Pick your battles, Tiresias. Pick your battles.

Hercules: What was that? You were whispering. It's hard to hear you when you do that.

Tiresias: I—could you answer the first question I asked? About why you need to record this whole thing?

Hercules: Oh sure. So Odysseus wants to record your date for, he said, "Don't tell Tiresias, but I don't trust him to follow through. So record it, but tell him it's for 'research purposes.'" So, Ty-Hercules, this is for research purposes.

10:41 AM
Tiresias: Okey dokey, then.

Hercules: He's pretty paranoid. Oh, whoops! I wasn't supposed to tell you the first part. I was just supposed to say the research-purposes part. Stupid, stupid, stupid.

Tiresias: Are you smacking your forehead? Stop that.

Hercules: Yessir, Ty-Hercules. What should I do instead?

Tiresias: Uh, pet Artemis?

Hercules: Yessir, Ty-Hercules.

Hercules: You know, that whole name is a mouthful. You mind me shortening it to Ty?

10:42 AM
Tiresias: *sigh* Yes, that's fine.

Tiresias: So if you're recording my date, can you tell me why you're recording this right now? Which isn't a date?

Hercules: Oh, so I figured we didn't have much time between your training to kill Medusa and when you actually meet Medusa. I'll be hiding in the bushes during your date. And sometimes I'm not good at technology and forget to hit record, so—

Tiresias: Okay, got it. So you're here to teach me how to murder someone.

10:43 AM
Hercules: Heeheehee, yessir! You're going to Hercules's School of Slaying and Awesomeness. First school I've ever attended.

Tiresias: You didn't go to school?

Hercules: With biceps like these, my dad had me work out every day. No excuses, you know?

Tiresias: I, um, words. Have none.

Hercules: So I guess the first—what do the teachers call it—lesson? Can you use a sword?

10:44 AM
Tiresias: Negatory.

Hercules: What?

Tiresias: No, Hercules. That means no.

Hercules: No? What did they teach you in school then?

Hercules: Can you fight with gastraphetes, dory spears, ballistae, a very sharp stick?

Tiresias: Wow, what DID I learn in school?

10:45 AM
Hercules: Pet, pet, pet, pet, pet the puppy.

    Tiresias: Let's just assume if you put a weapon in my hands, I probably don't know how to wield it.

Hercules: Huh, well in that case.

Hercules: Why don't you just jab her with this poison-tipped arrow Odysseus gave me to give you in case "that buffoon has never had weapons training"?

    Tiresias: Hercules, where were you hiding that?

10:46 AM
Hercules: Scratch, scratch, scratch, scratch the puppy's ears.

    Tiresias: Okay, I'm going to have to ask you to hand over the arrow before you resume petting my dog—Hercules, hand it over on the safe side, NOT WITH THE POISONED ARROWHEAD FACING ME.

Hercules: Whoops. Good thing I didn't nick you in the hand, eh?

    Tiresias: Yes. Okay, that should fit nicely in this large pocket inside my winter coat, but ... how do I even stab her? You can't discreetly pull a whole arrow out of your pocket and just jab someone when they're looking right at you.

Hercules: Huh.

10:47 AM
Hercules: I've got it!

Hercules: Stab her when she's looking AWAY.

Tiresias: Yes, Hercules, that's a grand idea except for the fact that it would be really hard for me to tell when she's looking away.

Hercules: Why's that?

Tiresias: I—just trust me on this, okay?

Hercules: Okey-day.

Hercules: Ooh, bruh, I have another idea.

10:48 AM
Tiresias: Should I be worried?

Hercules: What if I make a noise to distract her and then you stab her?

Tiresias: What sort—what sort of noise?

Hercules: OOOooooWopALooooNEEEENEEENEENEENEE-wopwomp

Tiresias: Um, I suppose that is *a* noise that would draw attention. What are you imitating?

10:49 AM
Hercules: Birds.

Tiresias: I—

Tiresias: Yes, that was very good, Hercules. Very birdlike.

You Matched!

Name: Arachne (Greek, Roman, whatever, it's all the same)
   Interested In: Monsters
   Bio: Athena is a sore loser, I said what I said. Former Lydian princess, current monster fashion icon. The best weaver to ever live, even if I am a spider now, thanks to Athena. Let's talk linen.

———

Name: Medousa (Greek), Medusa (Roman, preferred because everyone always refers to me that way)
   Interested In: Mortals and Monsters
   Bio: Yes, I have snake hair. No, the tusks and wings, though cool, are just rumors. Looking for online pals because I will turn you to stone in person, unfortunately.

Private Message

December 31

2:42 PM
Arachne: You ready to slay a hero?

> **Medusa:** He's not a hero, he's a prophet. I don't feel great about this.

Arachne: Well, I don't feel so great about hoisting myself into a tree like a common arachnid, but I got your back, girl.

> 2:43 PM
> **Medusa:** Right, I can see you doing that all the way from the parking lot. You know, you really didn't have to come.

Arachne: And let you off a man in a graveyard alone? What kind of friend do you take me for?

Arachne: OOF. Oof.

2:44 PM
Arachne: There. Do you have your microphone all set up?

Medusa: Of course. That's how I'm talking to you right now. What are we going to say if he notices my mic?

Arachne: Just tell him you're recording it for Echo and you should be fine. We aren't letting you go in alone.

2:45 PM
Medusa: We? Are there others in this chat?

Arachne: Royal we, girlfriend.

2:46 PM
Medusa: So let me get this straight.

Arachne: Yes, let's do the checklist one more time.

Medusa: He gets here.

2:47 PM
Arachne: Yup.

Medusa: We stroll off, away from any witnesses.

Arachne: Best for you to stay away from humans as much as possible anyway. Don't want to accidentally lose the veil.

2:48 PM
Medusa: And then I pull the knife out of this ... uh ... what is this thing called?

Arachne: Squee! I'm so glad you asked. It's called a fanny pack, or a bum bag, if you're in the UK. I really think they're making a comeback in mortal fashion.

Medusa: You know better than I do. Okay, so I pull the knife out of my fashion accessory and, well, stab him. And then run. Er, stroll away casually.

2:49 PM
Arachne: Simple as that!

Medusa: Right. Yeah. Okay.

Arachne: And I'll be right up here in this tree if anything at all goes wrong. Try to steer him in my direction.

2:50 PM
Medusa: You don't think this is … wrong?

Arachne: Medusa. It's kill or be killed. Don't you remember our past life?

Medusa: Yeah. I do. A little too well.

2:51 PM
Medusa: That means I also remember how often people got hurt by being in the wrong place at the wrong time.

Arachne: Trust me, hon. You're not Poseidon, taking advantage of people. And you're definitely not Athena, cursing people on top of their own misfortune. You're looking out for your friends. And I'm proud of you.

2:52 PM
Medusa: Thanks, Arachne. It might be a little conceited, but … I always hope that maybe, even without any divine gifts, we can do something to patch up all the damage done by the gods.

Arachne: *sniff* You're going to make me cry.

Arachne: Go get 'em, girl. Stick it to the heroes. For all of us.

Private Message

3:01 PM
Tiresias: So, you, um, are also recording this date for posterity?

Medusa: Haha, so Echo likes it when I record everything so she doesn't have to ask clarifying questions. Because, you know, she can't.

> **Tiresias:** Well I'm glad I don't have to hide this microphone in my jacket anymore. AND I'M DEFINITELY NOT HIDING ANYTHING ELSE IN THIS JACKET EITHER. HAHAHA. Anyway, here's my dog Artemis.

3:02 PM
Unknown Source: *bow-wow*

> **Tiresias:** What cliché dog noises, eh?

Medusa: Awwwww, can I pet her, or is she working?

> **Tiresias:** Oh, she failed her training to be my working dog.

But I decided to keep her anyway. Feels terrible to keep something based solely on what it can do for you, you feel?

Unknown Source: Bark! *lick, lick*

3:03 PM
Medusa: Of course! Look at this cutie. I could never give her up. Haha, lots of kisses! Oh, hey, careful with my, uh, not-at-all-suspicious fanny pack.

Tiresias: Oh, sorry about that. She failed training because she likes to investigate suspicious objects.

Tiresias: So anyway, is the graveyard nice? Wanna go for a walk about?

> **Medusa:** Yes, let's. We can find a, uh, place where there isn't a funeral currently taking place. Rest in peace, whoever you are. May the gods bless your crying family. Sorry, everyone.

3:04 PM
Tiresias: Ah, so that explains all the commotion when my Uber brought me here.

> **Medusa:** Funeral traffic. Don't worry, we're only slightly lurking by the funeral gathering. Oh, nope, the pastor saw me. Hi, pastor. Feels wrong to kill people in front of a ... I mean, let's walk!

3:05 PM
Tiresias: Sorry, didn't catch that last part. Someone was wailing.

Tiresias: Anyway, agreed. Let me get out my collapsible cane.

Tiresias: Okey-dokey, let's go! Do you mind holding Artemis's leash? She's pretty rowdy.

3:06 PM
Medusa: I would love to! Come here, girlie. Aw. You love your owner a lot, don't you? That's ... super unfortunate. I mean sweet!

Unknown Source: *woof*

Medusa: The other day I helped a doggie that looks a lot like Artemis find her forever home with a sweet little girl. Usually I worry about kids getting dogs for Christmas, but this girl was so serious about it. She even made a pledge, haha. Like a marriage vow of taking care of her puppy through sickness and health.

3:07 PM
Tiresias: That's adorable. My daughter used to love dogs.

Medusa: Oh yes, you had a daughter ... what was her name?

Tiresias: Manto. She was a prophetess, not a doctor, but she was very much the Hippocratic oath type. The pledge reminded me of that. That's great you get to impact so many lives.

Medusa: Man, she sounds great. I kind of wish I got to meet my kids, but they popped out of my severed neck when Perseus chopped off my head.

3:08 PM
Tiresias: Oh ... the miracle of life? Or death.

Tiresias: Gaia, this is going to be hard, Odysseus.

Medusa: Huh? Oh, hold on, Artemis. Don't pee on grave-stones, that's rude.

Unknown Male Source: Psst. Tiresias. Over here! In this really cool-looking tomb with the Grecian columns. Should I make them collapse? So I can bench press them? Heeheeheehee.

Tiresias: Be right back, Medusa.

3:09 PM
Medusa: Sounds good.

Unknown Source: Bark! Bark! Bark!

Medusa: Shh, Artemis. I know that's a really big spider in the tree, but she's friendly ... to me. And you. Not, necessarily, to your owner.

3:10 PM
Tiresias: Quick, Hercules, I think she's talking to a funeral guest or something. What are you doing hiding here?

Hercules: Yeah, so, hiding in case you, uh, don't have the guts to—

Tiresias: Kiss her, yes. Obviously. Herc, this is being recorded in our DM. She can probably read this.

Tiresias: What if she sees you?

Hercules: I'm here for the, uh, bird noises. Augh! Is there a spider in here?

3:11 PM
Tiresias: Do you—do you hate spiders?

Hercules: They're … all the legs … uh, nuh-uh.

Tiresias: Well, maybe go find another hiding spot. Here, let me help you find one.

Unknown Female Source: Girl, why haven't you made your move? There's no one around.

Medusa: Well, you know, the dog is here. I feel like we should keep it rated G. You can't just traumatize a doggo like that.

Unknown Female Source: Medusa!

3:12 PM
Medusa: SO, Tiresias, did you hear something rustling in that bush?

Tiresias: Haha. No, I most definitely did not shove a funeral guest under there. Did you know Roman names are so popular with the youth these days? Hence me talking to someone named Hercules.

Tiresias: Anyway, continuing our conversation from earlier.

Medusa: So what do you have going on at the theater?

3:13 PM
Tiresias: Oh yeah, a much better conversation than impending doom.

Tiresias: We're getting ready for a children's production. It's odd to have a production happening in January. But after the theater caught on fire in December, and we had to find a new place, we bumped the performance dates to mid-winter.

Tiresias: But it's been really fun working with the kids. They're doing *Annie*! Have you seen it? I know Persephone sometimes broke out the old projector in the Underworld. I, you know, listened to the movies. The songs were nice.

3:14 PM
Medusa: Aw, *Annie*. Yeah, Persephone started showing that one a couple decades ago. That's so cute that you're working with kids ... so ... wholesome.

Tiresias: And the girl playing Annie is actually a foster kid, so she really identifies with the lead role. I would love to foster someday.

Medusa: Oh ... yeah. I would too. Except I always worry about turning a child to stone. I try to be careful by wearing a veil, but imagine if it slipped ...

3:15 PM
Tiresias: Oh, for sure. But you've been a great mom to all those pets you take care of.

Medusa: That's true. I also often feel like a mom to my friend Echo. She has a hard time since she can only repeat what other people say. But I've been encouraging a lot of my friends to go to group therapy, and we're all getting better at communicating. It's like a weird little family.

Tiresias: Wow. That's wonderful. There's not a single person who has come back yet who doesn't have their own trauma. That's really selfless of you to help others when I imagine you're processing things too.

3:16 PM
Tiresias: Gaia, I can't go through with this.

Hercules: OOOooooWopALoooNEEEENEEENEE-NEENEEwopwomp

Hercules: OOOooooWopALoooNEEEENEEENEE-NEENEEwopwomp AUUGHHAUUGHH! SPIDER SPIDER SPIDER. BIG HUMAN SPIDER, AUGGGGH!

Medusa: What in the world ... is someone dying? Or is that ... a very strange-sounding creature?

Hercules: MUST RUN AWAY!!!

Unknown Female Source: Wow. Rude.

3:17 PM
Medusa: Uh, random spider I definitely don't know—do you know that person?

Tiresias: I—

Tiresias: Tiresias of Thebes, and Medusa of ... the ocean near Greece?

Tiresias: Anyway.

Tiresias: You have unsealed a horrendous fate for the heroes of old. For a monster and a mortal will be their undoing.

3:18 PM
Medusa: Uh ... that was a weird voice. Are you okay? You look a little pale.

Tiresias: Oof. What a headache.

Tiresias: Did I just prophesy? If so, they're getting shorter. Maybe to account for attention spans.

> **Medusa:** Wow, I think you did. And I guess something really bad is coming for "the heroes of old." Do you remember what you said?

3:19 PM
Tiresias: Oh, gee darn. Would HATE to see something happen to them.

Tiresias: And no, I don't. I suppose I could relisten.

Tiresias: But I would advise you, DON'T RELISTEN. Not because there's the name of a friend or anything in the chat. But because, you know, listening to prophecies can be harrowing for some folks.

> **Medusa:** Oh, no need to relisten! Really! The prophecy went something like, "Tiresias and Medusa, you've unlocked something terrible for heroes. They're going to be undone by a monster and mortal." Really vague prophecy stuff, not something you need to relisten to.

3:20 PM
Tiresias: Yeah, maybe we should just delete this conversation afterward.

Tiresias: Sorry, this has turned out to be a weird date.

> **Medusa:** Well, our whole situation is a little weird. Coming back from the dead. Meeting in a graveyard. At least we're pretty entertaining people, haha. But, uh, maybe we should head home. I need to check on Echo. She was going to have

a job interview today. Weird day for a job interview, but that's how fast food be, I guess.

3:21 PM

Tiresias: I'm sure she'll do great. I probably should get Artemis back. She's been tugging at the leash like crazy. She must see a rodent or something. Thanks for handing her back to me.

Medusa: No worries. Haha, bye!

Private Message

December 31

3:30 PM
Arachne: So. Um.

Arachne: You forgot me at the graveyard.

    3:38 PM
    Medusa: Oh gods, I just got home and saw this. I am so
    sorry! I'm coming right back!

Arachne: Nah, it's okay, girl. I made Echo come pick me up on her
way back from the job interview.

    Maybe Echo: Job interview.

3:39 PM
Medusa: Thank the Fates. I can't believe I just ... ran. I was so
stressed out about the whole thing, and I just wanted to get out of
there, and I can't believe I left you.

    Arachne: You choked. Happens to the best of us.

Arachne: I was pretty distracted by that screaming man, though. What happened?

3:40 PM
Medusa: Guys, he has a cute dog who failed guide dog training, he helps kids at the local theater, he wants to foster children ...

Arachne: And?

Medusa: And I think we have the wrong guy. I know he's in the hero chat for some reason, but maybe he just needed to give them a prophecy.

3:41 PM
Echo: Wrong guy. Wrong guy.

Arachne: Stay out of this, Echo darling. Medusa, people don't just hang out with heroes for fun. Heroes are the WORST. You only associate with them if you're up to something.

Echo: Echo darling. Worst. Worst.

3:42 PM
Medusa: What do you mean, Echo? Oh! You just had your job interview. Is that what's the worst?

Echo: That what's the worst.

Medusa: Oh no. I'm going to give you some phrases, and you repeat the one that's true, got it?

3:43 PM
Echo: Got it.

Medusa: Okay. I aced the interview. I got the job. The interview was okay. They're considering me. The interview was terrible. They said no. Uh, someone died, haha, and, uh, a volcano erupted!

Arachne: Haha!

Echo: The interview was terrible.

3:44 PM
Medusa: I'm sorry, girl.

Echo: They said no.

Arachne: Oof.

Echo: Someone died.

3:45 PM
Medusa: ...

Arachne: ...

3:46 PM
Medusa: Uh, are you guys almost back to the apartment? Because I think we need to untangle that one in person.

Arachne: Agreed.

Arachne: You're off the hook for now, Medusa. But once we figure this out, we're bringing your actions before the group chat!

3:47 AM
Medusa: I accept my fate.

Echo: Someone died.

Killer Bros

December 31

4:04 PM
Tiresias: For the last time, Hercules, there isn't a human spider on you.

Hercules: Are you sure???

Tiresias: Yes, see, I'm whacking you with my cane. No spider.

4:05 PM
Tiresias: And why are you recording this conversation?

Hercules: Sometimes the heroes like to play pranks, like putting human-sized spiders in my apartment. So I just want to have on record that there is *no* spider.

Hercules: So if there is, in fact, a spider ...

Hercules: I contractually can pound you in the face.

4:06 PM
Tiresias: Comforting. Now would you mind leaving my apartment?

Hercules: Wait, Odysseus has a checklist of items for me to go over as a "debrief" of the date. That's the other reason I'm recording this. Uhhh, here's the list, in my pocket.

Hercules: Question One: Would you consider the date to have been a success?

4:07 PM
Tiresias: Besides the part where you ran out screaming like a banshee, yes. I was enjoying getting to know Medusa.

Tiresias: Really enjoying getting to know her. Wow.

Hercules: Okay, writing that down.

Hercules: How do you spell banshee?

Tiresias: Just put down "yes."

4:08 PM
Hercules: All righty. Question Two: On a scale of one to ten, how much did Medusa scream when you killed her—

Hercules: Wait a moment. There's an asterisk by the first question.

Hercules: Asterisk: A successful date is defined by killing your date by the end.

Hercules: You didn't kill her.

4:09 PM
Tiresias: Nothing gets past this one.

Hercules: So would the date even be considered successful?

Hercules: There, there, Tiresias. It's okay that you're confused. You really did try your best to kill her. I didn't mean to scare her with my manly screaming.

Tiresias: Please stop patting my head.

4:10 PM
Tiresias: Thank you. And yes, I didn't kill her. But I would still consider it a success.

Hercules: I'm confused.

Tiresias: I mean, when else are you going to go on a date with someone who gives little girls puppies and provides support groups for traumatized, cursed beings?

Tiresias: I really hope I didn't blow it. Because man, I wouldn't mind meeting up with her again.

4:11 PM
Hercules: But you didn't kill her.

Tiresias: No, I—

Tiresias: Perhaps it would be best to move on to the next question?

Hercules: You got it!

Hercules: Question Three: On a scale of one to ten, how much blood spilled—

4:12 PM
Tiresias: Hercules, are there any questions that don't involve murder?

Hercules: Hmmm.

Hercules: Would a question about turning a monster into taxidermy fall under the category of killing?

Tiresias: I—words escape me.

4:13 PM
Hercules: Well, that's all the questions if we're ignoring the ones about murder. Odysseus wants screenshots of this conversation, too.

Tiresias: You know what, Hercules, scratch this recording. Don't send it to Odysseus. And don't tell him how the date went. Tell him I got sick or something.

Hercules: So.

Hercules: If I happened to have sent a bunch of screenshots of this conversation to Odysseus before you said that ...

Hercules: Would that be a bad thing?

4:14 PM
Unknown Source: *woof*

Tiresias: Oh fury.

PRIVATE MESSAGE

JANUARY 1

9:07 AM
Tiresias: I hope I didn't completely ruin our first date. I know men running out of bushes and screaming bloody murder can put a damper on things.

> 9:13 AM
> **Medusa:** It just adds to the atmosphere of a graveyard, you know?

Tiresias: Oh yes. That was, um, definitely planned.

> **Medusa:** Honestly, it was way more normal than the Fields of Asphodel. Although the wailing ... did bring back Underworld memories.

9:14 AM
Tiresias: Oh yes, what WONDERFUL memories.

Tiresias: You know, aside from the numerous lessons we got from Persephone, I do remember one other thing distinctly from our time there.

Tiresias: I was constantly thinking about how I would do things differently if I got a do-over.

9:15 AM
Tiresias: You know, like every movie about a person who gets transformed into their high school selves all over again.

> **Medusa:** I never thought I would get a second chance at life. You know, things weren't at all bad, pre-Poseidon incident. In fact, I think Athena and I got along pretty well. Not that she talked to me. But I was one of her priestesses for a while.

> 9:16 AM
> **Medusa:** But then everything went downhill. And I always wondered what life would have been like if I hadn't been turned into a monster before what is now considered legal drinking age.

> **Medusa:** America is weird.

Tiresias: I know, in Ancient Greece we drank wine like it was water.

9:17 AM
Tiresias: But I see what you mean. I honestly despised the fact that I had the gift of prophecy. Everyone hated what I had to say— mostly because I predicted how they would die. And that tends to be a buzzkill at parties.

Tiresias: I hate that you had to come back as a monster, and me, with prophecies. It doesn't really feel like a second chance if you bring that with you.

9:18 AM
Medusa: I know exactly what you mean. I may never get to be a normal mortal again, but I guess if I had, I wouldn't have my friends like Arachne or Echo or, you know, the whole monster girl squad.

Medusa: And for what it's worth, I think your prophecies are a gift. We never know what's going to happen to us in life, but you give people that chance. And even if we can't escape fate, knowing it all ends one day … I feel like it helps us live life to the fullest.

9:19 AM
Tiresias: Wow, you really think so?

Tiresias: I hadn't really thought about it as a gift … but I'll have to ponder that a little more.

Tiresias: And for what it's worth, I think your curse is pretty gift-y too. Snakes for hair is awesome. And there are quite a few people I wouldn't mind being turned into permanent statues.

9:20 AM
Tiresias: Actually, the other day, I ran across a post about how people are viewing you differently. Not as a monster, but as someone who was defending herself and other women.

Tiresias: I guess we should all see ourselves differently.

Medusa: Wait … really? Wow. Honestly, that's all I want in this new life. To help other people not feel as alone and monstrous as I did last time around.

9:21 AM
Medusa: I don't know how we all came back, but I'm glad both of us did.

Tiresias: You know what? Me too. I always thought if I was given a chance to come back, I'd help people see they can seize their fate, and the future isn't always set in stone.

Tiresias: That's why I love working with these theater kids. They can view theater as a way to escape bad home lives, bullying, you name it.

9:22 AM
Medusa: The future isn't set in stone ... I like it. I think our coming back is pretty good proof that even the end may not actually be the end.

Tiresias: So speaking of second chances ...

9:23 AM
Tiresias: I don't suppose we could give another date a chance. Maybe this time not in a graveyard. Unless you're really into that.

Medusa: You know, there's a botanical garden I've been meaning to visit. They have a greenhouse that's warm even in winter. With flowers, butterflies ... and there's also a herpetarium—an exhibit with reptiles.

9:24 AM
Tiresias: Well, I bet the snakeys love the warmth and some new friends.

Tiresias: Although I'm not sure about Bobart. He seems like a loner.

Tiresias: But this sounds like a great idea.

9:25 AM
Medusa: Great! It smells so nice in there, I think you'll love it. I'm free the day after tomorrow. :)

Tiresias: Sounds like a date! I have rehearsal tomorrow anyway, so that works best. See you on the third!

Monstrously Magnificent Maidens

January 1

10:02 AM
Scylla: So Echo *wasn't* the one who killed that dude, right?

Arachne: Where you been, girlfriend? You missed all the action last night of us figuring it out.

10:03 AM
Scylla: Chary and I were having a friend outing and eating sailors. We're so full.

Charybdis: *BURP* Yes, we are.

Echidna: Ladies, I believe eating modern mortals was against the rules in the housing handbook.

10:04 AM
Aglaope: There's a handbook?

Arachne: For once, I'm with Aglaope. That's news to me.

Echidna: I ... should not be surprised this group didn't read the handbook.

Scylla: So? Spill the tea on Echo.

10:05 AM
Aglaope: Do we have to?

Medusa: You traumatized her, Aglaope. You might as well tell the truth.

Aglaope: *sigh* FINE.

10:06 AM
Aglaope: So I may have gone to get a burger while Echo was having her interview.

Aglaope: And I might have said hi to Echo, *slightly* interrupting her interview, but only slightly, not enough to be a big deal.

Arachne: Omgs, get to the point.

10:07 AM
Aglaope: Wow, pushy.

Aglaope: Anyway, I took a bite of the burger, and when I tell you, the modern invention of burgers is so good ...

Aglaope: Well, I was so delighted I burst into song.

10:08 AM
Scylla: ... Okay? And?

Aglaope: Well the interviewer was a man, and driven mad by my siren song, he jumped into the nearest body of liquid.

Aglaope: Which happened to be the oil for the french fries in the massive deep fryer.

10:09 AM
Scylla: Oh my gods.

Charybdis: *urglblurgl* Holy Hades, that's disturbing even for me.

Lamia: HAHAHA.

Lamia: ... Oh, I mean, that's terrible.

10:10 AM
Scylla: So did Echo get the job?

Medusa: No, because the whole place turned into an active crime investigation. People running away screaming, swearing to never eat something deep fried again ...

Aglaope: It was a drama of Greek proportions.

10:11 AM
Echidna: Now that we have that out of the way—and I am sorry, Echo, dear—we need to get back to the subject Arachne has informed me we need to address.

Arachne: MEDUSA'S DATE.

Lamia: Ah yes, with the blind prophet. How was it, darling?

10:12 AM
Arachne: She DIDN'T kill him.

Charybdis: I'm used to sinking ships, but wouldn't a blind guy be pretty easy to kill?

Aglaope: Was he only pretending to be blind?

Scylla: In that case, she would have turned him to stone.

Aglaope: Oh yeah.

10:13 AM
Arachne: Ladies, let Medusa explain herself.

Arachne: Go on, Medusa. Tell us why you didn't kill him.

Medusa: I think we've made a mistake. This guy is not dangerous.

Lamia: All men are dangerous, friend. Never forget it.

10:14 AM
Scylla: Lamia, you're the one who kills and eats them.

Lamia: That doesn't negate my statement. Men are dangerous, I'm just even *more* dangerous.

Medusa: Tiresias works with children in a theater. He has a dog who failed service dog training, but he kept her anyway. He's been cursed by deities as much as we have. I think he's a good guy. The fact he's in the hero chat is probably a fluke. You know the app still has some bugs.

10:15 AM
Medusa: In fact, I've set up another date with him.

Arachne: YOU DID WHAT?

Echidna: Oh, that was not what I expected to hear.

Echo: You did what?

Charybdis: Wait, *not* to kill him? To just date?

10:16 AM
Medusa: That's right. To just date. I can't turn him to stone, he actually likes talking with me ... you don't come across a guy like that every day.

Echidna: Oh, Medusa. I'm so sorry to tell you this. But we've gotten more intel.

Medusa: Oh no.

10:17 AM
Echidna: Hercules has been seen coming and going from Tiresias's apartment. They appear to be friends.

Arachne: You know, one of the most famous heroes of all time? A member of the hero chat?

Medusa: ... Oh.

10:18 AM
Medusa: Maybe the heroes are easing up? No more monster killing?

Echidna: Three more disappearances that we know of, just since your date. I don't think they've had a change of heart.

10:19 AM
Arachne: You still there, girl?

Medusa: Yeah. I'm just disappointed, I guess.

10:20 AM
Lamia: Men tend to be, darling.

Echidna: I don't think you can trust Tiresias. He appears to be working with Odysseus, that conniving fox. How do we know any of the things the prophet told you are true?

Scylla: He may have made up the thing about the theater, and the dog.

10:21 AM
Arachne: And even if those were true ... mortals tend to treat other mortals a lot differently than they treat monsters.

Medusa: You all raise fair points. Of all people, I should know better than to trust men. Especially if he's in a group chat with people like Odysseus and Perseus ... and hanging out with Hercules ...

10:22 AM
Medusa: But then, why didn't he try to kill me last time? While he had the element of surprise?

Aglaope: Oh, I have an idea.

Arachne: A miracle!

10:23 AM
Aglaope: What if he's trying to become friends with you to figure out more about all of us? Everyone knows you have lots of monster friends. If he gets you to trust him, you might tell him about us.

Scylla: And then the heroes could swoop in.

10:24 AM
Arachne: ... Wow, that's actually a good theory.

Aglaope: I don't know why you would doubt me.

Echidna: It does seem like something the heroes would do.

10:25 AM
Medusa: That ... makes a whole lot of sense.

Medusa: Well, everyone. I'm still going on the date.

Medusa: But this time, I'm sending the heroes a message. Don't mess with my friends ... or you might have a deadly encounter with a herpetarium.

You Matched!

Name: Antigone (Greek, preferred, pronounced, an-tih-guh-knee. None of this Anti-Gone business)

Interested In: Mortals

Bio: My family history's a mess. It all started when my dad, um, married his mom. And it really went downhill from there. Yeah, so. If you swipe right on me, I'm concerned for you.

―――――

Name: Tiresias (Greek), Ty (American, because baristas have a hard time spelling the other one). No preference which you use.

Interested In: All Beings

Bio: I'm a prophet, so I can foresee many future conversations about art and dogs. Joined the app on the first day it was out, but apparently, it's important to include I'm also blind. Some people DMing me said so. So I'm blind. There. Anyway, let's talk about my dog. :D

Private Message

4:17 PM
Tiresias: Antigone?

Antigone: Ty? What's up? I haven't seen you since you prophesied my death and everything.

4:18 PM
Tiresias: Yeah, sorry, that happens a lot. I didn't mean to swipe for romantic reasons.

Antigone: Oh, same. I do wish this app had a way to connect with old friends, apart from the forums.

Antigone: Even if those old friends tell you you're gonna die.

4:19 PM
Tiresias: What are friends for, right?

Antigone: Ha. For sure.

4:20 PM
Tiresias: So did you join this app to connect with someone new? I know you and Haemon were madly in love, until, you know, both of you tragically died because your families didn't approve.

Antigone: I know, right? It was like an Austen novel, but with death.

4:21 PM
Tiresias: Austen novel?

Antigone: Persephone has quite the library in the Underworld.

Antigone: Anyway, I'm actually signing off DearHades pretty soon. Would you believe it? I found Haemon on my walk through Grove City College's campus the other day. They're also putting on a play about me. I guess they just held auditions for it to take place next term.

Antigone: The actress who is "me" is way too dramatic. Needs to tone back the eyeliner.

4:22 PM
Antigone: Tons of people are finding their other whole. Helps that Hestia stuck most of us in Pennsylvania where there's cheap rent.

Tiresias: Other whole?

Antigone: Sure. Didn't you read the DearHades mission statement? You don't need another person to make you whole. You just bring two wholes together to make them more than whole.

Antigone: And it seems the Fates were on my side. Because he and I connected again.

4:23 PM
Tiresias: That's great news! I'm happy for you.

Antigone: But as soon as I saw your profile I had to swipe.

Antigone: And thank you for being such a good friend all those years ago.

4:24 PM
Antigone: I know you didn't get much time with your daughter.

Antigone: So thank you for treating me like one, since my father was out of the picture.

4:25 PM
Tiresias: I—I don't know what to say.

Antigone: Sometimes wordless moments are the most beautiful.

Antigone: Best of luck on this app.

4:26 PM
Antigone: May you find your other whole.

Antigone has left the chat

4:27 PM
Tiresias: That's the problem. I think I have.

Heroes Before Monster-os
January 1

4:44 PM
Odysseus: You know, Tiresias, in my short time on this mortal earth—the second time around—I've had a chance to collect a number of heads from animals. Mostly from a man who sells taxidermy up in Indiana.

Odysseus sent a picture

Odysseus: Here's one of a buck.

Odysseus sent a picture

Odysseus: One of a moose.

Odysseus sent a picture

4:45 PM
Odysseus: Another of an elk.

 Tiresias: I'll have to take your word for it.

Odysseus: Do you know what creature's decapitated head I do not have mounted on my wall yet?

4:46 PM
Tiresias: The chat's awfully quiet. Where are Achilles and Perseus?

Odysseus: Oh, they are—what are they doing, Hercules? What's it called?

Hercules: Play fighting with swords?

Odysseus: LARPing. That's it. They've really taken to it.

4:47 PM
Odysseus: So it's just us three in the chat, I'm afraid.

Hercules: *gasp* Does this mean I get to be a part of this discussion?

Hercules: Permission to enter the chat, sir?

4:48 PM
Odysseus: Yes, as long as you serve as a mediator between myself and Tyler.

Hercules: Sir, yes sir.

Odysseus: Mediator, meaning you take my side in the argument, no matter what.

Hercules: Of course, sir. Be back in a jiffy.

4:49 PM

Odysseus: Good, now while Hercules is off bench pressing his chaise lounge, you want to explain to me why I don't have the head of a certain gorgon on my wall?

Tiresias: I've heard they're very tacky decoration.

Tiresias: It would ruin the feng shui.

4:50 PM
Odysseus: Witty.

Odysseus: But dodging the true question.

Hercules: No dodging. This is not dodgeball.

Odysseus: Finished bench pressing already?

4:51 PM
Hercules: Yessir, one hundred reps all done.

Tiresias: How—how is that possible?

Odysseus: Back to the question at hand.

4:52 PM
Odysseus: Would you agree, Hercules, as our mediator, that we made it very clear to Tiresias what he must do on his date with Medusa?

Hercules: I agree!

4:53 PM
Odysseus: And would you also agree we upheld our side of the agreement not to kill any more monsters, upon the condition Tiresias would slay the gorgon?

Hercules: You mean besides all the ones Perseus swiped right on?

Tiresias: I'm sorry, what?

Odysseus: Hercules, WOULD YOU AGREE?

4:54 PM
Hercules: Oh, yes, I agree.

Odysseus: And would you agree there's no excuse for such behavior, seeing we've given him the honor of being in the hero group chat in the first place?

Hercules: Oh boy, what I wouldn't give to be a permanent member of this group.

Tiresias changed his name to Odysseus 2.0

4:55 PM
Odysseus 2.0: And would you agree, Hercules, that it's quite ridiculous to ask a prophet—who is known for saving lives—to murder someone on a first date?

Hercules: Huh, I hadn't thought about it that way, but yeah, Odysseus 2.0. That does seem pretty lousy.

4:56 PM
Odysseus 2.0: And don't you think we ought to get to know those we choose to kill first? Before we go on murdering rampages? Maybe they're really a nice person deep down. Maybe everything we've been told about monsters isn't right.

Hercules: Wow, you're really starting to make a lot of sense.

Odysseus: Stop that.

4:57 PM

Odysseus: I leave for one minute to pour myself a glass of bourbon, and this is what I come back to.

Hercules: Oh no, this is so confusing. I DON'T KNOW WHAT TO BELIEVE ANYMORE.

Odysseus 2.0 changed his name to Tiresias

Tiresias: All I'm saying is we ought to think with our minds, not with our—

Tiresias: Swords.

4:58 PM

Odysseus: Dear me, thinking. Now that's my territory, isn't it?

Odysseus: Well since we're going to be using our minds, ponder this. If you don't kill her, there is no way to retrieve your daughter.

Tiresias: I do miss Manto.

Tiresias: I really miss her. But not enough to kill someone. She wouldn't want that. Manto wouldn't.

4:59 PM

Odysseus: Yes, because Medusa's been given a second chance, right? We all have. Correct?

Tiresias: Yes.

Odysseus: And it would be particularly heinous to steal

someone's second chance at life. Why, doing so would make someone nothing short of a monster.

5:00 PM
Hercules: And monsters are ... bad.

> **Odysseus:** Very good, Hercules. Do yourself a favor and reward yourself with several thousand more bench presses.

Hercules: Yes sir!

> 5:01 PM
> **Odysseus:** That should keep him busy for about ten minutes.

> **Odysseus:** Now, Tiresias, as we've established, you are hesitant to take away someone's second chance of life. Especially now that you've gotten to know this someone. They've become more human to you.

Tiresias: Where are you going with this?

> 5:02 PM
> **Odysseus:** Wonderful places, my boy.

> **Odysseus:** And you and I both would agree that if you knew someone well, it would be horrifying to see them perish too quickly.

5:03 PM
Tiresias: Yes?

> **Odysseus:** I ran into a wonderful young lady at Grove City College the other day. And would you believe it? Not only was she one of the displaced mortals from the Underworld.

Odysseus: But she so happened to find the long-lost love of her life.

Tiresias: Oh gods, no.

5:04 PM
Odysseus: Oh Gaia, yes. And I thought, "Wouldn't it be the most tragic thing for one of these young lovers to have an accident? After all, they died last time before they could even be married."

Odysseus: You would hate for an accident to befall poor Antigone, wouldn't you?

5:05 PM
Odysseus: After all, she was the closest thing you had to a daughter after Manto, correct?

5:07 PM
Odysseus: My, my, this silence is uncomfortable.

5:08 PM
Tiresias: You wouldn't.

Odysseus: Oh, you'd be surprised at the number of things that fall into the "I would" category.

5:09 PM
Odysseus: Now that we are understood, I'd like to see an actual murder attempt on the next date.

Odysseus: And you'd better follow through. I'm not one for waiting.

5:10 PM
Odysseus: After all, that's the thing about us Ancient Greeks.

Odysseus: We're known for our tragedies.

Killer Bros

January 2

6:33 PM
Hercules: Yooooo, Tiresias, why are you punching someone?

Tiresias: Me and the director are showing July and Pepper how to do the fight scene at the beginning of—

Tiresias: Is that Hercules's voice?

Tiresias: *sigh* Okay, everyone, take a fifteen-minute break.

6:34 PM
Unknown Source(s): "That was really fun." "That punch looked so real." "Ugh, I left my water bottle at home. Can I borrow yours?" "Ew, no, there's a drinking fountain in the hallway." "Ty is the best director ever." "How did he learn to fight like that?"

Tiresias: Hercules, why are you recording this conversation?

6:35 PM
Hercules: Sometimes I like to listen to these chats in my earphones at night and pretend I have friends.

Tiresias: That's—really sad.

Unknown Source: Who is this guy?

Tiresias: Oh, hey, Director, this is just a friend. He's helping me choreograph the fight scene at the beginning of the show.

6:36 PM
Director: Oh, nice to meet you.

Hercules: Hercules.

Director: Man, there's been a lot of Greek names going around lately.

Hercules: Actually, it's Roman—

Director: Anyway, Ty, I'm going to print off some things in the office. Think you can handle the herd when they get back from break?

Tiresias: No problem. Yep, go print some things. See you later.

6:37 PM
Tiresias: Is he gone? Dude, what are you doing here?

Hercules: Like you said, helping you with fight chor—whatever you said. Does this mean I can punch you?

Tiresias: Fake punch, sure. Now square your shoulders. The kids are back and will be watching from the seats, so we need to show them how it's done in the show.

Tiresias: Great, now tell me why you're actually here. Whoa, your shoulders are like rocks. I can't even squeeze them without hurting my fingers.

> 6:38 PM
> **Hercules:** Haha, that tickles. Okay stop it.

Tiresias: Ouch, okay. No more squeezing shoulders, got it.

> **Hercules:** Anyway, thought I'd give you another pep talk before you commit murder tomorrow. Why are you holding your hands over your ears?

Tiresias: Gaia, say it any louder, why don't you?

> **Hercules:** Okay … I THOUGHT I WOULD CHEER YOU UP BEFORE YOU COMMIT MURDER TOMORROW.

Tiresias: Don't worry, kids, Director Ty is in a play where people stab each other, haha … dude.

> **Hercules:** What? Oh, okay, you're motioning me closer.

6:39 PM
Tiresias: Okay, I'm going to throw a fake punch like this. When I do, I need you to react and act like I've punched you. It'll look real from the audience.

Tiresias: Now, I punch.

> **Hercules:** Oof.

Unknown Source: Heeheeheeheeee.

> **Tiresias:** You reacted the wrong way, didn't you? The kids are all laughing at you from the audience.

6:40 PM
Hercules: Ohhh, was I supposed to go the other way? That makes more sense.

> **Tiresias:** You know what, get on the floor. We're going to practice a headlock.

> **Tiresias:** Ow. Ow. Ow. Hercules, I'm supposed to headlock YOU.

Hercules: Oh, like this?

Hercules: That's a very good headlock, very convincing. But I'm not choking to death. I don't think you're doing it right. Your arm's all loosey-goosey.

> **Tiresias:** It's called acting. We're not supposed to do it for real.

6:41 PM
Audience: Heeheehee.

> **Tiresias:** Okay, I'm releasing you from the headlock and gonna address the kids, since this is a disaster.

> **Tiresias:** Hey, kids, that's how NOT to do the fight scene. Go ahead and practice singing "It's the Hard Knock Life" with your music director in the lobby. She'll have a piano ready.

Audience: "Did you see that dude?" "His huge arm could explode my whole head!" "I thought I saw a video of him somewhere bench pressing a couch." "Is that even real?"

6:42 PM
Tiresias: Now that they're gone ...

Tiresias: I don't need a pep talk.

Tiresias: I have to stab Medusa with a poison-tipped arrow in a botanical garden tomorrow, since Odysseus is now threatening the lives of my friends if I don't. That's not exactly something you give a motivational speech for.

Hercules: Duuude, you clearly never spent time in Sparta. Why are you pinching your nose?

6:43 PM
Hercules: And I thought this was supposed to be all worth it. What I wouldn't give to hold Megara in my arms again.

Hercules: She'd say something sassy.

Hercules: I'd kill some sort of monster for her.

Hercules: You know, typical romantic stuff.

Hercules: But after what happened with Hera, and what she made me do to Meg and my family, I—I— *sniffle sniffle*

6:44 PM
Hercules: Hoohoohoo! *sniffle sniffle sniff*

Tiresias: Are you—crying?

Hercules: No, it's just really dusty in here. *sniffle sniffle*

Hercules: But if I was crying, it's because ...

6:45 PM
Hercules: When I died, my mortal part got destroyed and my not-mortal part got sent to Olympus.

Hercules: And the whole time there, I kept thinking I didn't deserve to be in such a nice place because of what I did.

Hercules: I don't care that I couldn't control myself. My hands did it, Tiresias. MY hands.

6:46 PM
Hercules: So when my mortal part resurrected and was reunited with me, and I got brought here, I was so pumped. I thought I'd find Megara and explain everything.

Hercules: So the last memory I had of her wouldn't be her face looking at me all scared and—

Hercules: And then I couldn't find her, and— *sniffle sniffle*

Hercules: Odysseus says there probably isn't anyone else coming back unless we get some more gorgon blood and—

6:47 PM
Hercules: And I was the guy who stormed the gates of Hades with these very hands. These hands. And now all they can do is bench press things. Because if I'm not holding something ... I think about—

Hercules: *sniffle sniffle* Oh gods.

Tiresias: I ... there, there. Is that your shoulder?

Hercules: Yeah. *sniffle* Can't you tell? It's extraordinarily muscular. You had a hard time squeezing it earlier.

6:48 PM
Tiresias: So my date means something to you because it's your only chance to make amends for what you did? To get her back?

Hercules: *snuffle* Yeah.

Tiresias: Have you ever considered, Hercules, that YOU didn't do something? That something was done to you? Something way beyond your control.

Tiresias: And that we can only do so much with the fates we are given.

6:49 PM
Hercules: But ... it was my hands.

Hercules: I—think I need to go. Gotta hit the gym.

Hercules: Best of luck on your date tomorrow. Use those hands well.

Private Message

January 3

4:03 PM
Tiresias: So remind me again why you're also needing to record this date? Mine is because my, uh, friend—whose name is definitely not Hercules—wants to know how it went.

Tiresias: Thankfully he's not hiding in those leafy plants over there. This time. I guess he had to hit the gym again. I wonder if he sleeps there ...

Tiresias: But that also puts more pressure on me to follow through ...

4:04 PM
Medusa: I'm recording for my friend Echo again, haha. Communicating can be ... very difficult. Especially when trying to figure out if she killed a man or if it was someone else.

Medusa: Long story.

Tiresias: Yes, killing. Definitely what I want to be thinking about right now.

Tiresias: INSTEAD, let's think about how nice it smells in here.

4:05 PM
Medusa: I love all the tropical flowers. Should I describe some to you?

Tiresias: Sure, that would be great. It would take my mind off other things.

Medusa: Aw, I'm sorry to hear that. Well, there are lots of hibiscus flowers. Little ones that hummingbirds like to stick their beaks in. Oh wow, that's a bright blue one. No wait. That's a butterfly. Ooh, a Blue Morpho! I love those. When they have their wings closed, they're just brown, but when they open, iridescent blue!

4:06 PM
Tiresias: I don't know if we had those in Greece, from what I can remember, but you described it really well. It sounds beautiful. What else is there? Any more butterflies?

Medusa: So many butterflies.

Medusa: I think that's a Swallowtail. They're yellow with long black tail things on their wings. And Monarchs, beautiful red-orange. Oh! Hey, one just landed on me. Hold out your finger. Maybe I can transfer him over so you can hold the little guy.

4:07 PM
Tiresias: Like this?

Tiresias: Oh, wow. I feel the little dude. Wow.

Medusa: His itty-bitty feet feel so tickly. I'm not sure what he is. He's pale yellow and, haha, can you feel that? He's using his proboscis to taste your finger.

4:08 PM
Tiresias: Let's hope he doesn't like human flesh, haha.

Tiresias: You know, I always liked the idea of a butterfly. Not because of the transformation, but because the caterpillar has to go through so much to get there.

Tiresias: I remember a particularly disgusting lesson from Persephone about how the caterpillar essentially turns into goop before it turns into a butterfly.

4:09 PM
Medusa: Yeah, she was ... weirdly animated about that part.

Tiresias: Wow, you remember that one too? I wonder if we can get together with tons of displaced people and piece together all the missing parts.

Tiresias: Oh, did he just fly off?

4:10 PM
Medusa: Yes, he did. Aw, he's fluttering away with a little friend.

Medusa: Butterflies are so beautiful ... but so delicate.

Medusa: Easy to ... accidentally kill ...

Medusa: Hey, wanna go to the herpetarium?

4:11 PM

Tiresias: Sure, it is starting to get a little crowded in here. I can sort of feel the bodies pressing all around, and it's getting hard to hear in this echoey room. Besides, if we want to do something that would not be good for a lot of witnesses ... herpetarium sounds great!

Medusa: Right ... fewer witnesses ... and venomous snakes. Off we go!

4:12 PM

Tiresias: Shoot, it just got really toasty in here. Is Bobart liking the new environment?

Unknown Source: *hssssss*

Medusa: Shh, Bobart, you're not allowed to talk in public. We don't want to scare the mortals if they figure out there are a bunch of snakes under this hood.

4:13 PM

Tiresias: So I don't suppose you want to lean over the railing of one of these exhibits and pay really good attention to one of these snakes, do you?

Medusa: Oh! Uh, yeah, I was gonna ask you the same thing. Come along to this, um, black mamba exhibit. It looks like the lid is open for the keepers to feed him. I hear they, uh, have a really unique ... hissing sound. That you'll want to hear.

Tiresias: Sure, I guess I could do that because it would be really suspicious of me to say no ... here, snakey, snakey. WHOA!

4:14 PM

Tiresias: Good thing I gripped that railing. I could've

sworn someone in the crowd almost pushed me in. Can you imagine what would've happened?

Medusa: Wow! That snake is incredibly deadly and hungry. That would've been a disaster, haha.

Medusa: Hey, uh, part of why you tripped so easily appears to be because you're struggling to fish something out of your really deep pocket. Do you, uh, need some assistance?

> **Tiresias:** NO. Ahem, I mean, no, I was just digging out some ... uh, gum. Yes, that's what I just pulled out.

> 4:15 PM
> **Tiresias:** I hear it's good for American dates. There're supposedly all these commercials about it.

Medusa: Uh, yeah, sure. Hey, wanna check out the cobras?

> **Tiresias:** Depends, are they deadly?

Medusa: Um ... yes? But very cool.

> 4:16 PM
> **Tiresias:** Sounds perfect, but only if the cage is open. Because, dates are supposed to be thrilling, right?

> **Tiresias:** Since the arrow trick isn't working, maybe someone could accidentally get shoved in. Almost getting pushed gave me an idea.

Medusa: Uh, did you mutter something?

> **Tiresias:** Only that I'm SO HAPPY to be on this date with you. To the cobras we go!

4:18 PM

Medusa: Wow, it must be feeding time. This one is open too! You should lean forward to hear the, uh, um, unique wiggling sound? Yes. The wiggling sound.

Tiresias: That's a great idea, but here, is this your shoulder? Lean forward with me. I'd hate for you to miss it.

Medusa: Yeah, haha, that's my shoulder. Oh no, I accidentally tripped into you—oh no, you're falling into the ... wait, let go!

Tiresias: But don't you want to see the snakes even closer? Hey, stop pushing me. I know that's you. I can hear Bobart hissing.

4:19 PM

Medusa: Bobart, this is a stealth operation!

Tiresias: Gotta wrestle free. Use my knowledge from the fight scene in *Annie*.

Medusa: Stop ... wiggling ... like a cobra ... and ... get in there.

Tiresias: Not until you go in first!

4:20 PM

Tiresias: Wait a moment.

Medusa: Ugh, let go! Tuck and roll, Medusa.

Tiresias: Dang it, where'd you go? Hold up, you just said you were going to put me in there. You weren't ... trying to kill me ... were you?

Medusa: Me? What were YOU doing, pushing and pulling me like that? I knew it. I knew you would try to kill me. Gods, I'd hoped not, though.

4:21 PM
Tiresias: So ... what? You thought you'd get the jump on me first? Real classy, doing that to a guy who can't see.

Tiresias: I'm leaving, and you'd better not follow. Or I'll ... I don't know, smack your shoes with my cane. Sorry, that was really lame. But don't follow me.

Medusa: Fine. Leave. But if I ever see you again ...

Medusa: Well. I won't turn you to stone, cause, you know, I can't. But I'll try to push you into some venomous creature!

4:22 PM
Tiresias: Well, at least the venomous creature won't be you. Bye.

5:08 PM
Tiresias: ...

Tiresias unswiped Medusa

Heroes before Monster-os

January 3

7:12 PM
Tiresias: I imagine Hercules sent you screenshots by now?

7:13 PM
Odysseus: Yes, he's off grabbing some takeout for me. And the other boys—well, I can tell you they're definitely not off killing monsters they matched with. They are, hmm. What do young people do for fun these days?

7:14 PM
Odysseus: Ah, got it. They are "vibing" with the "homies" at some college-town restaurant where you pay by the taco.

7:15 PM
Tiresias: Okay, so you did see the screenshots that showed I attempted to kill her and she replied in kind? It was premeditated on her part too.

Odysseus: Yes, so it seems one of the monsters caught wind of what we were up to. A shame.

Tiresias: It was horrible. To try to take someone's life away when they just got it back.

Tiresias: So are we agreed on two things?

7:16 PM
Tiresias: One, that I was right all along that it was a bad idea to go on a date with Medusa. Because the whole time I felt awful about how she would feel knowing she was being used. And, well, knowing she would die and all.

Tiresias: And after feeling used on this date, I agree. It sucks.

Tiresias: Two, you can no longer threaten Antigone, since my life is in peril. I obviously can't go on any more dates with Medusa. So we're done here.

7:17 PM
Odysseus: I suppose we can agree on one thing.

Odysseus: It would make no sense for you to continue in your relationship with her.

Odysseus: So you are no longer of use to me at the present.

7:18 PM
Odysseus: However, I will keep you in this group chat for now.

Odysseus: Prophets can have use from time to time.

7:19 PM
Tiresias: Whatever, I'll keep this conversation on mute.

7:20 PM

Odysseus: This is agreeable to me. The less I hear from you is likely the better. Tell Antigone we say hi. And that she, and you, seemingly lucked out of more dire circumstances.

7:27 PM

Odysseus: Good, you already muted us.

Private Message

January 4

9:24 AM
Arachne: So you tried to kill him.

Medusa: Yup.

9:25 AM
Arachne: And he tried to kill you.

Medusa: Yup.

9:26 AM
Arachne: And ... neither of you succeeded?

Medusa: Yup.

Arachne: Girl, I'm fishing for more info here.

9:27 AM
Medusa: I was honestly having fun until we tried to kill each other.

Medusa: I know we have our monster squad. But sometimes I really miss being a mortal.

   Arachne: Me too, girl. I would give anything to walk into a cafe without everyone screaming.

9:28 AM
Medusa: I'm sorry. I didn't mean to be insensitive.

   Arachne: You're not, girlie. We all have our trauma. Let it out.

Medusa: I just hoped this second chance at life would be different. Instead, people see "monster" and immediately want to chop off my head again. It may be shallow, but I kind of hoped that ... well ...

   9:29 AM
   Arachne: Finish the thought, queen. Speak the truth.

Medusa: I hoped that maybe I could find love. My first life was over so fast. I never met my kids. I had to move in with Stheno and Euryale, and honestly they weren't very nice. I never saw my parents again ...

9:30 AM
Medusa: You girls are my family. But I also kinda wanted to have a family myself someday. Is that crazy?

   Arachne: It's not crazy. At all. That's a normal thing to want. Mortal or monster.

Medusa: I guess I know better now. I should go through and unmatch all these profiles Echo swiped right on for me.

   9:31 AM

Arachne: Hey, one bad prophet doesn't ruin all of Greek mythology. Maybe at least chat with a few people? And if you think you might like any of them, the squad can do research and figure out everything about them.

Arachne: Echidna is scary good at stalking people's online profiles.

9:36 AM
Medusa: Sorry, the puppies were trying to steal each other's food. I guess I could give it a shot. Worst case, I don't find anyone and I'm in the same place I am now.

9:37 AM
Arachne: That's the spirit! Knock 'em dead.

Arachne: Er, figuratively.

DearHades Squad

January 4

1:11 PM
Persephone: So, Hermes, about those packages you left at the mouth of the Underworld.

Persephone: My, uh, nervous plant habit may have gotten the best of me and …

Persephone: The packages are now lost in a lush jungle.

1:12 PM
Persephone: On the bright side, our ferryman of the dead, Charon, is very excited to be leading people on a "Cruise of the Deadly Jungle" across the River Styx. He said something about having to change the name due to trademark.

  1:13 PM
  Hermes: Those packages were from your mother, Miss Persephone.

Persephone: Oh, jolly, let me guess what was in them. Kale?

Hermes: I wouldn't know. I do not peep inside parcels.

1:14 PM
Hermes: But I suppose when I did peep inside the boxes ...

Hermes: There may or may not have been an unpopular vegetation by the name of "kale" in there.

Hermes: And a note on the package that may or may not have stated something along the lines of: "Give up yet?"

1:15 PM
Persephone: What the fury, Mom? You can't wait eight more months?

Persephone: Oops, sorry, Hermes, didn't mean to use that kind of language in here.

1:16 PM
Hermes: Ah, it's all right, miss. The Brits say far worse.

Hermes: But I'm actually quite relieved you messaged, because I've been up to my eyeballs today in damage control from Aphrodite and her shenanigans.

Persephone: Oh, Gaia.

1:17 PM
Hades: Hey, everyone. Just made it through the "jungle." Sweetheart, you really need to tone it back on the carnivorous plants.

1:19 PM
Persephone: Sorry, Hermes. We're back. I had to pry a human-sized Venus flytrap from his arm.

Persephone: The thing wouldn't stop singing about some dude named Seymour needing to feed it.

1:20 PM
Hades: Should I be concerned that your plant life is becoming sentient?

Hermes: Never mind the miracle of life, we have far bigger concerns on our hands.

1:21 PM
Hades: My hands that were just eaten by a plant would beg to differ.

Persephone: Like what, Hermes?

Hermes: Like these, I suppose.

Hermes sent screenshots

———

HERMES'S SCREENSHOT ONE

PRIVATE MESSAGE
JANUARY 4

8:03 AM
Aphrodite: Hello, Hermes.

Aphrodite: I wanted to speak to you.

8:04 AM
Hermes: I can't imagine whatever you would want to talk with me about, miss.

Aphrodite: See, I've known all British people to be very trustworthy and upstanding people. Anyone with an accent like that must be reliable and virtuous.

Hermes: I suppose that's one example of correlation versus causation.

8:05 AM
Aphrodite: And since you have a fake British accent, I figure, "That's close enough."

Aphrodite: Now, my father is taking too long in getting rid of that abomination of an app called DearHades. Perhaps you've heard of it?

8:06 AM
Hermes: Why no, miss!

Aphrodite: Oh, well you're not missing out on much. Hades—shifty guy as he always is—even had the audacity to lie and say you were one of the developers. Typical of him, right? First to lie about Persephone actually being in love with him, when Eros never flung an arrow of love at her for him.

8:07 AM
Aphrodite: Then to be deceitful about this.

Hermes: I am shocked and dismayed. Dismayed, I tell you.

Aphrodite: Well, I'm glad I put you to the wise. Maybe my husband Hephaestus can try to erase your names on that app store listing. They had the audacity to put him down as one of the developers too.

8:08 AM

Hermes: Will the suspense never cease?

8:09 AM
Aphrodite: I know two very true things now, Hermes, thanks to you.

Aphrodite: One, that you are a trustworthy deity.

Hermes: Obliged.

Aphrodite: Two, I'm always one for spilling tea, and I just can't contain all of these screenshots buried in my photos. May I share them with you?

8:10 AM
Hermes: I don't know. Privacy is an important part of the structure of society.

Aphrodite sent many screenshots

———

APHRODITE'S SCREENSHOT ONE

Aphrodite's To-Do List for Today (January 3)
   Task One: Bug Zeus incessantly about anything he's found wrong about the app.
   Status: Done.
   Task Two: After realizing Zeus has no intention of taking down DearHades, ask around for other people who are willing to take it down.
   Status: Done, reached out to Hephaestus and Iris.
   Task Three: When Hephaestus and Iris claim they don't want to "get involved," search for a chaos agent who is willing to wreak havoc in the app.

Status: In progress, will seek out a fury. Will also disguise myself as a profile in the app to find furies, since DearHades is so dang good at helping beings connect with one another.

————

APHRODITE'S SCREENSHOT TWO

YOU MATCHED!

Name: Aphrodite (Greek, preferred). Venus (Roman). Definitely not the goddess of love. That's just coincidentally my name.

Interested In: Chaos Agents, especially furies

Bio: I'm a huge fan of this app. Such a big fan that I wonder what would happen if it had some glitches introduced to it. Hahaha, just kidding. That would be really mean. But seriously, has anyone else ever wanted to see what would happen if some bugs got implemented? If so, let's talk.

Name: Furry Real Friend

Interested In: All Beings

Bio: UWU, you have found my profile *blushes* OWO OWU, let's be friends. Furry, but the technical term is feathery or avian. But furry is fine too. I know it would make more sense of an avian to have OVO in their profile, but I prefer OWO *ducks, ready to be hit by all the angry rotten tomatoes of Chads*

————

APHRODITE'S SCREENSHOT THREE

PRIVATE MESSAGE
JANUARY 3

10:04 AM

Furry Real Friend: UWU, you are very pwetty. *blushes and looks away shyly*

10:05 AM
Aphrodite: Yes, yes, so I've been told. Born out of seafoam and all. Let's cut to the chase. Can you or can you not mess with this app?

Furry Real Friend: OWO

Furry Real Friend: Mess with it? OWU

Furry Real Friend: But then I cannot talk to the pwetty lady. *flaps my feathers to try to woo the pretty lady with a bird dance*

10:06 AM
Aphrodite: You are a fury, yes?

Furry Real Friend: A furry, yes. UWU

Furry Real Friend: *clicks my beak and sighs, knowing the pretty lady probably won't take interest in wittle ol' me*

Aphrodite: Spell check not working on your keyboard?

Aphrodite: You are a chaos agent who can shapeshift and seek out the destruction of men?

10:07 AM
Furry Real Friend: I don't know about that ... *gasps, looking confused and bewildered*

Aphrodite: But you look just like a fury in your profile. You have wings and seem very birdlike.

Furry Real Friend: A furry, yes. *blushes*

Aphrodite: Why do you keep adding an extra R?

10:09 AM
Aphrodite: So I learned what a furry is.

Aphrodite: You dress in a mortal mascot costume and have conventions and competitions and things? Is that what a furry is?

Furry Real Friend: An oversimplification, but yes. OWO

10:10 AM
Aphrodite: How did you even get on this app? It's for Ancient Greek beings.

Aphrodite: Never mind. I'm looking for a fury, with one R. I shall leave you be, mortal in a bird costume.

Aphrodite left the conversation

Furry Real Friend: OWO

———

APHRODITE'S SCREENSHOT FOUR

YOU MATCHED!
    Name: Alecto, a Fury
    Interested In: Chaos, but I suppose All Beings if I have the time
    Bio: Just like mortal dating apps have bot accounts, immortal ones have beings like me on it. Up for a good time full of destruction? You know which direction to swipe. Oh, and if you ran into a furry, that was thanks to me. Decided to let him on the app for a bit of fun.
    Name: Aphrodite (Greek, preferred). Venus (Roman). Definitely not the goddess of love. That's just coincidentally my name.
    Interested In: Chaos Agents, especially furies

Bio: I'm a huge fan of this app. Such a big fan that I wonder what would happen if it had some glitches introduced to it. Hahaha, just kidding. That would be really mean. But seriously, has anyone else ever wanted to see what would happen if some bugs got implemented? If so, let's talk.

———

APHRODITE'S SCREENSHOT FIVE

PRIVATE MESSAGE
JANUARY 3

3:08 PM
Aphrodite: Alecto?

3:09 PM
Alecto: Afternoon, dear. How may I rain destruction on your day?

3:10 PM
Aphrodite: How would you like to mess with this app?

Alecto: It would be my pleasure.

3:11 PM
Alecto: How about some glitches and I let some more people who aren't Ancient Greek on the app—just like that Furry Real Friend?

Alecto: The more glitches, the more bad reviews the app will receive.

Alecto: The more bad reviews, the fewer customers.

Alecto: Sounds like a deal?

3:12 PM
Aphrodite: That sounds like a beautiful start.

————

HERMES'S SCREENSHOT TWO

PRIVATE MESSAGE
JANUARY 4

8:21 AM
Aphrodite: So, Hermes, what do you think? Alecto is planning to get started today. Full force on January fifth, once she gets back from her vacation in the Bermuda Triangle.

8:22 AM
Hermes: I think ...

Hermes: I think this could certainly put a wrench in things.

————

1:36 PM
Persephone: Wow, that was a lot of screenshots. It was like screenshot-ception.

1:37 PM
Hermes: What are your thoughts, miss?

1:38 PM
Persephone: I'm trying to process while also not creating more plants that can eat my husband.

Hades: Thank you.

1:39 PM

Persephone: We're already up to our eyeballs in chasing down all of Zeus's profiles. He's created several hundred accounts by this point. Always disguises himself as some animal, thinking a duck or platypus will somehow woo all the ladies.

> **Hermes:** In his defense, have you seen Perry the Platypus, miss?

1:40 PM

Persephone: And as much as I love the shades who are monitoring app activity ...

Persephone: I may have spent too much time in their education about different dog breeds. And not enough time on how to spot spammer accounts on dating apps.

> **Hades:** You didn't know, sweetheart. You only had three months a year to educate them. Even if their education *did* span thousands of years ...

1:41 PM

Persephone: Can this day get any worse?

> **Hermes:** Evidently it can. I've been receiving a great deal of updates from the shades, and ...

Persephone: And what?

> **Hermes:** A number of monster accounts are going dead. They will go on dates with mortals, and then their account activity just stops.

1:42 PM

Hades: Maybe they found their perfect match?

Hermes: Doubtful. The heroes who matched with them continue swiping afterward.

Persephone: Should we be worried?

Hades: Aphrodite talks a lot at the annual Olympus party I'm invited to once a year.

1:43 PM
Hades: From what I can tell from her conversations about human dating life now, many mortals keep their accounts active on dating apps, but may not regularly use them.

Persephone: Why's that?

Hades: Maybe they went on a bad date and decided to give the app a break.

1:44 PM
Hermes: One can hope that's what's occurring on DearHades. But we'll keep an eye on monster activity.

Hermes: If something more insidious is taking place, however ...

Persephone: Then we would need to shut down the app.

Hades: Are you sure—?

Persephone: Positive.

1:45 PM
Persephone: Darling, I love you dearly. And I will do whatever it takes to find two oddballs and stick them together on a date. Even if I have to go knocking on all the apartment doors in Grove City.

Persephone: To prove our eccentric love story is replicable and not a fluke to Demeter.

Persephone: But Ancient Greece was a dangerous place. For women, for monsters, for foreigners ...

1:46 PM
Persephone: And now that we've been given a second chance to do it all over, we CANNOT allow anyone's safety to be put in jeopardy.

Hades: I love you.

Persephone: I'm well aware, darling. For now, let's tackle one thing at a time. Starting with Aphrodite letting a bunch of non–Ancient Greeks on the app.

1:47 PM
Hermes: What's to do?

Persephone: We try even harder. I'll go in and personally boot as many accounts as needed.

Persephone: If Demeter and Aphrodite are so keen on taking down me and Hades, it must be a relationship worth fighting for, right?

1:48 PM
Hermes: To be honest, miss.

Hermes: All the best things in life tend to require the biggest fights to keep them.

You Matched!

Name: Hippolyta (Amazonian, preferred)

Interested In: Killing Men

Bio: Looking to take out a man, if you know what I mean. Queen of a group of female warriors—who occasionally get with men outside of our borders to produce more females. Men, swipe if you wish for your last days on this mortal world.

———

Name: Tiresias (Greek), Ty (American, because baristas have a hard time spelling the other one). No preference which you use.

Interested In: All Beings

Bio: I'm a prophet, so I can foresee many future conversations about art and dogs. Joined the app on the first day it was out, but apparently, it's important to include I'm also blind. Some people DMing me said so. So I'm blind. There. Anyway, let's talk about my dog. :D

Private Message

January 5

7:03 AM
Tiresias: Just got the notification that you swiped. It's rather early. Are you on the other side of the world? I know some people who got brought back moved back into the Mediterranean area. They felt more at home.

7:04 AM
Hippolyta: Listen, mortal man, here is the plan.

Hippolyta: I will send Pegasus to fly you to Themiskyra. He now lives here and enjoys our bountiful vegetation.

Hippolyta: You will arrive in my homeland and will prepare yourself for a duel of honor.

7:05 AM
Hippolyta: You will draw your sword. I, my arrow. Our battle will be committed to legends.

Hippolyta: I will spill your blood. It will water the ground. This is why our vegetation thrives.

Hippolyta: Then you shall die.

7:06 AM
Hippolyta: When you leave this mortal earth, the Amazonians will throw a feast in your honor. We shall eat a suckling pig and many meats. We do not make bread. For we do not belong in kitchens.

7:07 AM
Hippolyta: We shall then burn your body and scatter your ashes in the sea.

7:08 AM
Hippolyta: What time shall I send Pegasus to pick you up? Is three minutes enough time for you to get ready?

7:09 AM
Tiresias: Does this—does this tactic actually work on men?

7:10 AM
Hippolyta: We have thrown ten feasts within the last ten days.

Tiresias unswiped Hippolyta

You Matched!

Name: Medousa (Greek), Medusa (Roman, preferred because everyone always refers to me that way)

   Interested In: Mortals and Monsters

   Bio: Yes, I have snake hair. No, the tusks and wings, though cool, are just rumors. Looking for online pals because I will turn you to stone in person, unfortunately.

Name: Tiresias (Greek), Ty (American, because baristas have a hard time spelling the other one). No preference which you use.

   Interested In: All Beings

   Bio: I'm a prophet, so I can foresee many future conversations about art and dogs. Joined the app on the first day it was out, but apparently, it's important to include I'm also blind. Some people DMing me said so. So I'm blind. There. Anyway, let's talk about my dog. :D

Private Message

January 5

8:23 AM
Tiresias: Ugh, I thought we unswiped each other. Why is this app so glitchy?

Tiresias unswiped Medusa

You Matched!

Name: Narcissus
   Interested In: Narcissus
   Bio: I love you so much, Narcissus. You are more beautiful than anything in all the world. I would do anything for you, my beloved. My gorgeous, amazing Narcissus. Only here to match with other profiles I created for myself.

————

Name: Medousa (Greek), Medusa (Roman, preferred because everyone always refers to me that way)
   Interested In: Mortals and Monsters
   Bio: Yes, I have snake hair. No, the tusks and wings, though cool, are just rumors. Looking for online pals because I will turn you to stone in person, unfortunately.

Private Message

8:39 AM
Medusa: Hey, Narcissus. Didn't expect you to swipe on anyone but yourself.

Narcissus: Most beautiful man in all the world, how glad I am to behold you.

8:40 AM
Medusa: Nope, not man, not beautiful, and no beholding. You know Echo has swiped on, like, all of your profiles, right? Maybe you could stop being obsessed with yourself for two seconds and at least give the girl a proper rejection?

Narcissus: You are not me? :'(

8:41 AM
Medusa: No, but that's a good thing. You really need to talk to other people. I can give you the name of some therapists.

Narcissus: Am *I* a therapist? I would love to talk to myself. :)

Medusa: I have no idea what Echo sees in you.

8:42 AM
Narcissus: Pardon me, I have an appointment with my mirror. Ta-ta.

Narcissus unswiped Medusa

You Matched!

Name: Kirke, Circe (preferred)
    Interested In: All Beings
    Bio: Sorceress, girl boss, feminist icon. If you are Odysseus, I will turn your men into pigs again. Honestly, give me even the slightest provocation, and I will turn anyone into an animal. In case you didn't catch it the first time, I hate you, Odysseus.

———

Name: Medousa (Greek), Medusa (Roman, preferred because everyone always refers to me that way)
    Interested In: Mortals and Monsters
    Bio: Yes, I have snake hair. No, the tusks and wings, though cool, are just rumors. Looking for online pals because I will turn you to stone in person, unfortunately.

Private Message

January 5

9:17 AM
Medusa: Hey, Circe. I don't think we've really talked before. I see you hate Odysseus too.

9:18 AM
Circe: Are you here to ask about working for my company? If so, you should know I have a rigorous vetting process.

Medusa: Oh, no, sorry. I'm just trying to make friends.

9:20 AM
Circe: In that case, any enemy of Odysseus is a friend of mine. Is he still lurking around this app?

Medusa: And killing monsters, yes. Have you talked to him?

Circe: Ha! I've blocked him three times. So if by talking to you mean hurling my foulest insults at him before hitting block, then yes.

9:21 AM
Medusa: I'm sorry he keeps bothering you. We monsters are trying to keep an eye on his activity. A lot of monsters keep going missing.

9:24 AM
Circe: I'm sorry, but I'm terribly busy running all five of my companies. I don't really have time for chitchat. Was there anything else you needed?

Medusa: Oh. No, that's okay. I'll leave you alone, then.

Circe: Good. If you see Odysseus, tell him I hate him.

9:25 AM
Circe: Actually, tell him to come by my office so I can tell him in person.

Circe: I'm a bit peeved. He hasn't created any new accounts lately for me to block.

9:26 AM
Circe: Do you think he's lost interest?

Medusa: Um, maybe?

Circe: How dare he.

9:27 AM
Circe: That's it, I'm going to find him and yell at him in person.

Circe: Turn some people into pigs.

Circe: And then show him he doesn't need Penelope.

9:28 AM
Medusa: Wait, what?

Circe unswiped Medusa

You Matched!

Name: Hera (Greek, preferred), Juno (Roman)

    Interested In: Finding my lousy husband on this app

    Bio: Zeus, when I find you, I will kill you. For real this time. And anyone who is matching with him, I have plenty of curses brewing for you.

———

Name: Tiresias (Greek), Ty (American, because baristas have a hard time spelling the other one). No preference which you use.

    Interested In: All Beings

    Bio: I'm a prophet, so I can foresee many future conversations about art and dogs. Joined the app on the first day it was out, but apparently, it's important to include I'm also blind. Some people DMing me said so. So I'm blind. There. Anyway, let's talk about my dog. :D

Private Message

January 5

9:43 AM
Hera: Zeus, get your behind back home. Or so help me, I'll turn your behind into a pair of feet so they will walk you back up to Olympus.

9:44 AM
Tiresias: I'm so sorry, Hera, I accidentally swiped right. I couldn't even imagine ever dating a goddess. Being a mere mortal and all.

Tiresias: And do you start every conversation this way?

9:45 AM
Hera: Zeus is on this app in disguise. You can never be too sure.

Hera: How do I know you aren't my cheating husband?

Tiresias: I—I just am not? I'm not sure how to prove it.

9:46 AM
Hera: Fret not. I have a foolproof test to be sure whether I am speaking with a mortal or with my poor excuse of a husband.

Hera: I'm going to send one word, and I want you to send me the first word or phrase that comes to mind.

   Tiresias: Okay?

9:47 AM
Hera: Women.

   Tiresias: Women are cool? I don't mind talking with them?

Hera: You are not my husband.

Hera: At the mere sight of the word women, he goes into a frenzy and starts creating thunderstorms in the sky.

9:48 AM
Hera: As there were no thunderstorms in the Grove City area, where I suspect he is hiding and going on dates, you have proven yourself to be a mere mortal.

Hera: I will not curse you this day.

   Tiresias: Thank you?

9:49 AM
Hera: I will, however, curse whoever my husband is on a date with.

Hera: And the creators of this app.

Hera: After I punish Aphrodite for creating StupidCupid. As Zeus has over one hundred accounts on that app as well.

9:50 AM
Hera: Farewell.

Hera unswiped Tiresias

You Matched!

Name: Medousa (Greek), Medusa (Roman, preferred because everyone always refers to me that way)

    Interested In: Mortals and Monsters

    Bio: Yes, I have snake hair. No, the tusks and wings, though cool, are just rumors. Looking for online pals because I will turn you to stone in person, unfortunately.

———

Name: Tiresias (Greek), Ty (American, because baristas have a hard time spelling the other one). No preference which you use.

    Interested In: All Beings

    Bio: I'm a prophet, so I can foresee many future conversations about art and dogs. Joined the app on the first day it was out, but apparently, it's important to include I'm also blind. Some people DMing me said so. So I'm blind. There. Anyway, let's talk about my dog. :D

Private Message

January 5

9:54 AM
Tiresias: Argh, I'm sorry. The app keeps glitching and matching me with you.

9:56 AM
Tiresias: I'll unswipe again, but know I seriously didn't want to do it. To go through with what I was asked to do on the date. I—there's no explanation that will make it okay, but you were the last person I wanted to throw into a snake pit.

Tiresias unswiped Medusa

You Matched!

Name: Just a Handsome Duck (but I've been called many names)

Interested In: All Beings

Bio: I am a completely innocent but also a very attractive duck. I've been told I am irresistible to women with an almost godlike allure and pure masculine energy. You've never had duck like this before.

———

Name: Medousa (Greek), Medusa (Roman, preferred because everyone always refers to me that way)

Interested In: Mortals and Monsters

Bio: Yes, I have snake hair. No, the tusks and wings, though cool, are just rumors. Looking for online pals because I will turn you to stone in person, unfortunately.

Private Message

January 5

10:23 AM
Medusa: Okay, despite the shocking amount of red flags in such a short bio, I had to swipe.

Medusa: I don't remember a duck in Greek mythology, and I have so, so many questions.

> **Just a Handsome Duck:** Quack quack, beautiful.

10:24 AM
Medusa: Are you an actual duck? I know there are a lot of weird creatures in Greek mythology, but animals don't usually talk.

> **Just a Handsome Duck:** Does it really matter what I am, or does it only matter what we can be ... together? Quack.

Medusa: I'm beginning to regret my curiosity. You're not a real duck, clearly.

> 10:25 AM
> **Just a Handsome Duck:** Of course I am. Quack quack.

10:26 AM
Just a Handsome Duck: Don't leave, sweet thing. I imagine you've never had a duck lover before.

Medusa: You are certainly right. Honestly, the closest thing I can think of where something like that happened in Greek mythology was when a swan turned out to be ...

Medusa: Zeus.

10:27 AM
Just a Handsome Duck: Still interested? ;) ;) ;)

Medusa unswiped Just a Handsome Duck

You Matched!

Name: Eurydice

Interested In: Mortals

Bio: Really down for a man who freaking follows instructions. Yeah, I'm looking at you, Orpheus. I sneeze one time as we're leaving the Underworld—when you were specifically instructed not to turn around or I would die. But no. You had to turn around and say "bless you," sending me to an eternal grave because of it ... Also, I really like music.

———

Name: Tiresias (Greek), Ty (American, because baristas have a hard time spelling the other one). No preference which you use.

Interested In: All Beings

Bio: I'm a prophet, so I can foresee many future conversations about art and dogs. Joined the app on the first day it was out, but apparently, it's important to include I'm also blind. Some people DMing me said so. So I'm blind. There. Anyway, let's talk about my dog. :D

Private Message

January 5

11:12 AM
Tiresias: Hi, Eurydice. I know you swiped on me a while back, but I've been catching up on messages after a really unsuccessful matching with someone else.

11:23 AM
Eurydice: Sorry, just saw this. Good to hear from you, Tiresias.

11:24 AM
Eurydice: So this is awkward, but I'm actually probably deleting this app today.

Tiresias: Oh? Did you also have a bad experience on a date? Someone tried to kill you too?

Eurydice: Too? What? Are you okay? Who tried to kill you?

11:25 AM
Eurydice: And no, I actually found Orpheus on this app. Just when I'd given up all hope on my lover being one of the ones resur-

rected, I spotted him. We've been chatting all morning and plan to meet up soon.

Eurydice: And would you believe it? It was actually due to a glitch! I'd swiped on someone else and Orpheus's profile appeared.

Tiresias: A glitch?

11:26 AM
Tiresias: And that's amazing, Eurydice. I'm so happy for you! That's encouraging. I'd figured everyone who was going to return already did.

Eurydice: Indeed. I don't know when the cutoff is.

Eurydice: I don't know if they've stopped bringing people back, or if people are still returning. But there's hope for all of us, right?

Tiresias: Yeah. There are definitely some people I would love to see again.

11:27 AM
Tiresias: And I wonder if any of the heroes' lovers are back. Maybe if they are, they can stop this war on monsters.

Eurydice: War on monsters?

Tiresias: Long story, involving a gorgon and ... trust me, you probably don't want to know.

11:28 AM
Eurydice: Oh, speaking of gorgons, I remember something very distinctive from the resurrection process.

Tiresias: You do?

11:29 AM
Eurydice: For sure. Most people don't recall that part. They just remember waking up in some apartment in Pennsylvania with a pamphlet on the floor beside them that read "So You've Been Brought Back after Thousands of Years."

Eurydice: But considering I have a special connection with the Underworld, I tend to remember more than most people about that place.

11:30 AM
Tiresias: That's a blessing. I only recall bits and pieces. Mostly Persephone's lessons as she tried to educate us on human affairs. She spends nine months in the mortal world, so I'm sure she was itching to share everything she learned with whomever she could.

Eurydice: Most shades don't remember much. Especially if they landed in the Fields of Asphodel.

11:31 AM
Tiresias: The place where ordinary souls go to forget. I remember.

Eurydice: But I do remember two important details.

Eurydice: One, a god in full Greek armor was the one who brought us back. He must've stormed the gates of Hades.

11:32 AM
Tiresias: In Greek armor ... Ares?

Eurydice: Sounds about right. He's all for stirring up chaos and conflict. If he brought monsters AND mortals AND demigods AND whoever else back, that's a recipe for a brawl.

11:33 AM
Tiresias: What was the second thing you remember?

Eurydice: He poured something on us from an amphora jar. I don't think any of us needed more than a few drops. But one moment, he was flicking something dark and disgusting at my face. And the next ... I was in Pennsylvania.

Tiresias: Please tell me it wasn't gorgon blood.

11:34 AM
Eurydice: I don't know, my dude. It's not like Ares was like, "Flick, flick, you get some gorgon blood. And YOU get some gorgon blood."

Tiresias: But did it look ... bloody?

Eurydice: It did look dark brown, so it definitely wasn't water. And honestly, with everyone's theories about gorgon blood floating around this app, that's what I assumed it was.

Tiresias: Oh gods.

11:35 AM
Eurydice: What's wrong?

Tiresias: Do you happen to know how much is left? Gorgon blood—or whatever the brown substance was in that jar.

11:36 AM
Eurydice: I wish I knew.

Eurydice: Even if it takes a few drops per person, a ton of the Underworld has been emptied. And not all of us are living in Grove,

PA, mind you. I've heard of people on this app getting apartments in other cheap places. Like Westminster, MD. Conway, AR. Those were a couple that were mentioned.

11:37 AM
Tiresias: We have to hope there's some gorgon blood left. Maybe it can still be found in the House of Hades. Maybe we could bring back Megara and Penelope and ... Manto ... and all this monsters versus heroes stuff can stop.

11:57 AM
Eurydice: So sorry, Orpheus is distracting me. Best of luck. Maybe your person will come back. Maybe there's still some blood left.

Tiresias: Yeah maybe, I—

Tiresias: THE GATES OF HADES HAVE BEEN SHUT.

11:58 AM
Eurydice: Tiresias?

Tiresias: THE NATURAL ORDER OF ALL THINGS HAS BEEN DISTURBED. HEROES OF OLD, TREACHEROUS MONSTERS, MERE MORTALS HAVE RETURNED TO THE LAND OF THE LIVING.

Eurydice: Is this how you prophesy now?

11:59 AM
Tiresias: BUT NO LONGER. FOR ARES HAS BEEN FOUND IN THE UNDERWORLD, AND THE BLOOD OF THE GORGON HAS BEEN CONFISCATED.

Eurydice: Oh.

Tiresias: No longer shall shades return to the land of the living, except if a mortal or hero shall once again storm the gates of Hades with gorgon blood and release the souls of the departed.

12:00 PM
Eurydice: Well this is very awkward.

12:02 PM
Tiresias: Oh, my head. Eurydice, what did I just prophesy?

Eurydice: I don't know how to say this nicely.

Eurydice: But no one is coming back from the Underworld, unless you go and get 'em yourself. With some new gorgon blood. Since I guess Hades or Thanatos or whoever in the Underworld confiscated the other stuff.

Tiresias: Gaia.

12:03 PM
Eurydice: But who knows? Maybe your person isn't dead after all. Maybe they're still alive and kicking.

Tiresias: I want to believe that.

Tiresias: But I have this horrible feeling in my gut.

Eurydice: Ate too many tacos?

12:04 PM
Tiresias: That's what sucks about being a prophet.

Tiresias: You're almost never wrong.

You Matched!

Name: THOR (NORSE)
  Interested In: BRINGING THE THUNDER
  Bio: WIELDER OF THE MIGHTY MJOLNIR, PROTECTOR OF MANKIND, BRINGER OF THUNDER. I WISH TO ENJOY GOOD COMPANY AND FREE-FLOWING ALE.

———

Name: Medousa (Greek), Medusa (Roman, preferred because everyone always refers to me that way)
  Interested In: Mortals and Monsters
  Bio: Yes, I have snake hair. No, the tusks and wings, though cool, are just rumors. Looking for online pals because I will turn you to stone in person, unfortunately.

Private Message

January 5

1:03 PM
Medusa: Sorry, Mr. Thor, my friend Echo went through and swiped on every profile she came across. I didn't mean to bother you.

THOR: FRET NOT, SNAKE WOMAN, I ONLY WISH TO BEFRIEND ALL BEINGS AND INVITE THEM UNTO MY ALE HALL FOR A CELEBRATION.

1:04 PM
Medusa: Oh, that's nice. Um, I think we're from separate mythologies. I didn't know they opened it up beyond Greek beings. Is everyone allowed now?

THOR: EVERYONE IS INVITED TO THE CELEBRATION. EVERYONE. ESPECIALLY EVERY STRANGE CREATURE HAVING SOMETHING TO DO WITH SNAKES THAT I HAVE SWIPED UPON, NOT AT ALL HOPING THEY ARE IN FACT LOKI. I WILL FIND YOU, LOKI.

1:05 PM
Medusa: Oh yes, that's very nice of you, Mr. Thor. I meant allowed on the app.

THOR: BRING FORTH MORE MEAD. I ENJOY THIS GAME CALLED HIDING AND SEEKING.

1:06 PM
Medusa: Yes, well, I'm going to leave you alone now, have a very nice day.

Medusa unswiped Thor

THOR: IT APPEARS YOU WERE NOT LOKI. I WILL CONTINUE SEEKING.

You Matched!

Name: Ammit (Egyptian)

Interested In: All Beings, especially their souls

Bio: Nom nom nom, I'm hungry for some souls today. If you die, definitely swipe right on me. Because if your heart is heavier than the feather of Ma'at, the feather of truth, that means you're my next meal. Don't let the crocodile face, hippopotamus hindquarters, or lion's feet scare you away. I really am quite the catch.

———

Name: Tiresias (Greek), Ty (American, because baristas have a hard time spelling the other one). No preference which you use.

Interested In: All Beings

Bio: I'm a prophet, so I can foresee many future conversations about art and dogs. Joined the app on the first day it was out, but apparently, it's important to include I'm also blind. Some people DMing me said so. So I'm blind. There. Anyway, let's talk about my dog. :D

Private Message

January 5

1:32 PM
Tiresias: I really need to stop swiping when I'm tired and my brain isn't fully functioning.

1:34 PM
Ammit: What's the matter, sweetheart? Is your soul feeling a little downcast?

Ammit: I can lighten your load.

Ammit: Do you mind ripping your heart out of your chest so I can have my friend weigh it against a feather?

1:33 PM
Tiresias: You know what, I'm good. Thanks, though.

Tiresias: Also, what are you doing on this app? I thought it was for those in Greek mythology only.

Shade Admin has entered the chat

Shade Admin has removed Ammit's account

1:34 PM
Tiresias: Oh, um, thank you Shade Admin for vigilantly taking Egyptian soul eaters off this app. I'll be out of your hair now.

Tiresias has left the chat

1:35 PM
Shade Admin: Tiresias?

1:37 PM
Shade Admin: Why does your name sound so familiar?

You Matched!

Name: Tiresias (Greek), Ty (American, because baristas have a hard time spelling the other one). No preference which you use.

Interested In: All Beings

Bio: I'm a prophet, so I can foresee many future conversations about art and dogs. Joined the app on the first day it was out, but apparently, it's important to include I'm also blind. Some people DMing me said so. So I'm blind. There. Anyway, let's talk about my dog. :D

———

Name: Medousa (Greek), Medusa (Roman, preferred because everyone always refers to me that way)

Interested In: Mortals and Monsters

Bio: Yes, I have snake hair. No, the tusks and wings, though cool, are just rumors. Looking for online pals because I will turn you to stone in person, unfortunately.

Private Message

January 5

5:32 PM
Tiresias: It seems the app really wants us to talk, because it keeps glitching and re-matching us.

5:34 PM
Medusa: I guess. Since we're stuck in here again ... what did you mean you didn't want to throw me into the snake enclosure? You seemed pretty determined.

Tiresias: So I was set up on the date.

Tiresias: And I don't mean set up, set up, like the cute romantic movies where the man and woman end up dancing together and ... I don't know. Hercules was describing them to me yesterday and they made no sense.

5:35 PM
Tiresias: Anyway, I mean, someone set me up to murder you. And long story short, threatened someone I love. So I didn't have much of a choice.

Medusa: Huh. Those people wouldn't happen to be your posse of hero friends, would they? Like, Odysseus? *vomit emoji*

Tiresias: Ha. Friends is a loose term.

5:36 PM
Tiresias: Friends don't threaten to kill your friends. Unless, I suppose, in middle school. That is supposedly a rampant time for jealousy.

Tiresias: But yeah, how did you figure it out? Did the app glitch some screenshots to your group of monster boss babes?

Medusa: No, but they did see your name listed in the "Heroes before Monster-os" chat. Real classy name.

5:37 PM
Tiresias: Yeah, that's what happens when you let a guy with two brain cells figure out the group name.

Tiresias: I didn't know names were listed, but yeah, if you must know, they added me. I couldn't stand heroes in Ancient Greece. They were so cocky and just did whatever they wanted. Sort of like mini gods.

5:38 PM
Medusa: Names aren't usually listed, but something tells me Odysseus wanted everyone to know who was in his cool-guy squad.

Medusa: So they, uh, blackmailed you, huh?

Medusa: I guess that makes sense ... I did wonder why someone like you would be involved with the heroes.

5:39 PM
Medusa: Listen. I really, really didn't want to kill you either.

Tiresias: So did *you* get blackmailed?

Tiresias: Did someone threaten to eat you? Threaten to throw you into frying oil? I hear that's common.

5:40 PM
Medusa: No. I'm almost ashamed to say I wasn't blackmailed. But it seemed like, from the evidence ... See, a lot of monsters have been going missing. Killed by heroes.

Tiresias: Wait, really?

Tiresias: Odysseus swore he wouldn't kill monsters while I was going on dates with you. That was part of the agreement. That and he wouldn't kill Antigone if I managed to, um, follow through with my part.

5:41 PM
Medusa: Unfortunately for all involved, it seems he lied. Plenty of monsters went missing during our dates. And my friends pointed out that if the heroes wanted me dead, you would be the perfect person to do it, since I can't turn you to stone.

Medusa: And ... I guess it made sense. Because why else would someone want to go on dates with a snake-haired monster?

5:42 PM
Tiresias: Hold on, don't say that. It was extremely hard to go through with it because you're really incredible.

Tiresias: But this monster-going-missing stuff is serious. Don't you think we should get some admins involved?

Medusa: I think the admins have been really distracted with all the glitches and fake profiles. It may not be enough to just report it.

Medusa: We may need to go straight to the leaders of the Underworld.

5:43 PM
Tiresias: Yikes, that seems more like an in-person conversation. Hercules has talked about storming the gates of Hades ... and honestly, just mentioning it may alert an admin.

Tiresias: We may need to meet in person, just for privacy purposes. And logistics. I mean, when was the last time you tackled Cerberus?

5:44 PM
Medusa: I agree. We probably shouldn't talk about any specifics on the app. And not because it might get admin attention—that might actually be a good thing. But because with all these glitches, screenshots keep getting sent around. And to me, angry heroes are even scarier than Cerberus.

Tiresias: I bet that's a PR nightmare for Zeus.

Medusa: Ah yes ... Zeus. I met a not-Zeus-at-all duck the other day ...

5:45 PM
Tiresias: Well, I bumped into his wife. So, fun times. Can't wait for those two to find each other on the app.

Tiresias: But if we do meet in person, we have to promise each other something. I think it's fair to say both of us have trust issues.

Tiresias: How do we know we won't kill each other in person?

5:46 PM
Tiresias: I swore for our last date I wasn't going to follow through. Then Odysseus swooped in with the Antigone threat. So how do I know Echo isn't going to tell you to throw frying oil at me?

Medusa: So for the record, Echo wasn't the one who killed the guy in frying oil, despite what the tabloids might tell you.

Medusa: But anyway, maybe we need a neutral third party?

5:47 PM
Tiresias: Who did you have in mind?

Medusa: Well, I can bring Echo. She's not a monster, so I don't think she's particularly scary. And she remembers everything from every conversation she ever hears. So she can keep track of it in case we forget anything.

Medusa: Who do you want to bring?

5:48 PM
Tiresias: I like the idea of bringing another person each. Like a double date, to prevent murder.

Tiresias: I guess I could have Hercules tag along. I know he has a history with monsters ... but honestly, ever since he's been back, I don't think he's done anything like he used to. We've had some chats when he breaks down my apartment door and brings donuts. And I may be swaying his opinions on monsters.

5:49 PM
Medusa: Well, I don't know the real Hercules, but I love that Disney movie. So I think that's fair.

    Tiresias: Trust me, *he* loves the Disney movie too.

    Tiresias: This sounds like a plan. Where shall we meet? Preferably no graves, and no poisonous snakes. Sorry, Bobart.

Medusa: No one ever suspects something nefarious going down in a cute coffee shop. How about we go to Coffee Muses?

5:50 PM
    Tiresias: Yes, the coincidentally Ancient Greek–themed coffee shop that so happens to be in this very town.

    Tiresias: What day? The seventh? I have rehearsal tomorrow for a good chunk of the day.

    Tiresias: Unless you want to choreograph "You're Never Fully Dressed without a Smile."

    Tiresias: Don't worry. Everyone is dressed in more than a smile.

5:51 PM
Medusa: Ha! Well, it would be very Ancient Greek of them to do things without clothes. But yes, the seventh. Coffee shop. High noon, like a Western.

Medusa: And we'll figure out how to break BACK into the Underworld.

Reviews for DearHades in the App Store

Average Rating: 4.8 Stars

Aphrodite, One Star

This app sucks. So glitchy. Bot profiles. Would give zero stars if I could.

Io, Five Stars

The people on this app—except for many of the heroes, I will say—are accepting of cursed people. For those who don't know, I got turned into a cow thanks to Zeus. And then Hera sent a gadfly after me … You know what? You can just Google it. But the funny thing is, the app glitched and matched me with my long-lost lover Telegonus. Crazy, right? An app that finally glitched right. Telegonus has gone through quite the wringer, so I'm not sure if we'll hit it off right away. Could take a few years. But knowing love, it's worth the wait.

Eurydice, Five Stars

Wow. This app seriously delivered. I know some people mentioned in former reviews about it being glitchy, but honestly? I swear the glitches were delivered by the Fates or some benevolent being. Because they matched me with my long-lost lover. It was almost like Cupid himself had jumped into the app. Thank you, DearHades, for giving me another chance with Orpheus. We have quite a bit of catching up to do, so I don't foresee an engagement

190

for at least another year, haha. There's quite a bit of trauma to work through. But I think our future looks promising.

Narcissus, Five Stars

I keep swiping right on this beauty, who happens to look like me, haha. Great app. A little glitchy. Keeps trying to set me up with someone named Echo. But otherwise, solid.

Eros, One Star

Literally copied StupidCupid, and isn't nearly as good. And the founder Hades has a sketchy love life. Wouldn't trust this app for anything.

Bellerophon, Five Stars

Found my long-lost wife on here. Thank you, DearHades and whatever glitch that accidentally matched me to her! I know the app's mission is to set up two new people, so sorry, Persephone, if I couldn't help you with that, since I already knew my wife before this. Also, has anyone seen my winged horse Pegasus? Haven't been able to find him since I got brought back.

Read 1004+ More Reviews

Wanna Commit Murder with Me, Babe?

January 6

3:07 AM
Hades: Are you up, babe?

3:08 AM
Persephone: No.

Persephone: Why would you think that?

3:09 AM
Hades: Because I see the fridge light.

Hades: And because you just wrapped my feet in a bunch of vines. I ... definitely cannot leave my spot right now.

Persephone: I'm asleep. Zzzzz. And definitely not stealing the last of the pomegranate-flavored frozen yogurt from the freezer. No sir.

3:10 AM
Hades: Thank you for removing those vines.

Hades: Why are you up? You've been burning the candle at both ends. You're averaging three hours of sleep a night. Our room has been transformed into a jungle ...

Hades: I'm worried about you.

3:11 AM
Persephone: I know. I woke up from a nightmare and decided to read our app reviews.

Hades: Seph ...

Persephone: Yes, yes, I'm well aware that reading reviews is a great way to make someone stressy or depressy, but I had to know if someone met their match yet. I know we're only a few weeks in, but ...

3:12 AM
Hades: What?

Persephone: The reviews aren't bad. Aphrodite's glitches actually may be helping people find their true love. In fact, most of the one stars are just Aphrodite and her posse.

Hades: That's great!

Persephone: Uh-huh. Except for the part about the bet that two new people have to meet. No long-lost lovers or spouses. Since our app didn't originally put them together.

3:13 AM
Hades: Did your mother say those exact words?

Persephone: Yup. She laid out the agreement in an entire contract I signed when we made the bet.

Persephone sent a file

3:23 AM
Hades: Wow, that thing is extensive.

Persephone: Right?

Hades: It's twenty-eight pages long. My eyes are getting blurry just scanning through it.

Persephone: I may have eaten a few too many slabs of ambrosia before I signed it.

3:24 AM
Hades: Darling.

Hades: You know you can't handle much ambrosia. It goes right to your head.

3:25 AM
Persephone: Yes, I'm aware. But when your mother, for the one thousandth time, tells Zeus how she "worries for her daughter, being interloped with that horrible lord of the dead," you start shoving your face with ambrosia like it's baklava. And then suddenly, you're signing your life away on a twenty-something-page contract.

3:26 AM
Persephone: But the contract makes it plain and simple. Two NEW people have to match.

Persephone: So as great as the glitches are in reuniting people, it's completely up to our app to put two newbie whackos together.

Persephone: And get them engaged sometime early September, and—

3:27 AM
Hades: Babe, are you crying? You've wrapped vines around my feet again, so I can't leave my room.

Hades: Can you remove them? They've started singing Broadway tunes.

3:28 AM
Persephone: Ach, my plant life must be getting sentient again. It's probably better to just let them finish their songs, and then they slink away. They get sad when I murder them.

3:29 AM
Persephone: But yeah, I'm getting a little teary. Because how can we expect two people to propose to each other in that short amount of time?

Hades: Sweetheart, we're right by a Christian college.

Hades: Those students make premarital eye contact, and five minutes later, pop a ring out of their pocket.

3:30 AM
Persephone: *sniffle* Yeah?

Hades: Yes, and you and I got together much faster than nine months. People do it all the time.

3:31 AM
Persephone: Uh-huh, and that's the whole reason why Demeter put the one-year stipulation on this. Because you and I "rushed it. If it's replicable, then surely two people can get engaged in that

amount of time. In fact, I'm being generous. I could say they need to get married. But I'll be kind."

Hades: Goodness. You remembered all that while your head was all woozy from the ambrosia?

3:32 AM
Persephone: Oh no, she recorded the whole thing. In case I didn't believe her later that it happened.

Persephone sent an audio file

Hades: Three hours long, huh? I'll listen to that later.

3:33 AM
Hades: We may not be able to count the long-lost couples who are finding each other.

Hades: But these beings who came back have gone thousands of years without this type of love.

Hades: They're eager for it. They've been thinking about it for centuries.

3:34 AM
Hades: Surely there's a couple on our app, right now, who are hitting it off as we speak.

Persephone: I'm sorry for eating all the pomegranate fro-yo. Maybe we can grab more at the store later today? After we get some sleep and do some more admin tasks for the app.

3:35 AM
Hades: How about you take today off, and we do some self-care instead?

Persephone: But, babe.

Hades: The shades will handle it. There are quite a few that have really gone above and beyond the call of duty. There's Penelope. She's great at catching people with fake accounts.

3:36 AM
Hades: And Patroclus, who is amazing at customer service whenever someone has a complaint. He's probably the reason for half our good reviews.

Persephone: Yeah ...

Hades: Oh, and Manto. She's amazing at foreseeing any glitches in the code and has eradicated most of the threats from Alecto before they even happen.

3:37 AM
Hades: She may even be the reason people are matching with their lovers. She foresees it and redirects the glitch.

Hades: You're in excellent hands, darling.

3:38 AM
Persephone: Yeah, well, since today is a "self-care" day, I think you know what this means.

Hades: Horror movies and nerf gun battles?

Persephone: I can't wait to shoot you in the face.

Hades: I love you too, sweetheart.

Heroes before Monster-os

January 6

8:07 PM

Odysseus: Okay, before we get this meeting started, I want to clarify a few things. Hercules, Tiresias claimed to go on mute in this chat, so I need to make sure he's truly not receiving notifications.

8:08 PM

Hercules: Oh yeah, I broke into his apartment again yesterday to give him donuts.

Hercules: He showed me how the technology on his phone works.

Hercules: Whenever he gets a message, his phone reads it to him.

Hercules: But I also know this chat was blowing up yesterday with LARPing pictures from Achilles and Perseus.

8:09 PM

Hercules: And his phone didn't go off once.

Hercules: So I guess when he puts a conversation on mute, it really is ... almost like ... what's the word I'm looking for? Like the conversation can't speak to him.

Odysseus: Like it's mute?

8:10 PM
Hercules: Yeah, that's the word for it!

Odysseus: All right, second order of business, where is Tiresias tonight? Just so I know he won't be seeing any messages from this chat anytime soon.

8:11 PM
Hercules: I think he said something about rehearsals. Those run until nine or something.

Hercules: But I do know Tiresias will in fact yell at you if you ask if you can break the legs of the members of the cast.

Hercules: Apparently "break a leg" isn't meant to be taken for real.

8:12 PM
Achilles: Aren't there children in that cast?

Hercules: Oh, I was just going to break the director's leg. It's probably good luck, right? American customs are weird.

Odysseus: Thank you for answering the question about his whereabouts.

8:13 PM
Odysseus: Third order of business, did you manage to get Alecto to sign our W9 agreement so she can do some work for hire for us?

Hercules: You just said a lot of words I don't understand.

Odysseus: *sigh* Did Alecto agree to mess with the code? So we can delete conversations we don't want Tiresias to see?

8:14 PM
Hercules: Ohhhh, the fury? Yeah, so, funny story.

Perseus: BIRD.

Hercules: Great segue, Perseus. Thank you! This leads me right into the tale. So when you said to find a fury, my spell check or something messed up and connected me with someone who also looked like a bird.

8:15 PM
Hercules: He, um, how did he phrase it?

Hercules: *shakes my tail feathers at the himbo*

Hercules: And invited me to some convention or something.

8:16 PM
Hercules: I figured maybe the fury wanted to meet in person, since some people who came back aren't the biggest fans of phones and stuff. They want stuff to be like the good ol' days in Ancient Greece, where wars and famines were happening every other minute, and people had face-to-face conversations while stabbing each other.

Perseus: ANIMALS.

8:17 PM
Hercules: Right, thank you, Perseus, for keeping me on subject. So

I went to the convention and there were a bunch of people dressed up like animals.

Hercules: I got really confused. And embarrassed I hadn't brought a costume, so I went home.

8:18 PM
Hercules: Next thing I knew, the app glitched and set me up with a fury named Alecto.

Hercules: Anyway, long story short, I guess Alecto can, in fact, delete some messages. She says as long as you feed her some evil souls in the Underworld, she'll be happy.

> **Achilles:** That should be easy. Why don't we give her some of the monsters we've slayed in the last few days? They must be in Tartarus right now—the place of eternal torture.

8:19 PM
Odysseus: Good gods, Achilles, do you want the whole app to hear you?

Odysseus: Hercules, before we proceed, can you guarantee Alecto can delete conversation threads? As though it never happened.

> **Hercules:** I dunno, let me send you the email she forwarded to me.

Hercules sent a screenshot

8:22 PM
Odysseus: Goodness, Zeus has been hiring her to delete quite a few chats, hasn't he? That is satisfactory. Achilles, you may proceed with all your talk about murders and monsters.

Achilles: Right, so as I was saying, Alecto tends to live in Tartarus. So isn't she eating the monsters there? Surely we've provided some, er, snacks for her these past few days?

8:23 PM
Hercules: Snacks? You've been murdering monsters? I thought you were LARPing.

Perseus: Swords. Stabby stab.

Achilles: We *have* been, but that's also a cover for our liaisons with the monsters. They won't question why we're in full armor if we tell them it's a LARPing date.

8:24 PM
Odysseus: Are you uncomfortable with the fact we've been putting an end to a few abominations, Hercules?

Hercules: I ... no.

Hercules: I killed plenty of monsters back in the day, but ...

Hercules: Tricking them into thinking you're just going to play with swords on the date? That feels ... wrong.

8:25 PM
Hercules: Like Hera's mind control.

Odysseus: Ah, well, Hercules, considering you spent most of the days of your youth building muscles instead of brains, I think you ought to leave the topic of ethics to those who are more learned.

Perseus: Brains. Big brains.

Odysseus: Achilles, as you were saying.

8:26 PM
Achilles: Yeah, if you guys are going to interrupt Bridgerton, you might as well stop cutting me off mid-story.

Achilles: We've taken down a few monsters in the last few days. Want me to highlight some of the trophy ones?

8:27 PM
Odysseus: Why don't you pick a top three? To cut down on this conversation. Tiresias is only at rehearsal for so long.

Achilles: Number one.

Perseus: Singing bird.

Achilles: Yes, we took out a siren. First to tacos, then to death. Ironically, the tacos were her last meal and the murder weapon.

8:24 PM
Perseus: Two!

Achilles: Took out a satyr woman. Or I guess satyress is the right term. Not a monster, really, but we were bored and having a slow day. Why did I include her in the highlight reel?

Perseus: Death, death, death. Heeheehee.

8:25 PM
Achilles: Finally, we threw a serpentine female dragon into a venomous snake pit at some botany place. Which felt ironic, because, you know, dragons are also reptiles.

Hercules: Guys, do you need me to grab anything else?

Takeout, ice cream? LARPing costumes? I—I don't think I'm needed in this chat.

8:26 PM
Odysseus: What's the matter, Hercules? Can't stomach this talk? Have you gone too long without satisfying that bloodlust?

    Hercules: It's just … the satyress. She wasn't a monster. I know I'm not good at this ethics stuff, but it feels like she didn't deserve to die.

Odysseus: Ah, well maybe she wasn't a monster per se. But she certainly wasn't what you would call natural.

8:27 PM
Odysseus: She wouldn't have done well in this new world anyway. I don't even think they have satyrs or satyresses here.

    Hercules: I don't know, guys.

Odysseus: Has Tiresias made you soft?

Odysseus: You *do* realize if you want to be a hero like us, you must have the stomach for these sorts of things.

Multiple screenshots were sent

8:28 PM
Odysseus: Who sent those? What are these?

    Achilles: Are these … conversations between Tiresias and Medusa?

8:30 PM
Odysseus: Yes, recent ones, it seems. The app must've had another glitch and forwarded their private conversation to us.

8:34 PM
Perseus: Ooh.

Perseus: Tiresias is in trooouble!

Odysseus: Indeed, it appears he's setting up another get-together with the gorgon, with no intention to murder her on this date.

8:35 PM
Achilles: What's his deal? If she claims she isn't going to kill him, why isn't he going for it? Maybe he lied and will actually murder her?

Odysseus: Doesn't seem to fit his character.

Odysseus: Well, the lying does. Perhaps he attempted to deceive us.

8:36 PM
Perseus: Us?

Hercules: I don't know, Odysseus. He seems like the truth-telling type. His prophecies sorta force him to do that, to be honest.

Odysseus: Again, Hercules, you're not crafty like I am. Didn't have to be forged into surviving off illusions and trickery just to make it back home to Ithaca.

8:37 PM
Odysseus: What do you want to bet he staged the last date? Made it seem like they attempted to off each other so they could reconvene and plot against us?

Achilles: You mean they acted the whole thing out?

Odysseus: He is involved with the theater.

Perseus: Whoa.

> 8:38 PM
> **Achilles:** So what do we do now, boss? Take out Antigone to show him who not to mess with?

Odysseus: No, he's still useful. We don't want to be rid of someone who can foresee what's to come. Especially if we find ourselves in an all-out war.

> **Perseus:** War?

Odysseus: Yes, war. Whoever brought us back wanted to wreak havoc. Achilles, you ought to remember from the Trojan War that the gods will stir up conflict at a moment's notice.

8:39 PM
Odysseus: Achilles ... are you sobbing?

8:40 PM
Odysseus: Achilles, I can hear you all the way in my apartment. Don't even try to turn up your television. It still won't block the noise.

> 8:41 PM
> **Achilles:** The war just makes me think about my good friend. :'(

8:42 PM
Odysseus: Ugh, and just when I thought you'd manned up enough

to have this conversation with us in the group. You were doing so well, being so stoic.

Achilles: I'll be fine, just give me a moment.

8:43 PM
Odysseus: Wonderful, now while Achilles blows his nose excessively loud, we still have a greater use for Tiresias. He may not remember this, but during my travels to Ithaca, I ran across him as a shade.

Odysseus: Even in his ghostly state, he warned me about the future.

Odysseus: And a seeing eye is great strategy when it comes to battles.

8:44 PM
Odysseus: For now, we'll leave Antigone be.

Odysseus: But we do need some way to turn him against the gorgon. So that when we do go to battle, he won't hesitate to end a life if need be.

Hercules: Medusa's life?

8:45 PM
Odysseus: Yes, why don't the three of you come into my apartment? I know I don't let you in here often, but in case any of these messages leak, I don't want anyone figuring out our scheme.

Perseus: Partaaaay.

Achilles: I may or may not be in a snuggle blanket when I arrive. And I may or may not be in a green tea clay facemask. For ... manly purposes.

8:46 PM
Odysseus: Alecto, since we're paying you and all, do us a favor and delete this conversation thread for today. Wouldn't want it to fall into the wrong hands.

8:54 PM
Odysseus: BEFORE nine o'clock, Alecto. Or you won't get those souls you crave.

8:56 PM
Alecto: There are no monsters in Tartarus, Odysseus. Only the Titans.

8:57 PM
Alecto: Any rumors that there are monsters here are false. Hades takes pity on the monsters who have been cursed. Just like he took pity on Persephone when she fell into the greedy hands of a god who stole something precious from her.

8:58 PM
Alecto: I expect souls by the end of this.

8:59 PM
Alecto: If I receive none, I shall go after yours.

Alecto deleted the conversation thread for January 6

Echo's Notes

January 7

12:11 PM
Tiresias: Thank you, Echo, for recording this conversation via your, uh, voice. So that we can have a little privacy from DearHades.

Tiresias: And thank YOU, Medusa, for spotting the old man in the corner playing chess and suggesting Hercules play a game with him.

Tiresias: Because Hercules decided to discuss his workout routine with me on the rideshare over here, and by the time we placed our coffee orders, it didn't sound like he was going to be done anytime soon. And I didn't want this whole recording to be about "training" and "elliptical machines."

12:12 PM
Tiresias: So I'll just have to trust that one of you ladies won't kill me during the time it takes Hercules to play a game of chess and return to this convo—forgetting to tell me about his routine.

Echo: Won't kill.

Medusa: Right, we have a common cause. So let's get down to planning.

12:13 PM
Tiresias: Right, so, I guess first things first. You want to invade the Underworld to tell Hades what's going on with the monsters, in person, because admins and Hades are pretty unreachable in the app right now. Correct?

Medusa: Right. We need to tell them what's going on and fix this issue with the slaying of monsters.

Medusa: And I guess we could also ask why certain people have come back and others haven't? Not sure about Hades's logic there.

12:14 PM
Tiresias: Yeeeeeah, so about that.

Tiresias: I, um, had a prophecy the other day. Ares brought us back, because Ares likes to start wars. And bringing monsters and heroes back at the same time would, um, do that.

Medusa: What!

Tiresias: And … do you know how people are coming back? Because it's a little awkward.

Medusa: Uh, no …

12:15 PM
Tiresias: So you had some sisters, yeah? Or at least other women with snakey hairs?

Medusa: Sisters is a loose term, but yeah.

Tiresias: Anyway, um, Ares managed to get a jar of blood from one of them, from the days of yore. And sprinkled it on people.

Tiresias: But someone confiscated it. My bet is Hades. Eurydice thinks it's Thanatos.

Tiresias: Sooooo the only living gorgon with the blood to bring them back is sitting in front of me, probably drinking a Boba tea.

12:16 PM
Tiresias: And that's why the heroes, um, would prefer you not to be alive.

Medusa: I ... have no words.

Medusa: How long have you known this? Does everyone know but me?

Tiresias: Everyone has their theories. And as far as I'm concerned, I never told the heroes about the prophecy.

12:17 PM
Hercules: MY HORSIE PIECE STEALS YOUR HORSIE PIECE, ELDERLY MAN.

Tiresias: But I want to be clear that if we do go to Hades, and we do ask him to bring people back, we aren't going to kill you in the process.

Medusa: Well, I guess that's comforting? I'm concerned for the monsters here. But bringing more people back ... I guess that could be something we try for as well.

Tiresias: Yes, agreed. Honestly, if we brought the heroes' lovers back, they'd probably forget this whole monster-slaying thing.

12:18 PM
Medusa: Wow, you're right. As much as I hate to do anything nice for those scumbuckets, if it gets them to stop killing monsters, I'm on board.

Medusa: Although for you and Hercules ... I'd love to see Manto and Megara come back.

Tiresias: Yeah ... I—erm, I think we all would.

Tiresias: But if we're going to invade the Underworld, we have three major logistical issues on our hands.

12:19 PM
Tiresias: The first being Cerberus. I know you deal with dogs, but ever dealt with one with three heads?

Medusa: I can't say that I have, but Cerberus is my friend Echidna's kid. Maybe I can ask her what he likes.

Medusa: Monsters' children are kind of strange, to be honest. Not sure how a snake woman had a dog kid, but we don't question those sorts of things in Greek mythology.

12:20 PM
Tiresias: Indeed. And also we do have Hercules. As a last resort. He kidnapped Cerberus last time. Might as well bring him along for that safety net. And Echo, in case we get lost and need to keep up with communications.

Medusa: Agreed. Kidnapping doggy as last resort, and treats, toys, and belly rubs as first resort.

Tiresias: Our second logistical issue is Charon. We don't exactly have drachma on us. How are we gonna pay the ferryman?

12:21 PM
Medusa: Hmm. I wonder if he takes American dollars. I also have some Kohl's Cash.

Tiresias: I have a feeling Charon may not take that.

Medusa: Yeah, he probably shops at Hot Topic.

Echo: Have drachma.

12:22 PM
Medusa: What's that, Echo? Do you have drachma?

Medusa: Oh, chocolate coin drachma. Huh. Well ... we can try.

Tiresias: I hear it's pretty dark in the Underworld? Maybe he won't be able to tell?

Echo: Won't be able to tell.

12:23 PM
Hercules: GUYS, I JUST WON THE BEAUTIFUL LADY ECHO FIFTY DOLLARS. MY HORSIE MAN TOOK HIS QUEEN WOOD PIECE. AND NOW THE OLD MAN IS CRYING. I AM TRIUMPHANT.

Tiresias: Hercules, you know nothing about chess.

Hercules: Here's fifty dollars, Echo. Go get yourself at least two coffees with that.

Echo: At least two coffees. At least.

12:24 PM
Medusa: Uh, let's wait on that until we're done recording the convo. We need Echo to put it in her notes for us.

Tiresias: Yeah, make sure to screenshot it and send it to the sighties in the group. I'll relisten to it when I get home.

Tiresias: Anyway, the third logistical issue is Hades himself. Even if we did have gorgon blood—which we aren't using, I promise—I'm sure he'll be pretty mad at us for asking him to bring people back. So how do we handle that?

12:25 PM
Hercules: Ooh. What if—hear me out—we say please?

Medusa: That's a good first step, Hercules.

Hercules: I have many ideas. I'll let you know when I have more.

Medusa: Thank you, I appreciate it. As for Hades, I don't know … we may need to figure out what's in it for him.

12:26 PM
Tiresias: Maybe we play up the sympathetic lovers angle? Kind of like what Orpheus did before Eurydice sneezed on the way out of the Underworld?

Tiresias: I'm just hoping Thanatos isn't the one with the blood, because I hear he's scary.

Echo: Thanatos scary.

>**Medusa:** I don't like thinking about him. You guys are giving me chills.

12:27 PM
Hercules: That the grim reaper dude? Duuuuude. I never saw him in the Underworld, but even I would scream if I saw him. A manly scream. But a scream nonetheless.

>**Medusa:** Right, so, the lovers angle. Um, who are we pitching as the lovers who deserve to be reunited? Because even Hades can't be thinking, "Oh yeah, Odysseus is awesome, totally give him Penelope back."

Tiresias: True, but here's what I do know. People like Penelope, Patroclus ... the gods liked them. They were nice, not prideful.

12:28 PM
Tiresias: Maybe we try to talk more about them and why they deserve a second chance. And it doesn't just have to be lovers. Maybe if I tell all the reasons why Manto should return, it'll get Hades's mind off people like Odysseus.

>**Medusa:** I think that's a good idea. So they deserve to come back. As a bonus, no more killing monsters. I feel like Hades should be on board with that, since he seems like a relatively reasonable god. The monsters deserve a second chance.

12:29 PM
Medusa: I need a couple of days to get my affairs in order— get my shifts covered at the animal shelter and all that. But then I'm ready to storm the Underworld.

Tiresias: Ooh, yes, speaking of animals. Need to get a dog sitter for Artemis. And someone to cover for me at rehearsals.

Tiresias: Is two days from now, the ninth, too soon?

> 12:30 PM
> **Medusa:** The sooner the better. The longer we wait, the longer monsters are in danger.

> **Medusa:** I can't lose any more friends.

Hercules: I WILL BE YOUR FRIEND, SCARY SNAKE LADY.

Hercules: Come on, Echo, let's get you those two coffees! Yippee!

> **Echo:** Yippee!

Monstrously Magnificent Maidens, the Sequel

January 7

Group Information

Group Name: Monstrously Magnificent Maidens, the Sequel

Description: We're a bunch of monster ladies who gather to cheer each other on, spill tea, and keep each other safe. It's a rough world out there for monsters. Second iteration without one of our members, because we need to discuss her behavior.

———

9:18 PM

Echidna: Ladies, have any of you spoken to Medusa today?

9:19 PM

Arachne: Weirdly, no. Uh, what's with the new group chat? Who are we excluding?

Arachne: Ooh, just looked at the member list. Why you excluding my girl Medusa?

9:20 PM
Echidna: I think she's been acting a little suspicious. She was out today, I don't know where, and then she messaged me asking about Cerberus.

Aglaope: Oh yeah, he's your kid, right?

Echidna: Yes. And she was asking what sort of things he likes ... and if he has any weaknesses.

9:21 PM
Lamia: That does sound a bit suspicious. But why don't you just ask her directly? Secrets don't make friends. I should know. Secrets are how I secure my targets. :)

Arachne: Yeah, I'm not comfy talking about my girl behind her back.

Echidna: I did ask her. But all she said was that she was "just curious."

Arachne: Oh no, not curiosity. How sinister.

9:22 PM
Echidna: AND I asked her what made her think of it. And she said, "Oh, nothing in particular."

Arachne: Oh.

Arachne: All right, she's up to something.

9:22 PM
Scylla: Hold on, I missed a step here. How was *that* what translated to her being up to something?

Arachne: Medusa is a terrible liar. Remember when we exchanged gifts for that modern winter holiday not long ago? Anytime someone would catch her shopping, or hiding something, what would she always say if you asked her what she was doing?

> **Aglaope:** Ooh, I get it! "Oh, nothing in particular." Even if she was literally trying to sit on a pile of new yarn to hide it from Arachne.

9:23 PM
Echidna: Correct. Anyway, as I've been trying to ask, has anyone heard from her? With all this going on with app glitches and missing monsters, I'm worried she's planning on doing something reckless.

> **Arachne:** You know, I think the only one who has been with her today at all has been … Echo.

9:24 PM
Charybdis: *gloorpglup* Hey, Echo, are you here?

> **Aglaope:** @Echo

9:26 PM
Echidna: Echo? Please, dear, we could use your input. Are you here?

> **Echo:** Here.

9:27 PM
Arachne: Oh good. Where did you two go today?

> **Echo:** Go today?

Scylla: This is going to be painful.

9:28 PM
Echidna: Echo, is Medusa plotting something?

Echo: Is Medusa?

Arachne: Oh gods.

9:29 PM
Echidna: Arachne, you live close to Echo, right? Maybe you could go ask questions in person.

Arachne: Reporting for duty, Captain. I'll update you all once I find out more.

10:38 PM
Arachne: So after a LOT of persuasion that it's for Medusa's own good, and a good long time getting Echo to repeat the correct phrases ... I think Medusa is, um, taking up chess club?

10:39 PM
Echidna: Chess club?

Arachne: Yeah. Listen, it's REALLY hard to get a story out of someone by playing twenty questions. But from what I could gather, they went to a coffee shop and played chess with an elderly man.

10:40 PM
Echidna: Oh. Well, that's very in character for Medusa.

Scylla: Why was she lying, then? And why Cerberus?

Echidna: I don't know. It doesn't make sense.

10:41 PM
Arachne: Well, I do know one thing. We need to keep a close eye on our girl Medusa. I still get the sense she's up to something.

Arachne: And if our bestie is in trouble, even Tartarus itself can't stop us.

Heroes before Monster-os

January 7

11:03 PM

Odysseus: Hercules, please confirm Tiresias's messages are still on mute, and that he is not in a position to view our messages accidentally.

11:04 PM

Hercules: Dude conked out after a day of dates, rehearsals, and talks about invasions of the land of the dead. So I think we're A-okay. I think Perseus and Achilles are also down for the count. Slaying takes it outta ya.

> **Odysseus:** Did you make sure to send me the screenshots from the conversations? Since they distracted you by making you play a game?

> *Hercules sent several screenshots*

11:05 PM

Hercules: Echo was really nifty, being able to replicate the conversation and all. They sent it to all of us, so I don't think the game was a distraction.

Hercules: I believe that game with the horsey and other wooden pieces, Odysseus ...

Hercules: Is a calling.

11:06 PM
Hercules: They don't seem to know I'm listening in on the conversations for you. Although ... I'm not going to lie, Odysseus.

Hercules: Even though you said it was "so I can also have fun with them, and be pals with Medusa and Echo. And pretend to be part of their convo."

11:07 PM
Hercules: Because although I do that at night, when I relisten to all the messages and make-believe I have friends.

Hercules: It feels a little like spying.

Hercules: And I already feel really weird that Perseus and Achilles are killing randos all the time. It feels a little ... uncool.

> **Odysseus:** Like spying? Nooooo. I would never ask you to do that.

> 11:08 PM
> **Odysseus:** I simply like to be in the know. What are the kids saying these days? Wanting to know all the tea?

> **Odysseus:** What is with their obsession with tea, anyway?

Hercules: I don't know, but they're awful clumsy, spilling it all the time.

Hercules: So you're not having me spy on Medusa and Tiresias and Echo?

11:09 PM
Hercules: Because I'd feel real bad. Especially because Echo has these really pretty eyes, see.

> **Odysseus:** Yes, no spying. Only wanting to feel included. No ulterior motives.

> **Odysseus:** Now give me a few minutes to read through these messages.

> 11:14 PM
> **Odysseus:** So they're going to the Underworld, eh? With a gorgon who so happens to have the one cure to bringing back shades from the dead?

Hercules: Right??? :O But I think the most important takeaway is ...

Hercules: THEY INVITED ME TO COME WITH!!

11:15 PM
Hercules: Does this mean I have friends, Odysseus? My earthly dad back in the day said friends weren't allowed. They distracted me from bulking up the triceps.

> **Odysseus:** Erm, yes, friends. Hooray.

Hercules: I KNOW! I am so pumped. :D

11:16 PM
> **Odysseus:** But you know, Hercules? I'm feeling, um, pretty friendless right now.

Hercules: WHAT? Odysseus, I will be your friend in a heartbeat.

Odysseus: Yes, yes. I am keenly aware.

Odysseus: But I would also like to be friends with Tiresias and all the others too. Could you do me a favor?

11:17 PM
Hercules: Sure thing!

Odysseus: Could you record the conversations for me when you're in the Underworld? So I can feel like I'm a part of it?

Odysseus: I'll send a recording device to your apartment that should be able to pick up the conversation just fine and transfer it to my end.

11:18 PM
Hercules: Wow! Anything to make Odysseus also feel included.

Hercules: Man, I always thought real heroes were never lonely because they were so famous and popular. Mind blown.

11:19 PM
Odysseus: Two more things. One, I need you to stick as closely to Tiresias as possible.

Hercules: Like glue, with my new bestie.

Odysseus: Right.

Odysseus: Two, I have a feeling Tiresias may not do what he needs to do when he's in the Underworld.

11:20 PM
Hercules: And what does he need to do?

Odysseus: Something very brave and—well, I don't want to spoil the whole surprise. You do love surprises, don't you?

Hercules: Oh boy, do I!

11:21 PM
Odysseus: But to make sure Tiresias follows through with the surprise, I may need to feed you some lines. You'll have an inconspicuous earpiece as well, where you can hear me. Can you repeat everything I say to you?

Hercules: Can you repeat everything I say to you?

11:22 PM
Odysseus: Excellent.

Odysseus: Go invade the Underworld. Again.

Hercules: I will! I can't wait to figure out what the surprise is.

Odysseus: Oh, I'm sure we're all dying to. Especially a certain monster.

11:23 PM
Odysseus: Alecto, please delete this conversation thread.

11:47 PM
Alecto: Gaia, between you and Aphrodite, you people know how to keep a chaos agent busy.

Alecto deleted the conversation thread for January 7

DearHades Squad

January 8

10:47 AM
Hermes: Hades? Persephone?

10:48 AM
Hermes: I've been attempting to reach you for days.

10:49 AM
Hermes: Hades, please tell me you did not suggest Miss Persephone do a rousing game of Nerf gun battles. You know how she gets with those.

Hermes: They last for days. Weeks, even. And considering Persephone created a jungle in the whole of the Underworld ...

Hermes: You two could get lost.

10:52 AM
Hermes: Very well. Since you two insist on shooting foam darts at each other for days on end, I will simply leave some photos in here for you to come back to.

Hermes: Self-care is, indeed, important.

Hermes: But not when dealing with petty deities.

Hermes: As a petty deity myself, I should know.

Hermes sent several screenshots

———

HERMES'S SCREENSHOT ONE

PRIVATE MESSAGE
JANUARY 8

7:05 AM
Aphrodite: Hermes, I'm getting desperate.

7:07 AM
Hermes: I'm afraid I cannot help with that. You see, I already have quite a number of ladies falling all over me.

Hermes: They say I am quite the promiscuous little messenger god, I'll have you know.

Aphrodite: ...

Hermes: ...

Aphrodite: ...

Hermes: *jiggles shoulders*

7:08 AM
Aphrodite: Hermes.

Aphrodite: I'm desperate ... TO TAKE DOWN THE APP THAT IS COMPETING AGAINST MINE, NOT TO GO ON A DATE WITH YOU.

7:09 AM
Aphrodite: This is awful. They're surpassing reviews, downloads, everything.

Aphrodite: And the glitches Alecto introduced make people like the app more. I don't get it. Alecto *swore* she could stir up chaos. But it's almost like her glitches are getting rerouted, redirected.

Aphrodite: Whatever admin is doing that will face my wrath when I get the chance.

7:10 AM
Hermes: Perhaps you would do best to allow the app to run its course? Perhaps the two can work together and find ways to collaborate.

Aphrodite: Ew, Hermes. This isn't some kids' TV show where everyone ends up as friends in the end.

Aphrodite: This is politics.

7:11 AM
Aphrodite: And if I know anything about Ancient Greek politics, everything ends up in a war. If a beauty contest could cause the Trojan War, then surely someone trying to take away my job duties by pairing monsters and mortals unnaturally can face the consequences too.

7:12 AM
Aphrodite: If Alecto can't help me, then I'll use her computer to hack myself in and do things myself.

Hermes: You can—do that?

Aphrodite: Sure, I forced my techie husband Hephaestus to show me the ropes last night, before I let him get back to his coding projects.

7:13 AM
Aphrodite: Be right back, toodle-oo!

Aphrodite sent several screenshots

9:02 AM
Aphrodite: Game, set, match.

———

APHRODITE'S SCREENSHOT ONE

PRIVATE MESSAGE
JANUARY 8

7:14 AM
Aphrodite: Hey, sis, you getting rather peeved about this new app from Persephone and Hades?

7:16 AM
Hera: Ach, I still haven't yet located my husband on the dating enterprise. But I suspect these mysterious profiles of animals on DearHades have Zeus's name written all over them.

Hera: It irks me he didn't take down this app when he had the chance.

7:17 AM

Aphrodite: Listen, I love your husband—

Aphrodite: AND WHEN IS SAY LOVE, I MEAN AS A BROTHER. DO NOT SMITE ME.

Hera: Go on.

7:18 AM
Aphrodite: But I have a feeling we may need to take matters into our own hands. I'm planning to hack the app this morning and put out an admin announcement. To turn the monsters and mortals in DearHades against each other and to decrease the number of people on the app.

Aphrodite: And to prevent your husband from swiping on more people, obviously.

Aphrodite: That's the main objective. Not to see the app tank in downloads or anything.

7:19 AM
Hera: Yes?

Aphrodite: To do so, I may need to name-drop you.

Aphrodite: Say that you'll do something for some people on the app. Don't worry. I don't expect you to follow through.

7:20 AM
Aphrodite: But I have a plan that can kick Zeus, Hades, and Persephone in the gut at the same time.

Aphrodite: You game?

7:21 AM

Hera: I have tried nearly everything to locate Zeus.

Hera: I'll try anything at this point.

7:22 AM
Aphrodite: Good, I'll take anything.

APHRODITE'S SCREENSHOT TWO

Admin Announcement

Hey, everyone! This is definitely Persephone making this announcement. What would Persephone say? I love plants and kidnappers!

Anyway, Hades and I have done some evaluating of the app, and honestly? We made a BIG MISTAKE. Our bad. Humans and monsters really shouldn't be getting together, and well, it's downright abominable.

So we have a proposition for you. An all-out war. Between monsters and mortals.

I know, I know. Sounds crazy, right? But we have some INCENTIVES for whoever wins this battle.

Heroes: If you win and slay all the monsters—or enough to get the monsters to fly a white flag—we will bring back the rest of the mortals you miss from the Underworld. Hades TOTALLY agrees to this. You may have heard rumors that no one else is returning. But we can undo that. All you have to do is secure victory in this war.

Monsters: If you win, Hera has agreed to undo any curse placed on you. That's right. You'll be turned into a mortal again. Eradicate the mortals, or cause them to surrender, and my bestie Hera will transform you from a cow or spider or whatever into a living, breathing human.

And for those lame-os who are all like, "Oh, but I don't want to kill anyone. Doesn't a war seem extreme?" Let me riddle you this.

They will strike before you do. Without hesitation.

So why forego these incentives for the sake of HOPING the other side doesn't act outside of their selfish interests?

Let's make war, not love!

P.S. Some of my shade admins are not up to speed on protocols. So before they delete this announcement, I need you to do a few things.

One: Screenshot this and send it to everyone you can. Monsters and mortals alike. Share on social media, via messenger hawk, I don't care. Get the word out. You will have already received this announcement in your private messages on the app.

Two: Join StupidCupid. We've collaborated with Aphrodite to open some forums to mortals and monsters to create battle plans. Again, because we have such a large network of shade admins, not all of them are with the program, and they may boot you off Dear-Hades for conspiring together in battle. So jump on StupidCupid as a backup.

Three: Have fun. Us deities do like to watch a good war, so give us something popcorn-worthy.

———

APHRODITE'S SCREENSHOT THREE

StupidCupid's Mission

To find someone to make out with, duh. Why does a company need some gross, manipulative mission like a certain other app?

Our Story

Goddess of love Aphrodite and her son Eros (a.k.a. Cupid) want you to find your match. That's all. We're not here to waste your time with some long story.

How to Use StupidCupid

Swipe right, start talking.

Update

Forums are now available to discuss war plans. Monsters, head to "Monster Mayhem." Mortals, to "Hero Hub."

Make war, and make me proud.

_____

HERMES'S SCREENSHOT TWO

PRIVATE MESSAGE
JANUARY 8

9:12 AM
Hermes: I'm ... speechless.

9:13 AM
Aphrodite: Like it? The forums are already filling up like crazy. Something tells me that even though this app has only been active for a few weeks, DearHades has struck a chord with monsters and mortals.

Aphrodite: It's almost like this hatred has been brewing for thousands of years.

9:14 AM
Aphrodite: Ah, well, I must away. One does not start a war with cuticles like these. Must get to my manicure appointment.

_____

Hermes: Although Aphrodite needs a few loose bolts tightened in the brain, she may be right about one thing.

10:56 AM
Hermes: Gods have been relentless on humans and monsters alike —using them, cursing them simply for being in their pathways—

and the monsters and mortals have decided to shift blame to one another instead of to us.

10:57 AM
Hermes: I fear for what will happen if we do not act soon.

10:58 AM
Hermes: Perhaps we are already too late.

Echo's Notes

January 9

2:03 PM
Medusa: You recording for us, Echo?

    Echo: Recording for us, Echo.

Medusa: Awesome. Well. Let's ... storm the gates of Hades.

    2:04 PM
    Unknown Source: *WOOF*

Hercules: Must kidnap. Must kidnap.

    Tiresias: No, Hercules, that's a LAST resort. All right, Medusa, let's test your theory to see if it works. Go do your magic.

2:05 PM
Medusa: Hey there, Cerby. Who's a good boy?

    Cerberus: *Woof?*

Medusa: It's YOU! You're a good boy! You're doing such a good job!

Cerberus: *heh heh heh thump thump thump*

Tiresias: What's happening? Is he beating her to death with his paws?

2:06 PM
Medusa: Look at you panting and wagging your tail and definitely not beating me to death. Let me see that belly. Where's the belly?

Cerberus: *WHOMP*

Medusa: Oh yes, let's give you some nice scritches.

Hercules: I'm so confused. She's not kidnapping him. And yet, something is working. How?

2:07 PM
Medusa: Since we're friends, we can pass by, right Cerby?

Cerberus: *woof woof*

Medusa: That's a yes, guys!

Medusa: Thanks so much, buddy. I'll tell your mom you said hi.

Tiresias: That was surprisingly easy. No wonder Ares invaded the Underworld.

2:08 PM
Medusa: I get the impression heroes would just come in

swinging and ready to fight. Probably didn't think to offer belly rubs.

Hercules: Whaaaaaaat? I definitely did not do that.

Hercules: Echo, by the way, I did do that. But it was for love.

Echo: For love.

Tiresias: Well, whatever it was for, there's no way Charon will go as easy on us. He's a ferryman for the dead and won't take kindly to live folks.

Tiresias: Also, why am I tripping on a million roots? Did they grow trees or something since we left?

2:09 P.M
Hercules: It's like a jungle in here. Don't worry, Echo. I'm like Tarzan. Very brave.

Echo: Very brave.

Medusa: Huh ... interesting developments from the sidekicks.

Medusa: Anyway, is that the River Styx up there? And Charon ... in a safari outfit?

2:10 PM
Unknown Source: Hellooooo! Welcome to the Underworld Cruise of the Deadly Jungle! I'm Charon, your intrepid host!

Hercules: Does intrepid mean he's gonna eat us?

Medusa: Intrepid means he's, uh, brave and adventurous.

Medusa: Hello, Charon. Um, we're ready to pay the fare.

2:11 PM
Charon: The what? Oh! Yeah, the fare, don't worry about it. I can't wait to take you on this adventure! Everyone pile into the Charon Cruise Lines official watercraft!

Tiresias: Should I be very scared?

Charon: Watch your step, that's it. All aboard, all aboard!

Hercules: Are you going to describe things to us, safari man?

2:12 PM
Charon: Why, of course! Especially for our blind friend.

Tiresias: He means you, Hercules.

Medusa: *SNORT*

Charon: Alrighty-o, everyone, let's go!

2:13 PM
Charon: Welcome to Jumanji! Just kidding, haha, I just learned about that movie. I love The Rock. Anyway, here you'll see the unique forestation that sprang up only recently in the Underworld. Rumor has it Persephone grew the forest and may even be lurking about inside it!

Charon: Not that Persephone's lurking is scary—it's Persephone. But it sounds dramatic for the cruise.

Tiresias: Speaking of Persephone, we probably need to talk to her about that admin announcement that went up yesterday. Things have escalated.

2:14 PM
Charon: Ah yes, the war! I'm excited. I'm sure a lot of new people will be partaking in my cruise of these here jungles. Most fun I've had in millennia.

> **Medusa:** Um, yes. We are definitely not trying to avoid that happening. What a bummer it would be if a bunch of people DIDN'T die.

Hercules: Ooh, carnivorous plants. Bitey, bitey.

> **Medusa:** So have you seen Hades at least?

2:15 PM
Charon: As we round this bend, hold on to your hats! On your right, behold the gigantic Venus flytraps of Persephone.

> **Tiresias:** Are they singing?

Charon: On your left, uh, Hercules, don't touch the pitcher plants.

> **Hercules:** Awww, you're no fun.

Tiresias: But doesn't anyone else find it weird that one day Persephone and Hades set up this app and the next they suddenly want a war? That doesn't seem on brand.

> 2:16 PM
> **Charon:** What's that? Oh, I don't know. The two of them ventured into the jungle for a Nerf battle a couple of days ago, and we haven't heard from them since.

Medusa: So they're BOTH missing?

> **Charon:** Get ready for the rapids!

2:17 PM
Charon: Whee! Wheeeeee! Okay, just pretend they're rapids. It's really me rocking the boat, but close your eyes and you won't know the difference.

Tiresias: Um, yes we will.

Hercules: But if Hades and Persephone are gone, how will we find them?

Hercules: I know! We pretend to play a game of hide and seek. And then THEY find US.

2:18 PM
Medusa: Um, a very good thought, but I don't think they'll know we're hiding, which will make it a little hard for them to find us.

Medusa: I think it might be time to step out of the boat and go on a jungle adventure.

Echo: Jungle adventure!

Hercules: Bye, Mr. Safari Man!

Charon: Wait, Hercules, let me at least park the—

Charon: Oh. Okay. That was an impressive jump. For the rest of you, I'll dock the boat.

2:19 PM
Charon: It has been a pleasure, ladies and gentlemen. May you enjoy the rest of your quest. Wish I could join, but I need to go see if I have more cruisers to pick up.

Charon: Jumanji!

2:20 PM

Tiresias: Question: How on earth are we going to find Hades and Persephone if they covered the whole Underworld in a vast jungle? It's not like they're going to just pop up on the scene right in front of us.

Persephone: Ha! Two thousand and thirty-five points for me!

Hercules: That doesn't seem like a normal scoring system.

Persephone: Oh, hello there, everyone. Fancy meeting you here.

Tiresias: This doesn't feel convenient at all.

2:21 PM

Hades: Die, darling. Oh, erm, hello. We have guests. Very much alive guests.

Persephone: I can tell they're alive, Hades. Hello, all! Ooh, Medusa, I've missed our girl talks.

Medusa: Our what?

Tiresias: Hold up, Herc. She knows Persephone?

Hercules: Hello, Mr. Dead Man and Mrs. Dead Woman.

2:22 PM

Persephone: Oh, we're not dead, dear. You're a cutie. Always liked this one. Right, honey? Oh, you didn't for some reason. Don't remember why.

Persephone: WAIT. You all don't remember the Underworld very well, do you?

Medusa: Um, less than I realized, apparently.

Persephone: HADES. WE MUST GIVE THEM A TOUR.

2:23 PM
Hades: Erm, I mean, right now? In the middle of our battle?

Medusa: That does seem strange in the middle of an all-out war.

Persephone: Haha, don't be silly, I'm winning by a thousand points anyway.

Medusa: Uh, Tiresias, do you think points means dead people?

Tiresias: Um, maybe?

Hades: Darling, your shooting Charon didn't count.

2:24 PM
Hades: So am I taking all these people on a tour?

Persephone: Oh no, dear. You take the boys, I'll take the girls. We need girl time! Also, you're kind of stinky. Too much running around in the jungle.

Hercules: Hooray, girl time! Can I join you?

Tiresias: Um, no, Hercules.

2:25 PM
Persephone: I love this guy. Anyway, you boys have fun. Echo,

Medusa, come with me! I can't wait to show you what we've done with the place.

Persephone: And Hades, don't forget to show them my favorite addition!

Persephone: It starts with an "i" and ends with a "ce cream."

   Hercules: Awww, man, we'll never guess it.

2:26 PM
Hades: Right-o. Gentlemen, let's go tour the land of the dead, shall we?

   Medusa: Uh, we kinda had something to talk to you about—

Persephone: Let's go!

Echo's Notes

January 9

2:53 PM
Medusa: Wow ... Persephone ... you walk ... fast.

Persephone: Some might call it floating more than walking. Come on in, we can have pomegranate tea in the kitchen! Sorry this isn't a tour with the boys, but I thought we needed some time to catch up.

Echo: Catch up?

2:54 PM
Persephone: Neither of you probably remember much, but you were two of my favorite shades in Asphodel. Excellent students. I do hope you remember my lessons, though. They would've been quite useful for being alive again.

Medusa: Right, being alive again. On that topic—

Persephone: Tea for you, Echo.

2:55 PM
Persephone: And for you, Medusa.

Medusa: Oh, thank you. Uh, this isn't the kind of pomegranate that makes you have to stay in the Underworld, right?

Persephone: What's that? Oh. No, no, no. Normal pomegranate. I love chatting with you two, but not enough to steal away your time in the mortal world! Besides, you'll be back here soon anyway.

2:56 PM
Echo: Back here soon?

Medusa: Um, is that a threat?

Persephone: Haha! You two are so silly. No, I just mean you'll die again someday. Everyone ends up in the Underworld eventually. Kind of comforting, honestly. Mortal lifespans are so short, but they'll see their loved ones again soon enough.

Persephone: Well. Unless their relatives are evil and get sent to Tartarus.

2:57 PM
Persephone: And in Asphodel, they don't really remember much.

Persephone: Hades and I are working on improvements and updates.

Persephone: Anyway! I bet you're here about the blood.

Medusa: Um, kind of, but more importantly—

2:58 PM
Persephone: Ohhhh, you're here about love.

Medusa: What?

Persephone: I understand, honey. Come here.

Medusa: I don't think a goddess has ever hugged me before.

Persephone: You're scared to fall in love. Scared to trust a man.

2:59 PM
Medusa: I'm just going to, uh, extricate myself and sit on this barstool at the counter. I mean, you're right, but that isn't really what matters.

Persephone: I think it does matter, Medusa. You've met a very nice guy who likes you, and you like him. And yet, instead, you've tried to kill him. Why is that?

Medusa: Er, Persephone, I really appreciate this, but there's a much bigger issue at stake here. Heroes are killing monsters. We were hoping we could talk to you and Hades. Maybe if the heroes could get their loved ones back, they would stop coming after monsters.

3:00 PM
Echo: Loved ones back?

Persephone: Oh, I don't think giving the heroes their lovers back is an option.

Medusa: But all of us came back. Why not use the blood and bring more back?

Persephone: Well, first of all, we don't have it.

Persephone: Thanatos does.

3:01 PM
Echo: Thanatos!

Medusa: Oh no.

Persephone: And he may have destroyed it by now. People aren't supposed to leave the Underworld. It causes all sorts of problems. And moral dilemmas.

Medusa: What sort of moral dilemmas? I feel like the only dilemma here is that my friends are being killed.

Persephone: I don't mean to be insensitive, but I'm kind of a nerd about this, so buckle up.

3:02 PM
Persephone: If only a limited number of people can come back, who deserves it? Should it be random? Merit based?

Persephone: And what happens for people who have moved on? Now they have old lovers, old enemies, back again? What sort of chaos does that cause?

Persephone: And if you know you could come back again, doesn't that cheapen the value of life? If you have more than one life to live, death doesn't matter so much. And we tend not to value things that are easily replaceable.

3:03 PM
Medusa: Okay, yes, I understand. These are important topics. But Lady Persephone, monsters are dying now. And more are going to die with this w—

Unknown Source: *CRASH*

Persephone: Oh, don't worry, Echo dear, people trip on roots all the time here. Let me get you another teacup.

3:04 PM
Persephone: Anyway, all this to say, life ends for a reason, and the best thing to do, I think, is to live your one life as well as you can. And, if you're me and Hades, improve the afterlife.

Medusa: Please, Persephone, I—

Unknown Source: *Yap! Yap!*

Persephone: Hold on! Dog incoming. Hi, cutie! Hades loves dogs. This one has only one head. Hi, puppy.

3:05 PM
Persephone: So let's talk about why you're having a hard time focusing on Tiresias and instead have made saving the monsters your sole focus. And pet a puppy.

Medusa: Oh, yes, uh, okay. Hi, puppy. Awww. You are a cutie.

Persephone: It wouldn't have anything to do with guilt, would it? Maybe ... you don't think you're actually even going to have a relationship?

Medusa: Well. I mean. I can't, can I?

Persephone: Interesting. Elaborate.

3:06 PM
Medusa: If I can bring people back ... bring Manto back ... don't I have a duty to do it?

Persephone: Hmmmm. Indulge me, if you will.

Medusa: Did you just ... put on spectacles to look more scholarly?

Persephone: Let's say you die. People get brought back. Then what? They die again.

Persephone: The heroes have to go through this all over again. Who are they going to kill next time? Who will they sacrifice because they haven't learned to move on?

3:07 PM
Medusa: I guess ... I didn't really think of that.

Medusa: But honestly, I don't really expect anyone, even Tiresias, would understand. I trusted Poseidon once. He was a god, after all. A powerful god. So when he said he just wanted a temple tour ...

Medusa: When people want something, they'll do anything to get it.

Persephone: Whew, this is getting dark even for the Underworld.

3:08 PM
Medusa: Aw, Echo. Thank you. Be careful while hugging me. You don't want to accidentally see my face. Aw, and thank you for the kisses, Underworld puppy.

Persephone: First of all, my husband and I prank Poseidon once a year because he is a horrible person and deserves it and so much more, so I'll think up a particularly terrible prank just for you.

Persephone: As long as you don't tell anyone we're the ones who do it. I think he still suspects Hera.

Medusa: My lips are sealed.

3:09 PM
Persephone: Second, I know how tempting it is to believe the worst of everyone, especially after a traumatic experience. And girly, you went through a lot.

Persephone: Honestly, first time I saw Hades, I was scared. My mother always told me to watch out for gods. My father is Zeus—godly family trees are weird—and let's just say my mom wasn't a huge fan of him.

Persephone: She still doesn't trust Hades. And because of her temper tantrums, we all suffer for it.

Persephone: But there's no one like my husband. He's sweet, kind, brilliant, and of course, devilishly handsome.

3:10 PM
Persephone: I'm glad I gave him a chance.

Persephone: I think you shouldn't give up on yourself. Or Tiresias. You're worthy of love, girl. And you don't owe your blood to placate immature heroes who haven't learned how to deal with their emotions in healthy ways.

Persephone: Grief is the price of love. But for those who truly love … it's worth it.

Medusa: I … *sniff* … thank you.

3:11 PM
Persephone: Of course. And we'll keep this chat to ourselves, cool? Definitely not tell my mother. Because this is NOT MEDDLING. You two met ON THE APP.

Medusa: Uh, okay? I've never met Demeter.

Persephone: Great! Anyone want to go get some ice cream?

Medusa: Uhhh, yes, but that should probably wait. This has been a great talk, but especially after what we've discussed, I'm very confused.

Medusa: Why are you and Hades starting a war?

3:12 PM
Persephone: Um ... what?

Medusa: Here, this announcement you made.

Persephone: Can I read that?

3:13 PM
Persephone: So.

Persephone: I did not write this.

Medusa: Thank the gods. So you can undo it?

Persephone: Well. In theory ... but this seems to have spread pretty far.

3:14 PM
Persephone: Come on, ladies. It's time to stop a war.

Persephone: Shades! Someone bring me a phone charger! I need to talk to Hermes!

Group Message

January 9

4:32 PM
Hercules: Change group name to Dead Dudes.

Hercules changed group name to "Dead Dudes"

Hades: For the last time, Hercules, just because you're in the Underworld does not mean you're dead. Am I dead?

Hercules: The group name stays.

4:33 PM
Tiresias: Also, thank you Hercules for not recording this while Hades walked us through the Tartarus portion of the tour. Otherwise, the whole page would've just been "AAAAAAUGAIIIIGAH."

Hades: Kronos is a drama king.

Hades: Remind me again why your friend is recording this conversation?

Tiresias: He likes to relisten to them at night. I don't ask questions.

4:34 PM
Hades: Right, well, after that harrowing experience in Tartarus, let's start with something significantly better. How about a peruse of Elysium, since neither of you went there?

Hades: Hercules, your deity part went straight to Olympus after you died, correct?

Hercules: Yessir. Let's go!

Hades: And he's skipping.

Hades: What a character. I don't know why I was peeved with him the last time he invaded the Underworld.

4:40 PM
Hades: And here we are. Tiresias, it won't seem all that distinctive from Asphodel. The only difference is it's a little cleaner and people remember more stuff.

Unknown Source: Ice cream! Get your pomegranate-flavored ice cream right here.

Tiresias: What's that?

Hades: Oh, yes, well, you may have been wondering why Persephone started a school in Asphodel in the first place. And you may not remember, but you also worked a job when you were here too.

Tiresias: Vaguely. Did it have something to do with theater?

4:41 PM
Hades: Indeed, you directed some of the best shows Asphodel has ever seen. Medea—starring Medea. Antigone —starring Antigone. I will say you had an issue with type-casting.

Tiresias: Huh. So people have jobs here.

Hades: If they want them, yes. When Persephone got down here, she noticed people were lacking purpose. Those in Elysium just lounged on sofas all day, and those in Asphodel just wandered aimlessly, wailing. They still DO wail. Probably for tradition's sake. So she gave them things to do. School—where Persephone split her time teaching between Elysium and Asphodel—jobs, hobbies.

4:42 PM
Hercules: The ice cream guy isn't accepting my payment of chocolate coins.

Hades: No problem, how many scoops?

Hercules: *gasp* I can choose more than one? Back on earth, thousands of years ago, I was never allowed to have dessert. No excuses.

Hades: That'll be three scoops.

Hercules: Oh wow, oh wow, oh wow.

4:43 PM
Hercules: Mm, oh Tiresias, you have to try this.

Tiresias: No, really, I'm—yes, Hercules. When you smashed it against my face, it tasted very nice.

Hades: In addition to their jobs, we've had some shades commit to some overtime by helping us with the app. Everyone who works a job or helps with DearHades gets golden drachma, which can be put toward treats like the ice cream. We, of course, still give food, clothing, shelter, etc. to those who don't work. Because we don't want to make that their ultimate purpose. That's bad enough in the mortal world.

4:44 PM
Tiresias: Well, that was very expository, Hades.

Hades: Ah, here's one of the Elysium shades now. How's it going, Patroclus?

Patroclus: Putting out a lot of fires, Hades.

Hades: Considering you used to deal with Achilles, you're well suited for the job. If you don't know, Tiresias and Hercules, he is an excellent baker and cook full time. He's been giving a few new hobbies a go.

4:45 PM
Patroclus: Actually, Hades, we've been trying to get a hold of you. There's something in the app you should—

Hades: Later, later. Persephone will kill me if I don't finish this tour.

Hercules: Here comes the ice cream chariot, Tiresias. Chuggachuggachugga—

Tiresias: Yes, that's very good ice cream. Why don't you eat the rest for me?

4:46 PM
Hades: We may have to speed up this portion of the tour. Why don't we head to Asphodel and meet up with the girls after?

Hercules: I can't believe I get to eat all three scoops.

4:53 PM
Hades: Welcome to Asphodel.

Unknown Source: Oooooh.

Hades: And there's the wailing. You must feel right at home, Tiresias.

Tiresias: A little TOO at home.

Unknown Source: Can I interest you boys in any street tacos? They're apparently all the rage in the mortal world. Pretty lame if you ask me. Nothing compares to a good bread dipped in wine.

4:54 PM
Hercules: No thanks, I just had—Megara?

Tiresias: Hercules, you're shaking like an earthquake.

Hercules: I just ... does she recognize me, Hades? I'm afraid if she does.

Hades: Most people probably won't recall you here.

Tiresias: I'm remembering something. Odysseus once approached me when I was a shade. He had to spill some of his own blood for my memories to resurface. Maybe we need to do that to get Megara to remember Hercules?

Hades: Absolutely not. We just had the floors waxed.

4:55 PM
Hercules: I have beef jerky in my snack bag. Would that work? I'm scared she'll remember me, but I'm more scared if I don't try.

Hades: I seriously doubt—

Hercules: Here's some beef jerky, Meg.

Megara: Buddy, what is your problem? Why are you chucking chunks of meat at m—Her—Hercules?

Hercules: You remember?

4:56 PM
Megara: Bits and pieces, yeah.

Hercules: Bad bits and pieces?

Megara: When you're on this side of eternity, all of it is good. I missed you.

Hercules: I missed you too. I'm sorry you didn't get brought back.

Megara: You mean those losers who up and went for a second-go-around in that stinky mortal world? No. Herc, I love you. So much. But there's a reason I wouldn't do it all again.

Hercules: Yeah?

4:57 PM
Megara: Yeah, because I wouldn't change a thing about the first time.

Megara: Every good piece, every bad bit, all of it made me who I am now.

Megara: Give me those hands and let me hold them one last time.

Hercules: You can—actually hold them? I thought shades were—

Hades: Immaterial? Persephone also had me change that. Otherwise, we wouldn't be able to have that very-much-material pomegranate ice cream. Their biology doesn't work the same way mortals do, so they don't need food to survive. Since they're already dead, survival isn't really a thing. But it's nice to be able to have food anyway.

Hercules: Her hands are so nice.

4:58 PM
Megara: So are yours. They always were.

Hades: Tiresias, why don't we leave them be and continue our tour of Asphodel?

Tiresias: That seems wise ... so these shades you employ, what all do they do on the app?

Hades: Anything from booting out Norse and Egyptian deities to deleting Zeus's numerous accounts. Aphrodite has given us quite the headache.

Unknown Source: Ooooh.

Tiresias: I recognize that wail.

4:59 PM
Tiresias: Hades ... please, tell me that isn't Manto.

Hades: ...

Manto: Ooooh.

Unknown Source: *whomp*

Hades: Tiresias, you've collapsed. Are you all right?

Tiresias: I'd hoped. I'd hoped she'd also left this place.

5:00 PM
Hades: Perhaps we could grab some of Hercules's beef jerky. Maybe you could have another conversation with her?

Hades: Oh, Tiresias, I didn't mean for this tour to make you cry.

Hades: Shall I grab the jerky?

Tiresias: Please, I don't think I could handle it. I—I—

Tiresias: TIRESIAS, I SPEAK TO YOU.

5:01 PM
Tiresias: THE DAUGHTER, WHOM YOU CALL MANTO.

Tiresias: SHALL NEVER RETURN TO THE MORTAL WORLD.

Tiresias: SHALL NEVER PASS INTO OLD AGE.

Tiresias: Shall never see the light above the surface of the deep.

5:02 PM
Tiresias: Hades, please.

Tiresias: Please tell me I didn't prophecy what I think I just did.

Hades: ...

Hades: I wish I had better words.

Hercules: Hey, everyone, Megara just said goodbye, but I think we should be wrapping up this tour soon. She has to deal with the admin announcement in the app. It keeps popping up, even though the shades are deleting it.

5:03 PM
Hades: What admin announcement?

Hercules: Duuuuude, you don't know? That's the whole reason we came down here. To ask you to stop the war between monsters and mortals.

Hades: What war?

Hercules: Why is Tiresias on the floor, crying?

Hades: Hercules, what war?

Hercules: Oh, well, here's the admin announcement in the app.

5:04 PM
Hades: Shoot, Aphrodite.

Hades: And I have quite a few unread messages from Hermes. How long have we been at this Nerf gun battle?

Hades: Would you two excuse me? I need to make some calls.

> **Hercules:** Why are you crying, Tiresias? Is it because of that wailing shade over there?

Manto: Oooooh.

> **Hercules:** Do you want some beef jerky?

5:05 PM
Tiresias: Hercules, please just go.

> **Hercules:** What happened?

Tiresias: What's happened is our mission here is a complete failure. I just had a prophecy that Manto isn't coming back.

> **Hercules:** But I thought your mission was to bring back Penelope and Patroclus and—

Tiresias: So I can watch Odysseus get everything, and I—?

> **Hercules:** Oh, he's crying again.

5:06 PM
> **Hercules:** Tell you what, I'll go ask Hades nicely if he can sprinkle some of that bloody blood on this shade over here. Be right back. I'll turn off the recording so you can cry in peace, my dude.

5:11 PM
Hercules: So, um, news.

Hercules: Apparently Hades didn't confiscate the blood from Ares.

Hercules: Thanatos did. Ooh, that name makes me shudder.

Hercules: And Hades doesn't know where Thanatos hid it. In fact, he said it could be destroyed at this point.

Hercules: So the only way we could bring them back is—

5:12 PM
Tiresias: By killing Medusa, which we aren't going to do, so.

Hercules: Maybe we could just prick her finger? Like at the American doctor's office?

Tiresias: It has to be blood from a dead gorgon. Asclepius back in the day said he used the blood from a dead one.

Hercules: Lemme go ask Hades. Keep crying, buddy.

5:16 PM
Hercules: So, um, is there a plan B? Because plan A would require Medusa to be dead as a—well, dead person.

Tiresias: Why do the gods hate me?

Hercules: Oh, buddy, they hate everyone. But—

Hercules: "Consider, Tiresias, how close Persephone and

Medusa seemed when we entered the Underworld. It's almost as if they knew each other before this."

5:17 PM
Tiresias: What do you mean? And why did your vocabulary just change?

Hercules: "It changes when I ponder deep matters."

Hercules: "Now, back to the subject at hand. They seemed as though they were friends. And it does strike me as odd that Persephone absolutely needed to pull Medusa aside to discuss some business."

Tiresias: What are you saying? Are you saying they're working together?

5:18 PM
Hercules: "Precisely."

Tiresias: It seems like a stretch.

Hercules: "Not if you think about it. What if Hades was lying about Thanatos knowing where the blood is? What if Persephone and Medusa have been in charge of it this whole time?"

Tiresias: What do you mean?

Hercules: "Medusa insisted you come down to the Underworld. Perhaps to conspire with Persephone. Persephone probably used the blood to create an army for her app so she could win a bet with her mother."

Tiresias: But I had a prophecy that the blood got confiscated.

5:19 PM
Hercules: "Perhaps it had. And perhaps that is why Persephone and Medusa are speaking now. To formulate another
plan. Have you considered how easy it was for you to invade
the Underworld? Almost as if Persephone let you walk
right in."

Tiresias: It did seem easy.

Tiresias: But even if Persephone and Medusa were working
together, why is that a bad thing?

    Hercules: "Because, Tiresias, that would make her in
    charge of who came back."

5:20 PM
Tiresias: You mean Manto.

    Hercules: "Yes. And she is likely not bringing back Pene-
    lope, Patroclus, all of them, as leverage against the heroes.
    To meet the demands of monsters."

    Hercules: "Maybe she's withholding Manto because she
    wants to use you for your prophetic abilities. Those come in
    handy when it comes to the subject of war."

Tiresias: War, like the admin announcement said.

5:21 PM
Tiresias: So if she's been playing double agent this whole time, we
can't do much about it, can we?

    Hercules: "There is something YOU could do."

Tiresias: What? Kill her? Even if she betrays us, that still feels wrong.

> **Hercules:** "Very well, think about it from a practical perspective. If she laid down her life, she could bring back the lives of so many others. She knows this. She is being selfish by refusing to sacrifice herself to resurrect loved ones. Why?"

> **Hercules:** "Because monsters enjoy watching the suffering of others. Why I—I mean, Odysseus—witnessed it first-hand. A cyclops tore my—his—men limb from limb. Simply because they so happened to run into the wrong cave."

5:22 PM
Hercules: "How do you know she doesn't delight in your tears? In your suffering? That every time she says your daughter's name, she does so with a smirk? Knowing it feels like a punch in the gut to you."

Tiresias: WHY DON'T YOU KILL HER THEN, HERCULES?

> **Hercules:** "My, my, what a temper."

5:23 PM
Hercules: "And Hercules—I mean, I—would be inadequate for the job. Even if Medusa didn't pull off her veil and sunglasses as a defense mechanism, I have been having a weird enlightenment period where I don't want to use my hands to murder monsters."

> **Hercules:** "Which will hopefully be at an end soon."

Hercules: "But for now, you must be the one to slay the gorgon. And bring back so many shades who left the mortal world far too soon."

Tiresias: Like Manto. But the prophecy I just had—

Hercules: "Prophecies do not always come true if mortals wield their own destiny. Surely we can take hold of your destiny now."

5:24 PM
Tiresias: Manto wouldn't understand at first.

Tiresias: But maybe I could convince her over time that a sacrifice was worth bringing her back. Bringing all of them back.

Tiresias: Gaia knows I would give my life for her at this very moment.

Hercules: "And Gaia knows how selfish Medusa is for refusing to yield hers."

5:25 PM
Tiresias: Gods, I can't believe I'm going to do this again.

Hades: Do what again?

Hercules: Uhhh, use the restroom? Poor guy's got a tiny bladder.

Hades: No time for that. Just got off the phone with Hermes and Persephone, and we need to move.

5:26 PM
Tiresias: To where?

Hades: Olympus. We need to convince the gods to stop a war.

Wanna Commit Murder with Me, Babe?

January 9

6:31 PM
Hades: Are you sure they're going to be okay, left in the waiting room?

Hades: I know my brother is weird about mortals being on Olympus, but I honestly had no idea that rude receptionist wouldn't allow them past the lobby.

Rude Receptionist: 'Ey, I'm not allowed in Olympus either. If I can't go, they can't go. Simple.

Persephone: They'll be fine. Better here than with Charon, who's gone all plant-cruise happy. He's even gone so far as pushing some shades into River Styx to tell them to "look out for the piranhas." Which would be bad if he did that to one of the very-much-alive people in the lobby.

6:32 PM
Hades: True.

Hades: Which brings me to my next question. Why are you recording this, darling?

Persephone: Zeus and Hera have a history of going back on their word, so if we have their words on paper—or screen— that they'll stop this war, they can't back out.

Hades: Good thinking.

Rude Receptionist: Zeus'll see you now.

Hades: Are you all going to be all right?

6:33 PM
Tiresias: Hercules is going to keep us occupied by explaining the intricacies of chess.

Hercules: So you see this one that looks like a horse? Well apparently, it isn't a horse. Confusing, I know.

Hades: Have fun. All right, Seph, let's go in.

6:35 PM
Persephone: Shoot, they remodeled. I miss the "everything is made out of clouds" motif.

Persephone: Now it's all gold. Gold lamps, gold roads, gold thrones that Hera and Zeus are sitting on in front of us right now. Tacky.

Hera: We CAN hear you, you know.

Hades: Darling, we talked about inside voices.

Persephone: Yeah, well, inside voices are meant for inside people. And lemme tell you, Hades, I am an outside person.

Hades: Brother, it is so good to see you.

6:36 PM
Zeus: You're looking a little pale.

Hades: I mean ... we don't get sunlight in the Underworld. But yes, if you must know, I feel a little woozy. Seph and I can't be gone from the homeland too long or our health will take a serious toll.

Hera: Great, that means a quick meeting.

Hades: Glad you understand. All right, let's cut to the chase. Zeus, I was wondering if you—

Zeus: No.

6:37 PM
Persephone: Excuse me?

Hades: You didn't even let me finish what I was going to say.

Zeus: I consulted with Hera beforehand, and she said whatever you ask, I have to answer no ... OW. Hera, why did you just elbow me in the ribs?

Hera: Because you weren't supposed to say that part out loud, dimwit.

Persephone: Listen, there's a war about to happen, and it has Hera's name all over it.

Hera: How dare you!

6:38 PM
Hades: Sweetheart, what did we say about accusing the queen of the gods of inciting wars?

> **Persephone:** Accusing people is one of my side effects of being away from the Underworld too long, babe. You know this.

Hades: That's not a thing.

Hades: Zeus, Hera, you know we're not ones to approach Olympus unless we have something dire on our hands. And Hera, although we don't believe you're causing a war—right Persephone?

> **Persephone:** Hmph.

6:39 PM
Hades: Hera's name was on this admin announcement.

Hades: Here, take a look at my phone.

6:40 PM
Hades: Zeus, I need you to show it to Hera, too, so she can see the message.

Hades: What are you—?

6:41 PM
Hades: Zeus, are you creating ANOTHER profile on DearHades? On my own phone?

> **Zeus:** ... No.

Hades: Give me that back.

Hades: Hera, in summary, since I apparently need to confiscate this device, Aphrodite hacked our app and pitted mortals and monsters against one another.

Hades: She's claiming if the monsters win the war, you'll undo any curse placed on the monsters.

> 6:42 PM
> **Zeus:** Really? Wow, how big of you, Hera. You must be going to those anger-management classes I recommended.

Hera: I have done nothing of the sort.

> **Hades:** Hera, we imagine you didn't conspire with Aphrodite, so we need you to step in and disband any notion you'll provide this prize to the victors.

> **Hades:** Aphrodite name-dropped me, so I can already tell them I won't bring back loved ones. Partly because Thanatos is in charge of killing people, not me.

6:43 PM
All: *shudder*

> **Hades:** But also because I don't intend to endorse any kind of war of this nature.

> **Hades:** Will you go on record and say you will have nothing to do with this war? Or better yet, that you will punish anyone who does participate?

Hera: I—

6:44 PM
Hera: I shouldn't get involved. Shouldn't interfere with mortal affairs.

Persephone: Ugh, good gods.

Hades: Seph, let me handle this. You're about to squeeze that golden cup in your hands to pieces.

Persephone: Gaia, what the fury is wrong with these people?

Hades: While my wife is mumbling to herself and definitely NOT KILLING THAT GOLDEN PLANT. Seph, put it down.

6:45 PM
Persephone: Hmph. I'm doing it because I want to, not because you told me to.

Hades: Hera, might you explain *why* you've chosen not to interfere, when throughout history you've gotten yourself involved in things that had nothing to do with you?

Persephone: What did we say about minding our temper, darling? Ooh, look at you clenching your fists.

Hades: Side effects.

Hera: Simple, Hades, I have not been a fan of your app since its inception. Nor any other dating apps of the Olympian sort. It makes certain people forget about fidelity and—Zeus. Zeus, where did you get that burner phone?

6:45 PM
Zeus: Uhhh.

Unknown Source: *whiiiiiish*

Persephone: Did he just chuck his phone into outer space?

> **Hera:** As I was saying, this seems like it's your problem, since it came from your app.

Hades: Yes, it did come from our app.

> **Persephone:** Ooh, now he's gritting his teeth. I love it when you get angry, darling.

6:46 PM
Hades: And that's why we're trying to get you to say, on record, that you won't reverse the curses placed on the monsters … and that you do not endorse this war.

> **Hera:** Eh, I'll do nothing of the kind.

Persephone: So you DO endorse this war, and DO plan to remove all curses?

> **Hera:** Eh.

> **Hera:** I'm sure you'll think of something else.

6:47 PM
Hades: How about you, Zeus, king of the gods?

Hades: Your wife seems to be really dodgy about this whole thing. I'm starting to think maybe she did collaborate with Aphrodite.

Hades: You gonna just sit here and let her walk all over you? When you could stop this war with the snap of your finger?

Zeus: Well, I, er, uh—

Persephone: Shoooooot, look at that killer glare from Hera.

Zeus: I do not wish to get involved in this matter either. If mortals and monsters choose to wage war, what of it?

6:48 PM
Hades: It's a wonder you two ever ended up king and queen of the earth.

Hades: Come on, Seph, let's catch the first bullet train back to the Underworld. I'm not dealing with this asinine conversation.

Persephone: Whoa, shouldn't we go out the lobby? Why are you heading toward the exit doors that way?

Hades: And deal with that condescending receptionist? No, we're leaving, and on our terms.

Hades: Go ahead and shut this recording off.

11:23 PM
Persephone: But darling, what about the lobby—

ECHO'S NOTES

JANUARY 9

6:39 PM
Hercules: And that's how you get checkmate in fifteen moves.

Tiresias: Uh, Echo, why are you recording this?

Echo: Recording ... checkmate?

6:40 PM
Medusa: I think she means she's interested in learning chess and wants to take notes.

Echo: Take notes!

Tiresias: May have been better to turn it on about ten minutes ago, Echo, but I suppose we can leave it on for listening material for Hercules tonight.

Hercules: Yay, Echo's pretty voice will be in my ear! But you are not actually in my ear, Echo. That's not how it works.

Echo: In ear. Echo.

6:41 PM
Medusa: Wow, get a room, you two.

Hercules: Silly Medusa, we already are in a room. It's called the waiting room.

Tiresias: Yeah, and I wonder how long we're going to be waiting. Do you think they'll convince Zeus and Hera to call off the war?

Medusa: Persephone said she had a plan.

Tiresias: Yeah, what else did she say? You two seem pretty close.

6:42 PM
Medusa: Oh ... yes. Well, apparently we knew each other in the Underworld. I just didn't remember much, because, Asphodel. We, uh, just talked about ... stuff. Girl talk.

Hercules: Girl talk. Oh, the mysteries.

Tiresias: Herc, do you think she's being a little too dodgy? Like she doesn't want us to know something?

Hercules: What was that? It's so hard to hear you when you're whispering.

Tiresias: Nothing, haha. No need to yell in the lobby, pal. I was just saying you're very good at chess.

6:43 PM
Tiresias: Since chess is all about being secretive. And not giving away your strategy.

Hercules: I don't remember being good at that, but okay!

Hermes: Mail delivery.

Rude Secretary: Buddy, what the Hades is this? Envelopes are falling all over my desk.

Hermes: So I guess Zeus unswiped a lot of girls on that app, to block them from communications.

6:44 PM
Hermes: So they've decided to write their thoughts. Um, very angry thoughts, in letters. Some may be bewitched.

Rude Secretary: Yeesh, I'll need my letter opener to sort through these. Better diffuse any potential curses before they get to Zeus.

Medusa: I wouldn't be too upset if a certain duck got cursed ...

Echo: Duck?

Medusa: I'll tell you about it at knitting circle.

6:45 PM
Tiresias: Yes, speaking of knitting circle and monsters ... Hades said something interesting about the gorgon blood Ares had been using.

Tiresias: Apparently, Hades didn't confiscate it.

Tiresias: Thanatos did.

All: *shudder*

Tiresias: So I can see why the heroes are so anxious to tap into that blood supply of yours, Medusa. Because your blood is the only way to bring back tons of people.

6:46 PM
Tiresias: I can only imagine the burden of knowing laying down my own life could bring so many others back to life.

Tiresias: Let's discuss.

> **Medusa:** Right ... so many others.

> **Medusa:** People who might deserve to come back ...

> 6:47 PM
> **Medusa:** Disrupting the balance of life.

> **Medusa:** Yup. Interesting stuff. So, Hercules, what happens next in chess?

Tiresias: Oh, I hate to do this ... Gaia, why do I have to do this. How can I even do it? Maybe the letter opener?

> **Hercules:** While Tiresias is whispering not suspiciously, I'd love to tell you about all the reasons why the pawn pieces are like little friends. You mustn't underestimate them.

Rude Secretary: Well, it's time for my fifth meal break. Hope no one moves this letter opener right on top of this stack of envelopes.

> 6:48 PM
> **Hercules:** While Tiresias is getting up to stretch or something, let's talk about the queen and how she can do anything she wants. Remember, ladies. You are queens. Especially you, Echo.

Echo: Queen. Anything.

> **Medusa:** I think I just saw hearts in her eyes.

280

Hercules: Oh good, Tiresias is back. I thought I heard a bunch of letters collapsing back there.

6:49 PM
Hercules: How were those stretches, buddy? Did you work those quads?

> **Tiresias:** Yes, very muscular quads. Um, Medusa, is that Hades coming out of that door over there?

Medusa: What? That's … a blank wall …

> **Echo:** LETTER OPENER!

Medusa: Wha—ah! Tiresias, what are you doing?

> 6:50 PM
> **Tiresias:** Dang it, stop squirming, I—uh, stretches?

Medusa: With a sharp object stabbing toward my neck? You could hurt Bobart!

Medusa: Wow. I thought we were past this. You're really going to try to kill me again?

Medusa: Persephone said there were good mortals in the world … I'm starting to doubt it.

Medusa: Besides you, Echo, but I think you're a nymph or something, so you're good.

> **Echo:** Echo a nymph.

6:51 PM
Medusa: Thank you, that's good to know.

Tiresias: Well, you can thank muscles over here for giving me the idea.

Tiresias: He was getting all philosophical and very uncharacteristic. But he told me enough about you not to trust you.

Medusa: Is this because I didn't tell you what I talked about with Persephone?

Tiresias: I mean partly, but it was enough to confirm what he told me. And if I don't strike first, someone else will.

6:52 PM
Tiresias: Come on, Hercules, let's get out of here.

Medusa: I knew it. I knew all men were backstabbers.

Hercules: He did try to stab you in the front, though.

Medusa: Come on, Echo. We're going to join some monsters.

Medusa: Maybe a war is just what we need, after all.

6:53 PM
Hercules: Can we not go on the bullet train with them? Because that'll be, you know, pretty awkward.

Tiresias: I know Apollo rides his chariot past here around now. Used to serve him back in my past life. Let's wait for him to swing by.

Tiresias: Ladies, feel free to be on your way. Let's hope we don't bump into each other. Because if we do—

Hercules: What are you doing with that letter opener? You keep moving it back and forth in a horizontal line in front of your neck. What does this mean?

Medusa: It's exactly what I'll do to HIM if I see him ever again.

6:54 PM
Hercules: Open his letters?

Hercules: Aaaand, they're gone.

Admin Announcement

Everyone who is still on the app, THE LAST ADMIN ANNOUNCEMENT WAS A HOAX. For real, people, when would I ever say I enjoyed being kidnapped?

Not that I was ever kidnapped in the first place. Darling, yes, I know, I'll stick to the point and edit the copy later.

Please spread the word to the StupidCupid forums. Hades and I have attempted to create accounts there, but Aphrodite has hired many more furies to boot us out. She also seemed to catch on that Hermes, Hephaestus, and Iris played a role in developing our app. Because Iris's rainbows have turned into tornadoes. Hermes's letters keep exploding in his bag—causing major shipping delays.

And Hephaestus texted us on a burner phone and claimed his wife put him "in timeout for going behind her back and creating a competing app."

With our coding team down for the count, and shades only able to do so much without them, we don't know how long this app is going to last with all the new glitches the furies are introducing.

So screenshot this and send it to every hero and monster.

Please do not go to war. Hera will not follow through on her end of the deal—uh, take our word for it. Because she may deny it.

And Hades will certainly not bring back loved ones. That's not even his job. That's Thanatos's.

Gods-speed in stopping this war and putting an end to unnecessary bloodshed.

Monstrously Magnificent
Maidens

January 10

8:53 AM
Arachne: Good morning, ladies. That was a very productive emergency knitting circle we had last night.

Scylla: You mean the one where Medusa and Echo spilled all the REAL tea about what they've been up to? Not that I'm salty about that. At all.

8:54 AM
Medusa: I am sorry, you guys. I should've been truthful. If I had, I could've avoided a lot of heartache.

Medusa: But all that is behind us. I don't care if Hades and Persephone weren't the ones who put out that admin announcement. We're holding whatever gods did it accountable. Hera is going to lift our curses.

Arachne: Yeah, she is! Because we're gonna kick some hero booty!

8:55 AM
Echo: Kick some hero booty?

Lamia: Echo darling, you need to forget about Hercules. It was all a trap. He and Tiresias never cared about you two.

Echo: Never ... cared.

8:56 AM
Medusa: I don't think that's necessarily true, Echo. Hercules did seem to like you. But that doesn't matter anymore. The heroes are out to kill us, and we need to strike first and win this war.

Scylla: At least she isn't talking about Narcissus anymore. That's one good thing to come out of this.

Echo: Isn't talking about Narcissus. Anymore.

8:57 AM
Medusa: Wow, Echo, you're getting even better at using your own punctuation. You just continue to improve!

Echidna: Yes, excellent job, Echo. But let's focus, snakelets. Scylla, Aglaope, Charybdis, you've been networking with other monsters, correct? Setting up alliances?

Aglaope: Lots and lots of them. There are a ton of monsters in the mythos.

Charybdis: *glugalorp* Yes, luckily that's something I can do, considering I'm a whirlpool and it's pretty hard to get myself anywhere but the water. I won't be of much use in a fight. :(

8:58 AM
Echidna: Yes, I'm sorry about that, Chary. But you have been a huge help in networking. I'm not sure how a whirlpool operates a phone, nor how you've participated in our knitting circles, but that's a plot hole we will gloss over.

Scylla: She Skypes in to knitting circle and spins yarn into balls for us to use next time.

Aglaope: Oh, that's why the yarn is wet so often.

8:59 AM
Medusa: Do any of you actually pay attention to what's going on in knitting circle? Aglaope, do you even know the names of Scylla's dogs?

Aglaope: Scylla has dogs?

Scylla: ...

Scylla: Part of my body is made up of dogs, Aglaope. You never noticed this?

9:00 AM
Echidna: Ladies, back on track. Arachne, did you confirm the location of the battle?

Arachne: Sure did. Apparently there's a barren cornfield outside town where everyone is planning on gathering. Today is a prep day, and tomorrow we're going to hold the actual battle.

Medusa: We're coordinating when we're all going to get together and try to kill each other?

9:01 AM
Arachne: Just like the old days, line up and go for it. I think everyone is too impatient to wait around and assassinate each other. That's not as fun for the gods to watch, either.

Medusa: Makes sense, continue.

Arachne: So there's a monster chat on StupidCupid where everyone is planning to set up the details. Echidna and I have already joined. I think everyone is afraid the shades will shut down any chats here.

9:02 AM
Medusa: They likely will. Hades and Persephone are trying to stop the war. Which I appreciate. But it's too late now. Monsters deserve their curses lifted, and heroes deserve to get sent back to Hades.

Arachne: I sure would love to be human again. Being a spider has its perks, but I'd like to be able to go out for coffee without everyone screaming.

9:03 AM
Echidna: I'm glad we have this hammered out. Continue to reach out to all the monsters you know, everyone, and send them to StupidCupid and the "Monster Mayhem" forum. I'm one of the admins, so I'm vetting to make sure no heroes get in.

Arachne: Just an unsettling number of farm animals. Hera especially seems to have liked turning people into animals. I think a lot of these didn't even get recorded in the myths. I met two or three chickens already this morning.

9:04 AM
Medusa: Okay, everyone, let's all make StupidCupid accounts if we haven't already.

Medusa: It's time to go to war.

StupidCupid <3

January 10

New: Forums!
   Forum Name: Monster Mayhem
   Description: Battle planning, serious recruits only. Heavily vetted. Must be willing to battle on January 11.

———

9:25 AM
Echidna: Welcome to all our new members. As a recap, let's go over our upcoming battle strategy.

   Chicken: Bawk bawk!

Lamia: May I request all non-speaking entities keep comments to themselves or make use of a translator?

   9:26 AM
   Echidna: Admin approval granted.

Chicken: Bawk bawk! See translation: Bawk bawk!

Lamia: Ah. That was … actually what they were saying.

Chicken: It's an expression of excitement in our culture.

9:27 AM
Echidna: Let's get this ball rolling. We're going to begin our attack with an aerial flyover, with all of our flying friends dropping rocks and other missiles then wheeling back around. Don't hang out too long, just do a flyby, drop, and go. We just want to throw them off.

Seagull: Heeheehee, we seagulls make our own projectiles.

Arachne: …

Echidna: I don't want to know more. Arachne, you weren't kidding about the number of animals.

9:28 AM
Arachne: Hey, people got turned into animals a lot.

Echidna: Anyway. After the aerial flyover, our cavalry—any horse people, fast people—will advance on their flanks, while our tanks lead the frontal charge. We want to try to surround them.

Aglaope: We have tanks?

9:29 AM
Medusa: No, Aglaope, that's just a term for tough, brawny fighters. Usually used in contexts like D&D. Remember when we tried to play that one time?

Aglaope: Oh yeah. My characters died a lot.

Scylla: You kept jumping off cliffs to see if you could roll a nat 20 to fly.

Aglaope: Oh yeah. And Echidna was mean and said even a nat 20 didn't matter if my character didn't have wings.

9:30 AM
Echidna: FOCUS, ladies.

Chicken: Hold on, did I see the name Medusa pop up? That's a big advantage right there. All she has to do is look at people!

Medusa: Chicken is right, Echidna. I think I should be leading the tanks.

Echidna: Leading? I don't know, snakelet. You're a little ... squishy.

Arachne: Excuse you?

9:31 AM
Medusa: It's a D&D term. It means you have low hit points. Easy to kill.

Arachne: Oh. I wasn't very good at that game either.

Seagull: Wait, this is a real battle, right? This isn't a Dungeons and Dragons campaign?

Echidna: This is a very real, very serious battle, everyone. I stayed up all night outlining strategies. Let's please stay on task.

Medusa: I know I'm not a large monster, or one with tough skin or large tentacles, but I have to be at the front.

Otherwise, one of our people might turn around and look at me.

9:32 AM
Cow: Why is that bad? Is she ugly?

Chicken: No, you fool, if you look at her face, you turn to stone.

Cow: Ohhhh. Makes sense.

Scylla: Chicken seems a little more intelligent than the other cursed animals.

Chicken: As Diogenes once said, "Behold, a man!"

9:33 AM
Echidna: You do have a point, Medusa ... and anyone who tries to kill you will have to look at you ... but what about shooting at you from afar? Arrows? Even guns?

Arachne: Oh, update on the guns thing, our spies have discovered the heroes will only be using ancient Greek weaponry. Otherwise it will ruin the "heroic aesthetic."

Echidna: Okay, not guns then. But everything else.

Medusa: I appreciate the concern. But in the end ... if I die, it might not be the worst thing. Some of you, my core knitting circle ladies, know why that is. The most important thing is that our side recovers my body first, and under no circumstances, the heroes. Arachne has an amphora ready.

9:34 AM
Arachne: I still disagree with this Plan B. Very strongly.

And I think you should be careful—and it WOULD be a terrible thing if you die. But I also have your back, always.

Arachne: And some very large Tupperware containers. Couldn't find an amphora on such short notice. Sorry.

Medusa: I appreciate the effort, and the support.

Echidna: As much as I don't like it … fine. Medusa will lead our frontal charge. With plenty of armor on.

9:35 AM
Lamia: This is all good … but where are we getting weapons and armor?

Medusa: I think Echidna has been LARPing. She made some connections.

Echidna: Haha, not, not actually LARPing, just talking to some people … in a very cool, very not weird and nerdy way …

Echidna: But yes, I have many friends who make armor and weaponry.

9:36 AM
Arachne: Own your passions, queen.

Cow: She's a queen?

Chicken: Of course she's a queen. I think. Were you always this easily confused as a person?

Cow: I'll have you know I was a student of Plato in my first life before being cursed to this form.

Chicken: Ah, makes sense.

9:37 AM
Echidna: So with our three divisions of aerial, cavalry, and tanks ... that's about it. We don't really have enough creatures for much more than that.

> **Charybdis:** *glurpglolob* And if anyone wanders over to the ocean, I can pull them in.

Echidna: Yes, very good.

> **Cyclops:** So ... that's it? We just charge forward?

9:38 AM
Aglaope: Wait, we have a cyclops? Since when?

> **Scylla:** Nobody knew about it until just now, I think.

Cyclops: NOBODY? WHERE?

> **Lamia:** Well, I'm always delighted to kill some men. I think we have an excellent plan.

9:39 AM
Echidna: Good. In that case, nothing can stop us tomorrow. The tidal wave of monsters will crash upon the heroes.

> **Medusa:** And we will be avenged.

Wanna Commit Murder with Me, Babe?

January 10

10:10 AM
Persephone: I don't think the admin announcement is doing much good.

Persephone: I disguised myself as a chicken for the Stupid-Cupid app, to see how much the forums have progressed. They booted me, since there was another chicken and I was therefore "suspicious."

Persephone: But I got enough of a glimpse to know what's going down.

10:11 AM
Persephone: Babe, they're already going to wage war tomorrow.

Persephone: I'm sure you're still conked out from our late-night journey back to Olympus to retrieve the four people we left in the lobby.

Persephone: But Echo and Medusa were on the monster

chat. We can only assume at the very least Hercules has entered the war too.

10:14 AM
Hades: Sorry, just finished catching up.

> **Persephone:** You're good. Take your time. I know you need about thirty minutes to actually get out of bed. I'm fine with texting.

> **Persephone:** I made the executive decision to shut down the app this morning.

10:15 AM
Hades: You WHAT?

> **Persephone:** No need to shout, darling. Our new admin announcement keeps getting pulled down by glitches, and most people have evacuated to StupidCupid. They know by now the war isn't endorsed by us—I've seen posts all over my social feed this morning.

> 10:16 AM
> **Persephone:** They just don't care.

> **Persephone:** They want bloodshed.

> **Persephone:** And I couldn't keep the app up if it served as an instrument for ruining more lives. We can't be like the folks on Olympus. We have to be better.

10:17 AM
Hades: I'm sad it came to this, but I'm proud of you. We can figure out a plan B once we stop this war thing.

Persephone: Ha. Well, good luck convincing a couple to get engaged after all this. Even though we can just as easily set it back up, I doubt we'll have any takers.

Persephone: Also, things have gotten worse with Demeter.

Hades: How?

10:18 AM
Persephone: Hermes delivered a non-exploding package this morning. The first thing to draw my suspicion, since Aphrodite cursed all the developers of our app. Poor Iris and those tornadoes.

Hades: So that's why there was a class-five tornado going through Oklahoma in January. That was all over social media.

Persephone: Yes, dear.

10:19 AM
Persephone: So I opened the package—no sender—and it was loose-leaf pomegranate tea.

Persephone: I got so excited, because you know how it relaxes me.

Persephone: Anyway, I broke open one of the packets, poured it into a strainer to put in my teapot—but just before I began boiling water, I noticed something strange about the loose-leaf tea mixture.

Persephone: It had bits of green in it. Dark green.

10:20 AM
Persephone: Kale, Hades. Demeter sent me kale disguised as tea.

Hades: Are you positive?

Persephone: She posted on social media this morning an Olympian news article on DearHades and how it incited a war.

10:21 AM
Persephone: I think she caught on to the fact our app failed. So she thought she'd try to sneak me some kale to finish the deal nine months early.

Hades: Permission to stab your mother?

Persephone: Oh, babe, always granted. You know I love it when you get stabby.

10:22 AM
Persephone: But before committing matricide, I think we need to develop a game plan for this war.

Persephone: Our app won't work, and Aphrodite won't let us on StupidCupid. I think we need to resort to drastic measures.

Persephone: We need to get Thanatos involved.

10:23 AM
Persephone: Wow, I heard your gasp all the way in the kitchen.

Hades: Are you positive, Seph? You know he can be ... a lot to take.

Hades: And if we're talking about stab-happy people, he will murder everyone without hesitation. There's a reason why I don't let him into the Underworld much. He just deposits the souls at the entrance, and we handle the rest. And even that can be too much.

10:24 AM
Persephone: It's a last resort, I know.

Persephone: But we don't have many options. We're not the type of deities to go in there and kill people ourselves. And I don't know enough about the situation to make an informed decision about who should die and who should live.

Persephone: We put Thanatos on grim-reaper duty for this reason.

10:25 AM
Hades: What if he kills everyone? And there's no one left to play matchmaker for? What about your bet with Demeter?

Persephone: I—

Persephone: I know the Greek god thing to do would be to put our romance before everything else. Even if that meant letting people get hurt, killed, cursed.

Persephone: And believe me when I say I want to be with you for all eternity.

10:26 AM
Persephone: But I believe love means sacrifice.

Persephone: And if we have to give up time together to make sure we put an end to this war, then I'll take one week a year with you over an eternity together knowing their blood is on our hands.

10:27 AM
Hades: We'll find a way. We always do.

Hades: I have your back, even in this decision. I will always have your back.

> **Persephone:** Well, give it back, because I need a spine to face Thanatos.

10:28 AM
Hades: Once I get up, we'll schedule an appointment with him.

10:29 AM
Hades: Gaia have mercy on our souls.

KILLER BROS 2.0

JANUARY 10

11:02 AM
Odysseus: Wonderful. Thank you, Hercules, for setting up a private chat between yourself and Tiresias in the StupidCupid app. This will keep any chatter between you two out of the hero forums. I'm glad the app formats are roughly the same.

Odysseus: Are we recording now?

    Hercules: Yessir!

11:03 AM
Tiresias: Two questions.

Tiresias: One, why are we in a grove of trees in the MIDDLE OF JANUARY?

Tiresias: Two, why are we recording? My ears are numb from the wind, so I may not have caught that.

    Odysseus: We have tents set up. We intend to camp out the night before the battle.

11:04 AM
Tiresias: Couldn't we have, I don't know, stayed at the hotel half a mile away?

> **Odysseus:** We want this to be an authentic Ancient Greek battle, Tiresias. Men used to camp in the woods before the day of war. None of those pillow mints or cute towels in the shape of ducks and other animals.

Perseus: DUCK TOWELS.

> **Odysseus:** Yes, thank you for that contribution, Perseus. Why don't you go ahead and polish those LARPing swords of yours and leave us alone?

Perseus: SHINY.

> 11:05 AM
> **Tiresias:** LARPing swords? Will those even be effective?

Odysseus: Oh, the boys use real swords for their LARPing adventures. Doubles as a murder weapon for when they take the monsters on dates.

Odysseus: As for your second question, it helps to have a prophet nearby during a battle.

11:06 AM
Odysseus: Men used to travel for miles to consult the Oracle at Delphi before battle.

Odysseus: But since the Oracle is no longer living, we consider you to be the second-best thing. Hercules has the chat running to make sure we have any prophecies you utter on record.

Odysseus: You'll make sure to screenshot those and send them to us, right, Hercules?

Hercules: Anything to be counted as a hero, Odysseus.

11:07 AM
Odysseus: Right, yes, well, if you are valiant in this battle, we may consider bumping your role up to unpaid intern.

Hercules: Not—not hero?

Odysseus: No, you haven't quite earned it yet. But maybe someday.

Hercules: Huh.

Odysseus: While Hercules slumps and tosses me the most pitiful glare—

11:08 AM
Unknown Source: Ohhh.

Odysseus: And Achilles wails from the tent, reminiscing about his days in the Trojan War, why don't you two start a fire and begin cooking lunch for all the boys, eh?

Tiresias: Boys? Are there no females fighting with the heroes?

Odysseus: HAHAHAHAHA. What a good joker you are, Tiresias.

11:09 AM
Odysseus: But speaking of dangerous females, we need to re-strate-gize how we will approach the battlefield with a gorgon able to turn any of us to stone.

Odysseus: I'm thinking hoplite formation, with our shields, well, shielding our eyes.

Odysseus: But I may pick Jason's brain on this. He and I are often on the same wavelength.

Odysseus: Farewell, and I'll be back in a half-hour or so for the lunch you make me.

11:10 AM
Hercules: Huh, I thought after all that I would finally get to be a hero. I don't know how much more I can do.

Hercules: This is starting to be harder than those twelve labors.

Hercules: Mind grabbing me some wood for the fire?

Tiresias: Ah, the ground is full of snow.

11:11 AM
Tiresias: How are these sticks? Good enough?

Hercules: Thanks.

Tiresias: I doubt they'll burn, because they're wet from the—

Tiresias: Wow, what a blast of heat. I guess you got it going already, eh?

11:12 AM
Hercules: I'm gonna go grab some steaks out of the cooler I sneaked into my tent.

Unknown Source: Ohhh.

Hercules: I know Odysseus wants me to slaughter one of the cows in the monster camp and use that to feed the men, but I just decided to buy some steaks at Aldi.

Hercules: Do you think he'll notice?

11:13 AM
Tiresias: I think he'll get so mad he'll demote you to unpaid-unpaid intern. So far down that ladder you'll start having to pay him to work the job.

Hercules: Heeheehee. Yeah, he would do that, wouldn't he?

Tiresias: Hercules, why are you doing this? You like Echo, and you aren't killing monsters this time round. You do know Odysseus is dangling the position of hero in front of you just to get you to do what he wants, right?

11:14 AM
Tiresias: Hercules?

Hercules: Yeah, I sorta figured.

Hercules: I may not have much in the way of brains and smart stuff.

Hercules: But I know people can often see a strong person and be like, "Huh, let me ask them to do everything for me until I've used up all their strength" sort of thing.

Tiresias: Weak people like to use strong people. You're right.

11:15 AM
Hercules: But I could ask you the same thing.

Hercules: You don't seem like the stabby type. Except for that weird incident with the letter opener.

Tiresias: Okay, so one, Odysseus isn't having me fight anyway. He wants me to hang back in the trees until they can draw Medusa in here. If they haven't stabbed her first, they'll give me the honor.

Tiresias: Dang, that steak smells good.

11:16 AM
Hercules: Thanks, I grabbed some garlic salt from Aldi too.

Tiresias: Two, the reason I even tried to kill Medusa—the most recent instance—happened because you argued me into it.

Hercules: About that ...

Unknown Source: Ohhh.

Tiresias: Achilles must be having a rough go of things in that tent.

11:17 AM
Hercules: Um, that's not Achilles. There's a shade approaching.

Unknown Source: Ohhh.

Tiresias: I know that wail.

Tiresias: Manto, what are you doing here?

Manto: Ohhh.

11:18 AM
Hercules: I think Odysseus said something about the cornfield

being near one of the portals to Hades. He mentioned they have a heyday with it during Halloween with the haunted corn maze.

Manto: Ohhh.

Hercules: Maybe she got alerted by the blood in the steak?

Tiresias: Manto, I—

Manto: Ohhh, wow, it's cold. Why isn't he wearing a jacket?

11:19 AM
Hercules: Me? Oh, my dad used to tell me that doing pushups would keep me nice and warm in the winter. "No need for goatskin coats." See, one, two ... three ... brrr. Okay, time to grab my coat.

Manto: He dove into a tent.

Tiresias: That would explain the weird flapping noise right by my ear. He's going to burn the steak.

Manto: Let it burn. It's helping me remember.

Tiresias: Oh, right, the beef jerky. In the Underworld, that helped Megara remember things too.

11:20 AM
Manto: Dad, why are your eyes glittering with tears?

Tiresias: It's just so cold out here.

Manto: Then go inside.

Tiresias: See, I'd like to, but we're about to start a war. And we're apparently not allowed to stay in a hotel, because it would ruin the authentic—

Manto: A war? What for?

11:21 AM
Tiresias: Well, it's very complicated and would take well over 50,000 words to explain, but the short of it is we have to kill some monsters to bring you—and several others— back from the dead.

Manto: Dad.

Tiresias: Now I know it sounds barbaric, but I figure you didn't get to live a long life during your first time on earth. And it's completely unfair a person like me—who lived well into his old age—got a second chance.

Manto: Father.

11:22 AM
Tiresias: And I knew you would push back, but maybe someday you'll understand why we had to end one life to bring back many.

Manto: DAD.

Manto: I don't want to come back.

Tiresias: You—you don't?

Tiresias: But you spent your short-lived life as a war captive. I wanted so much more for you. You really don't want to return?

11:23 AM
Manto: Some ... some days I do. I think about how I could've worded things better in certain situations. Went for that daring kiss from my first crush, instead of letting him ask out an Amazonian princess. May he rest in peace.

Manto: But ending someone's life so I can come back for a few decades just isn't—doesn't make sense.

Manto: After all, we all end up in the same place.

> **Unknown Source:** *szzzzz*

11:24 AM
Manto: Sorry, had to flip over the steak. It was bothering me, the uneven char on one side.

> **Tiresias:** But Manto, I don't deserve this second chance. You—

Manto: Don't either. No one does. We get one life, Dad. And if we get another, then it comes at the mercy of the gods.

Manto: Give me those hands, they look blue.

> **Tiresias:** I—I can't.

Manto: Give me those hands.

> 11:25 AM
> **Tiresias:** Yours are so warm.

> **Tiresias:** I can't— *sob*

Manto: It's okay to cry. It means I was loved a great deal by you. I am *still* loved a great deal by you.

Manto: But if you bring me back by killing someone, that's not love. It's some sort of cheap substitute.

11:26 AM
Manto: And I will see you again before you know it. We'll direct plays again side by side in Asphodel.

    Tiresias: We did that?

Manto: Uh-huh. Hades and Persephone are working on remodeling how things work, since Hades hadn't been the original one to set up the Underworld.

Manto: They'll help our memories to return and stay.

Manto: But while your memory is good, please remember this talk.

11:27 AM
Manto: And since you've been given this second chance … make it count for the both of us. Don't throw your life away in some pointless war.

    Tiresias: I'll remember. I promise.

Manto: I'd best be going. Can't stay out of the Underworld too long.

Manto: See you soon.

    Tiresias: Soon.

11:28 AM

Hercules: Whew, sorry for the delay. Achilles brought a whole trunk of LARPing costumes, and I simply had to try on all of the—my steak!

Hercules: I may sneak Odysseus this one. You don't think he'll notice? Steaks are supposed to be all black, right?

Tiresias: Hercules, I can't fight in this war.

Hercules: Sure, you won't. Odysseus is having you hide in the trees back here. You only have to stab Medusa if she—

Tiresias: Hercules, my daughter just visited me.

11:29 AM
Tiresias: I've been going about this all wrong.

Tiresias: Even if Medusa's blood can save lives, it isn't worth it. That's too big of an ask for her, and those lives only last a few decades. We all end up in the same place.

Tiresias: I shouldn't have let you talk me into stabbing her with the letter opener.

Hercules: Um, so about that ...

11:30 AM
Hercules: Odysseus was feeding me the words to say.

Tiresias: Sorry, what?

Hercules: I only did it because I figured one more task for him would finally get me the title of hero. But we saw where that got me.

Tiresias: I need to find a way to contact Medusa.

11:33 AM
Tiresias: Dang it, why can't I access DearHades?

Hercules: Oh, because they took it down. This morning.

Tiresias: Shoot. And they heavily vet the monster forums.

Tiresias: Any way we can go across no-man's-land and talk to Medusa? Explain everything?

Hercules: No can do.

11:34 AM
Hercules: The monsters sent us a list of rules for the battle earlier. If anyone marches onto the battlefield before the appointed time, the monsters will send someone to eat them. I think they mentioned a cyclops.

Tiresias: Nobody can get past a cyclops on an open cornfield.

Hercules: Especially not Odysseus. He sure went white as a sheet when he read that one off the list.

Tiresias: So what do we do? If I wait until tomorrow, I have no guarantee Medusa will even get to this grove of trees. Not with the Hoplite formation jabbing spears in her direction.

11:35 AM
Hercules: Dude, the only way you could get to her earlier is if you were on the actual battlefield yourself.

Hercules: Which, you know, would directly disobey Odysseus's orders.

Hercules: So at this point, I'm game for that.

11:36 AM
Tiresias: How many LARPing costumes did Achilles
bring?

Hercules: You know what, Ty? I think I spotted one in there that's
just your size.

Wanna Commit Murder with Me, Babe?

January 10

1:01 PM
Persephone: Okay, babe, you've got this. We're just gonna approach Death himself, ask him not to kill everyone—but to threaten to kill anyone who continues the war after we issue a warning—and then we'll get some nice impossible burgers on the way home.

1:02 PM
Hades: Warning?

Persephone: Yeah, I'm thinking of you strolling up to the battlefield all cool and stuff. What screams cool? Does a feather boa scream cool?

Hades: Seph.

Persephone: And you twirl that feather boa in your finger-tips as you point to the nearest screaming hero and go, "Hey, you, killing is not nice."

1:03 PM
Hades: Oh my gods.

Persephone: And then they will of course acquiesce, and we'll all be friends again.

Hades: So I know you've been watching a lot of mortal-kids' TV shows lately ...

Hades: But I have a feeling it will play out a little differently.

1:04 PM
Persephone: You're right. A feather boa isn't intimidating at all.

Persephone: How do you feel about clogs?

Hades: Why are you recording our voices?

Persephone: Same deal with Olympus. We want to make sure we can hold Thanatos's word against him if he says he'll do one thing and then does another.

Persephone: Plus.

1:05 PM
Persephone: That eccentric receptionist's voice is just too good not to capture on audio.

Eccentric Receptionist with a Cool Accent: Ope, just gonna scoot on past you right there to go get some more ranch dressing for my chicken.

Persephone: So foreign. So wow.

Hades: Darling, she's from Ohio.

1:06 PM
Persephone: I was surprised, too, to learn Thanatos's office was in Cleveland. But I guess it makes sense. Ohio feels like death. Too bad we haven't visited him until now.

Hades: Yeah, well this office is giving me the opposite of death vibes.

Persephone: I know what you mean. The furniture is so chic and hip. I was under the impression we'd be sitting in coffins in the waiting area.

Hades: And all the employees are in bright colors. Are we sure we didn't stumble into Iris's office instead? You know, the goddess of rainbows slash now tornados?

Persephone: Pretty sure. She had a tornado blow through her place earlier this morning. Considering we're not spotting cows flying past us, probably not Iris's business.

1:07 PM
Eccentric Receptionist with a Cool Accent: Ope, so sorry to keep you waiting. This is usually Thanatos's lunch break, you see. He eats the same thing every day—

Persephone: The bones of children?

Eccentric Receptionist with a Cool Accent: Bratwurst with a wedge salad. So he can feel like he ate healthy that day.

Persephone: Even worse.

Eccentric Receptionist with a Cool Accent: Follow me.

1:08 PM
Persephone: Okay, babe, just breathe. You got this. You got this.

1:09 PM
Persephone: Don't hyperventilate and puke all over the floor. That's bad for business meetings.

1:10 PM
Persephone: And don't accidentally strangle Thanatos with a plant.

Hades: Are these ... pep talks supposed to be for me?

Persephone: ... Sure?

1:11 PM
Eccentric Receptionist with a Cool Accent: Whew, and that's the tenth door to get to him. He knows he can deliver quite a shock, so best keep him behind a lot of walls.

Persephone: Just breathe, just breathe.

Eccentric Receptionist with a Cool Accent: And I am so giddy to present to you ...

Unknown Source: *squeak*

Eccentric Receptionist with a Cool Accent: Thanatos.

1:12 PM
Hades: Gulp.

Persephone: *heavy breathing noises*

Thanatos: OMGs, are these my BFFs from the Underworld? Persephone, girl, what is up? I love what you've been doing with your hair, girl.

Hades: Yep, he's a lot to take in.

Persephone: That glittery jacket of his could just blind you, couldn't it?

1:13 PM
Thanatos: What are you two whispering for? Y'all know if you have some tea, I want it spilled. I am the god of tea, you know. And, well, death, but mostly the gossip stuff.

Thanatos: Marcella, can you please get these lovely folks some chairs? Something comfy? Would you two like an Arnold Palmer? OMGs I'm so sorry to be eating this messy salad in front of you.

Hades: You—your desk is literally immaculate right now.

Thanatos: Hades, wow, that was such a nice thing to say. Thank you.

Persephone: Did he just put his hands in front of his heart?

1:14 PM
Unknown Source: *scree*

Thanatos: Thank you, Marcella, for putting those chairs down. Now, you two, please sit and spill all the tea. Do you mind if I finish the rest of this salad? Been putting a lot of monsters in the grave lately, and that can give one quite the appetite.

Hades: Yes, the chair is, um, very plushy.

Persephone: So Thanatos, I'm sure you've heard there's a war coming up.

1:15 PM
Thanatos: Girl, whew, don't even get me started on thinking about that. You're gonna make me all sweaty. See me swipe my hand across my forehead in a dramatic fashion?

Hades: We, uh, see that.

Thanatos: Marcella is getting a right migraine about all the paperwork that's gonna be involved tomorrow.

Thanatos: Marcie, we haven't had a war like this since when?

Marcella: Aw, gee, maybe the Trojan War?

1:16 PM
Thanatos: And that one lasted a good ten years. But heroes these days want it fast. What happened to death comes slowly, for goodness' sake? Doing death well takes time, people. It's an art.

Hades: Right, so.

Persephone: Since you'd like to avoid that much paperwork, would you be open to stopping the war?

Thanatos: Girl, hold up, you're about to give me a heart attack.

1:17 PM
Thanatos: Let me get this straight.

Thanatos: You mean to tell me you want to interfere with what I do?

Thanatos: Because that is some straight-up audacity, I'll tell you what. And usually I like a powerful woman—and I suppose a man too, Hades—but I just don't know, y'all, how to feel about this.

Hades: Yes, yes, we apparently like stepping on toes, according to Aphrodite.

Persephone: But here's the thing, Thanatos.

1:18 PM
Persephone: From what we can tell, this war was started by heroes—to kill an innocent gorgon. To bring more people back from the dead than what has already been done.

Thanatos: Girlfriend, woo.

Thanatos: Don't even get me started. You see me fanning myself?

Hades: We, um, still have working vision.

Thanatos: Let me tell you, my blood downright boiled when I confiscated that blood from Ares. The sheer *audacity* of that dude. Thinking he could traipse right into the Underworld and undo my work. Good thing I destroyed that amphora, am I right?

1:19 PM
Hades: Yes, exactly.

Hades: And if we don't put a stop to this war, and if the heroes come out on top, they're going to take Medusa's blood, storm my gates, and resurrect more shades.

Thanatos: Dang, this tea is boiling. I love it! Don't you just love it, Marcie?

Eccentric Receptionist with a Cool Accent: Sure thing, boss.

Thanatos: But I don't love the idea that they'll undo my life's—well, death's—work. It's not their place.

1:20 PM
Persephone: Tracking with you, my dude. And so—

Thanatos: Girl, preach.

Persephone: —Hades and I can't exactly go onto the battlefield and kill any offenders. We wanted to come straight to the source and see if you'd be willing to step in tomorrow and issue a warning for them to stop fighting.

Thanatos: Wow, okay, this is a lot to process.

1:21 PM
Thanatos: Okay, tell you what. Marcie, grab a notepad.

Eccentric Receptionist with a Cool Accent: Got it.

Thanatos: Okay, Marcie, write this down. Tomorrow, kill all the people on the battlefield.

Eccentric Receptionist with a Cool Accent: Done and done.

Hades: Hold on. All of them?

1:22 PM
Thanatos: Well, sure, it gets rid of the problem in time for my four o'clock massage. Because, Hades, my friend, you don't know how stiff these shoulders have gotten. Oof. Enough tangles in my muscles to fill a Gordian knot.

Persephone: So, Thanatos ... um, we were hoping you could only kill a select number of people. Mostly the offenders who perpetuate the fight after we tell them to stop.

Thanatos: Hold on. Hold on. This tea is so much to take in, y'all.

Persephone: Maybe we walk through it step-by-step?

1:23 PM
Thanatos: Giiiiirl, you a mind reader? You need a promotion.

Persephone: Well, I'm Queen of the Underworld already, so—

Thanatos: Step one, I march onto the battlefield all intimidating. Marcie, mention to the wardrobe team to do the number in black rhinestones and spikes. You know, my killer suit.

Marcie: Ya, killer suit.

Persephone: Yes, that's correct.

1:24 PM
Thanatos: Step two, I make an announcement to stop the fighting, or else. Look at this fist I'm making. It's scary, isn't it?

Persephone: Yes, very scary. And right on with the next step.

Thanatos: Step three, kill everyone.

Persephone: I—no. Oh, Gaia.

Thanatos: Hold up, where did I go wrong?

1:25 PM
Thanatos: I may have to contact the Fates about this. Marcie, contact the Fates about killing everyone tomorrow.

Marcie: Fates, massacre tomorrow, you got it!

Hades: This could take a while ...

GROUP MESSAGE

JANUARY 11

6:45 AM
Medusa: Why do I feel like we should be singing a musical number about it being a good day to die?

    Arachne: Are you at the battlefield yet?

6:46 AM
Medusa: We're on the way. Echo is driving. She's in this group chat too, since we'll probably get separated during the battle and I want to make sure we can reach each other.

    Arachne: I just got here, and my dude, the heroes literally camped here last night. That's so unnecessary.

Medusa: Of course they did. It's literally hardly even a drive from our apartments. They're so extra.

    6:47 AM
    Arachne: Speaking of extra, starting the battle at seven in the morning is ridiculous.

Medusa: I'm glad we at least negotiated away from the "battle begins at the first light of dawn" nonsense. How would we even be able to tell when that is exactly? All of them should take up theater.

> **Arachne:** Echidna wants to know if you have your armor and weapons.

6:48 AM
Medusa: Yes, very heavy armor. I will be well protected. I can't have leather armor like Echo?

> **Arachne:** Echidna says to stop complaining or she won't let you fight on the front lines after all.

Medusa: Okay, okay. See you soon.

6:55 AM
Medusa: Okay, Echo, I've turned our chat to voice chat so we can all talk during the heat of battle.

> **Arachne:** Echo and I can mute ourselves unless we need you. But you should keep yours on. You're going to be in the most precarious position, and I need to know if I need to come rip off some heads for you.

Medusa: That works for me. Echo, remember what to do if you're in trouble?

> **Echo:** Trouble!

6:56 AM
Medusa: Yes, that's good. Literally just say anything you can.

> **Arachne:** What if she has to say "croissant" or something

because that's the last thing someone said? She needs some-thing to say that would be heroic last words.

Medusa: Why ... why would anyone say croissant on a battlefield?

Echo: Croissant.

Arachne: See? You just did.

6:57 AM
Medusa: Pfft. Both of you, stop giggling! And stop making me giggle! This is serious!

Arachne: I'd much rather our last interaction be laughing together. I love you girls so much.

Medusa: I love you guys too. So no dying, okay? Not allowed.

Arachne: And the same goes for you. Be careful out there, okay? You're worth too much to us to lose.

6:58 AM
Medusa: Bring it in.

Unknown Source: *CLANG*

Medusa: Haha, armor hugging is a little awkward.

Medusa: All right, off to battle.

Medusa: Gaia help us all. I'm going to turn this off for now.

7:01 AM
Unknown Source: CHARGE!

Medusa: Oh wow. Look at that unified hoplite formation. Oh, we're running now. It's hard to run in this much armor.

Medusa: No one get in front of me! I'm about to unveil my face.

Unknown Monster: You got it.

7:02 AM
Unknown Sources, Multiple: AHHH—!

Medusa: They should not have peeked around their shields. I feel like that was the point.

Unknown Source: *CRASH CLANG* AHHHHHH!

Unknown Hero: Okay, Tiresias, look for Echo's pretty eyes. Echo will be close to Medusa.

Tiresias: Hercules, I can't look.

Hercules: Why? Ohhh, because you don't want to get turned to stone. Me neither. Let's just say random things. And if someone echoes them, that's where she'll be.

7:03 AM
Hercules: I love Echo.

Hercules: Um, I love donuts.

Hercules: And sometimes, the occasional croissant.

Echo: Croissant. Love.

Medusa: Echo, are you okay? Die, fiend! Oh. Tiresias.

Medusa: Uh, still ... die?

7:04 AM
Tiresias: Later, later.

Tiresias: There's been a misunderstanding. Which I know happens in pretty much every book, but since this isn't a book, it's a for-real misunderstanding.

Unknown Source: *stab, stab, stab*

Tiresias: Hercules, are you stabbing monsters?

Hercules: No, there's a wasp. And I don't know how it's alive in January. I WILL PROTECT YOU FROM THE WASP, ECHO!

Medusa: One moment, I must turn these people to stone.

7:05 AM
Medusa: Yes, that wasp is one of our allies. Hercu—oh. Sorry, Mr. Wasp. He was a carpenter once.

Medusa: Well, Tiresias, you'd better start talking. Don't know if you can feel that, but it's my sword, pointed right at your throat.

Tiresias: Wow, yes, definitely could not feel that at all.

Tiresias: That was sarcasm. Everyone knows what a sword feels like.

Tiresias: Okay and now it's digging deeper. Listen, I was visited by my daughter. Um, Odysseus lied to me? Um, sorry, it's hard to think with a blade about to crush my esophagus.

7:06 AM
Medusa: Ugh, fine. I'll put it down. Oh hey, buddy. We're talking. Go away. Yup, you're stone now.

Tiresias: So I can't send you screenshots, which would clear this up way sooner, but basically. Daughter died, Odysseus lied, I cried. Sorry, Hercules brought a bunch of picture books into the battle tent last night to cheer Achilles up, so I keep thinking in rhyme.

Tiresias: What I'm trying to say is I was wrong. And there's no easy way to apologize on a battlefield for a murder attempt.

Unknown Source: *shing, clang, stab*

Tiresias: But we need to find a way to stop this battle.

7:07 AM
Medusa: Did the heroes put you up to this too? Is it another trick?

Hercules: I WILL NOW PROTECT YOU FROM THIS BEETLE, ECHO!

Echo: Protect.

Medusa: Echo, are those literal hearts in your eyes? No, don't look at me. Ugh, I'm going to put my veil back on.

Echo: Hearts. Eyes.

Medusa: Maybe we should step away from the battle for a moment. It's too chaotic to talk here. And I'm pretty vulnerable with my veil on. I don't want to turn Echo to stone. Or Hercules too, I guess. For now.

7:08 AM
Hercules: I CAN'T HEAR WHAT SHE SAID OVER ALL MY SHOUTING, BUT I THINK SHE JUST PUT HER VEIL BACK ON.

Tiresias: Hercules, is there someplace safe we can take them?

Hercules: Hmm, open plain, open plain, barn, open plain. Got nothing.

Tiresias: Okay, lead us to the barn. Protect Medusa from the front. Echo, grab my arm, and we'll be in the back.

Unknown Hero: Hey, where are you going?

Tiresias: Bathroom break?

Unknown Hero: Oh, okay, but come back here after so I can stab you.

7:09 AM
Medusa: He pointed at me, by the way. You have your hero battle armor on, Tiresias, so I assume they know you're with them.

Tiresias: Oh, is that what this clunky stuff is? I thought it was a suit.

Tiresias: Again, sarcasm.

Tiresias: But that may work to our advantage. Let's head to the barn. How close are we to it, Hercules?

7:10 AM
Hercules: Oh it's real close. All we have to do is encounter
Odysseus and Perseus and Achilles who are standing right in front
of it. Hi, guys!

> **Odysseus:** Hercules, you were supposed to stay back in the
> grove of trees with—Tiresias, is that you?

Tiresias: ... No?

> **Medusa:** Is this another trap? Really? The heroes are
> waiting in front of the barn!

Tiresias: Um, yes, a trap. Haha. We are taking her into the barn to
stab her. Don't worry, Odysseus, we've got this. No need to
interfere.

> **Hercules:** Dude, that's not what we're doing at all. I
> thought the plan was to protect her in the barn.

7:11 AM
Tiresias: Wow, Hercules, what a joker. Haha. Okay, anyway, off to
the barn we go.

> **Odysseus:** Mistake to put that veil back on, Medusa.
> Perseus, mind grabbing that little friend from the back?

Perseus: KIDNAPPING.

> **Tiresias:** Hey what are you—ow!

Hercules: Wow, right in the jaw! Echo, no!

> **Perseus:** HAHA.

Medusa: Echo!

7:12 AM
Odysseus: Wonderful, now I'm going to hold your friend right in front of me so you can't tear that little veil of yours off. That way she turns to stone too if you make a careless mistake. Are we understood?

Perseus: Ohhh, SMART!

Achilles: Patroclus would've done better.

Tiresias: What happened? Where's Echo?

Odysseus: Hercules, now's your moment. I need you to stab Miss Gorgon here and you can finally achieve that hero status.

Hercules: If this is what heroes do, it's not worth the price.

7:13 AM
Tiresias: Wow, profound.

Odysseus: So that's a no. Of course he'd choose now to be a philosopher. All right, option two. Tiresias, last chance for your daughter Manto. And since you're conveniently wearing armor, would you stab Medusa?

Tiresias: I ... will, but I need you to help me find her. She moved away from me.

Odysseus: Boy, she's right in front of you.

Tiresias: Over here?

Odysseus: That's literally the opposite direction.

7:14 AM
Tiresias: Oh, being a blind battle warrior is just so hard. I don't know if I can do it without a guide. Back in Ancient Greece, I had a child guide me.

Medusa: This is kind of an embarrassing way to die.

Odysseus: For Gaia's sake, fine, I will guide you to her.

Hercules: He let go of Echo.

Hercules: ECHO I WILL SAVE YOU. Take that, Perseus!

Perseus: Ow!

Hercules: Take that, Achilles!

7:15 AM
Achilles: Dude, no need to punch me. I literally don't want to be in this battle anyway. I'm outta here. Peace.

Hercules: Huh, ran out of people to punch. Echo, look away in case Medusa tears off her veil thingy. I'm whispering this so Odysseus doesn't hear. Not because I like whispering. I do not.

Odysseus: And you swing the sword like so.

Medusa: This is a ... strangely romantic trope. Holding a sword together. Beautiful.

Medusa: That is sarcasm. As Tiresias likes to clarify.

Odysseus: Okay, now I'm going to walk you to her, since she's being an idiot and just standing there.

7:16 AM
Tiresias: Gaia, it sure would be a shame if someone removed a certain head covering at this very moment.

Medusa: Ohhhh.

Unknown Source: *RIP*

Many Snakes: *HISS*

Medusa: Take that, Odysseus! Even Bobart hates you!

7:17 AM
Tiresias: And now his stone hand is wrenched around my bicep forever. Can someone break this thing off?

Medusa: Let me put my veil back on before you help him, Hercules.

Echo: Hercules.

Hercules: We were looking at a butterfly, what happened?

Unknown Source: *SMASH*

7:18 AM
Tiresias: Thank you, sir.

Perseus: ODYSSEUS IS DEAD. MUST MURDER SNAKE LADY!

Unknown Source: *crack! boom!*

Hercules: Is that thunder? Does that happen in January in cornfields?

Medusa: What's that appearing in the sky?

7:19 AM
Thanatos: Where is my megaphone ... ah! Here it is.

Thanatos: Heeeey, mortals and monsters, it's Thanatos! I'm here to slay.

All: AHHHHHHHHH!

Thanatos: Yeah, I thought this outfit was pretty fabulous. I'm really slaying it. But the screams, you are all too kind.

Thanatos: Anyway, everyone, this party is NOT a vibe. I killed all of you already, and this just makes me sad. No appreciation for my art. All of you alive again? Tragic.

Perseus: SCARY GUY GONNA KILL US ALL.

7:20 AM
Thanatos: Aw, thank you, Perseus. I do think my glitter is absolutely TERRIFYING-ly gorgeous.

Thanatos: Anyway, time to kill you all. Ta-ta!

Persephone: OMGs, Thanatos, we've been over this. You are not supposed to kill everyone. Remember? We legit ordered a whole buffet and charcuterie board yesterday. And somewhere in the middle of consuming the cheese board, you finally said you would only kill a select number of people.

Medusa: How many gods are going to appear in the sky today?

7:21 AM
Hades: I am Hades, and I am here. That is all.

Thanatos: Hey, girlfriend! Hey, girlfriend's boo! Hold up, hold up. I don't get to kill ALL of them? Honestly, this is making my shoulders tight again. I need to do some yoga.

Persephone: Great, so while he's doing that, y'all, here's the deal.

Persephone: Yes, very nice tree pose, Thanatos. My plants appreciate it.

Persephone: This war is not supposed to happen. And if it continues, Thanatos will slay—and yes, also slay—anyone who keeps fighting.

7:22 AM
Persephone: The whole point of the app was to bring together mortals and beings who would've been enemies in a past life.

Persephone: Me and Hades? Well, I can tell you a certain kale-obsessed goddess didn't approve. But we are happy. And that's what matters. All we wanted was for you to find your own happiness.

Unknown Source: *shoooosh*

Hercules: Is it raining kale?

Persephone: Very nice, Mom. So are we clear? If you continue to fight each other, Thanatos has free rein to take any of you down.

Medusa: Arachne? You hearing this?

Arachne: Loud and clear, girl. I'm telling the other monsters to stand down.

7:23 AM
Hercules: Perseus, Jason, and idk the dudes who aren't turned to stone yet. Are you hearing this?

Perseus: We do.

Perseus: BUT WE STAB ALL THE MONSTERS ANYWAY. YAAAAAAA!

Unknown Sources: YAAAAA!

Thanatos: Seriously, guys. This noise. Killing my vibe. I guess I'll have to kill you too.

Unknown Sources, many: *THUD*

7:24 AM
Thanatos: *sigh* Just having people fall down dead isn't part of my usual art. Kind of plebian. But oh well.

Persephone: I think it was beautiful, Thanatos.

Thanatos: Awww, thank you, queen. Anytime you need someone to slay, call me up.

Thanatos: Anyway, ta-ta. I have a hair appointment I need to get to.

Hades: I don't think I'll ever not be scared of him.

Persephone: That's okay, darling, you were very brave.

7:25 AM
Echo: Darling. Very brave.

Medusa: Hercules, I think she's talking to you.

Hercules: OMGs, Echo, I can't believe you think I'm brave. I think you're pretty and smart and a lot of other things too.

Echo: A lot of other things. Hercules.

Medusa: Aw, Tiresias, they're going in for a hug. And a smooch. Okay, this feels like I should not watch anymore.

7:26 AM
Tiresias: Yeah it, uh, sounds like they're going for it.

Tiresias: So I hope you caught on that we were not, in fact, trying to trick you. I know I've given you many reasons to doubt me. With trying to kill you, like, twice.

Medusa: Three times. But, I mean, I've tried to kill you too.

Medusa: On the plus side, it can only get better from here, right?

Tiresias: Oh for sure. Now, I don't expect you to forgive me, but maybe we can start fresh?

7:27 AM
Medusa: A fresh start. I think we could all use it.

Medusa: And no more heroes this time.

Tiresias: I'm, uh, I think I'm getting a prophecy. Right now, actually.

Medusa: Oh no. Is something terrible going to happen? Worse than *shudder* Thanatos?

Tiresias: I'm, uh, seeing into the future and, ah yes. There you are. And there I am. And where are we?

Tiresias: Ah yes, that Ancient Greek coffee shop. Yes, the name is still Coffee Muses. In fact, it's in the near-distant future. Tomorrow, in fact!

7:28 AM
Medusa: Now that's a prophecy I'm happy to help make come true.

Persephone: Well, love, we've obviously shut down the app for now. We can boot it up again and see if the monsters and demigods—and I guess whomever Thanatos didn't slay— may have a fighting chance at winning that bet for us.

Hades: You see those two down there?

Persephone: Those two making out? Hercules and Echo?

Hades: No, the other two. Tiresias and Medusa.

Hades: I think we have a fighting chance, Seph.

7:29 AM
Persephone: Well, if we have to place our bets on some-one ... I think we have more than the Fates on our side. Now let's get out of this kale rain.

Medusa: And since it's really weird to listen to gods talking about your love life ... I'm going to turn off our voice chat for now.

From Seph to Mom

~~Dear the Bane of My Existence,~~
~~Wassup, Mom,~~
~~Dear Please Stop Sending Me Kale Care Packages, Woman,~~
Dear Mom,

You've not been responding to texts, so I figured I'd write the old-fashioned way. You always were a little bit more ~~old-fashioned~~ vintage than I was.

Just got off a battlefield today and made the mistake of writing in pen instead of pencil. Much harder to ~~corect~~ correct mistakes.

Speaking of mistakes, I know I don't have a couple for you quite yet. Not an engaged couple, anyway, but I do have some promising prospects. Two couples. I talked with Hercules after the battle, though, and I guess he and Echo are going to take things "slower." Ironic considering how long they kissed, but Hercules still needs to get over Meg. And Echo has traces of Narcissus she needs to forget.

Medusa and Tiresias, though, they certainly give a ~~godess~~ goddess of spring hope. I may or may not disguise myself as a barista tomorrow on their date. Although I hear Achilles has already applied for the newest barista position.

Hope that kid learned from his mistakes. The last time he was on earth he died young because he was so brutal on the battlefield.

I even saw him crying near the barn when Thanatos departed. It seems like his murdering spree has gotten to him. Hercules was patting him on the back and comforting him.

I think the gods can learn a thing or two about mourning when we make terrible decisions.

Anyway, upon reflecting on the battle, and Thanatos's interesting costume choices, I realized some reasons why you held on so tightly when I made the decision to stay with Hades:

• ~~You love control~~

• You didn't have the greatest relationship with Dad.

You didn't talk about him much, and I didn't know how much you were hurting. And some part of me understands you wanted to protect me from all that aching too.

Medusa taught me a lot about recovery and nursing old wounds in our talks in the Underworld, and even when she got a second chance. She's still learning to trust Tiresias.

~~And it doesn't help that he tried to kill her.~~

So I don't know if they'll make it to the twelve-month mark with an engagement ring. You'd better bet your bottom dollar I'll be dropping heavy hints to Tiresias by the time we get to June (and no, this doesn't count as interfering, because ... reasons), but if they don't end up getting engaged ... I understand.

I now understand why you set the terms of the bet the way you did. Because you felt like I rushed into this thing. And although some couples can make it work, most need much more time.

• You're my mom.

So of course you'd cling to me as tightly as possible. I can only imagine the joy on your face when you heard my first cry, my first words, my first everything.

Tiresias has taught me a lot about that too.

The way he struggled with his daughter getting left behind— Hades told me so much about his reaction. And I'm sure with every trip I make to the Underworld, a little piece inside you ~~breaks~~ shatters too. So I'm betting you made this bet because you were worried that if I could spend every waking moment with Hades, you'd never see me again.

That's just not true. It isn't.

You'd better believe I'm getting on that bullet train up to Olympus. Participating in spring and harvest festivals with you. Going through the haunted corn maze in October in Pennsylvania, like we always do.

Because I'm your daughter, and you're my mom.

And when you let go, you'll always find me coming back to you.

Because that's how life works.

That's how family works.

That's how love works.

Love always comes back to you, no matter how far it travels.

Love,
Seph

From Demeter to Persephone

Dear Persephone,

The bet is still on, but perhaps my original mindset is not. I don't know when you blossomed from such a young seed into a beautiful woman, but maybe I misjudged Hades. Because you've become so wise after all your years spent with him.

Performance reviews from the Underworld have gone up exponentially in the past few centuries, and I can't help but think you played a hand in all of that. Something about you and Hades works better together. Not like two halves, but two wholes.

Although I still have my trepidations about your—union—I do think we could learn a lesson from you two up here on Olympus.

Know that I will never stop being proud of you. Hear those words again: I am proud of you. Always have been.

And I cannot wait for you to come back to me—bet won or lost.

Sincerely,
Demeter (your mom)

KILLER BROS

JANUARY 12

10:24 AM
Hercules: Yooooo, Tiresias, they have the DearHades app up again. I'm not going to use it for dating, duh. But we can now talk to each other.

Tiresias: Okay, two things.

Tiresias: One, you are literally in my apartment, where we're talking face-to-face. So I have no idea why you're even recording this.

Tiresias: And two, aw, you didn't break my door down this time.

Hercules: Yeah, the lady at the front desk gave me another key. She figured I was couch surfing or something here.

10:25 AM
Tiresias: So I smell donuts.

Hercules: Sorry, dude, Echo and I ate most of them. She went with me to the gym earlier and took some videos of me. Come look.

Tiresias: Listen, I don't want to hear videos of you grunting as you lift eight hundred pounds at a—

Unknown Source: Aaaah ooOOOoh.

Tiresias: Is she singing? That's gorgeous.

10:26 AM
Hercules: She's listening to songs off-screen and singing covers. But look at the number of views on that thing.

Tiresias: Um, Herc ...

Hercules: Already got over ten thousand. It's blowing up with comments.

Hercules: I know that fast-food thing didn't work out for her, but she mentioned something about building our Beats_and_Barbells channel to something called monetization. I don't know how she managed to get that word repeated, but she did.

10:27 AM
Hercules: Oh, wait, I know!

Hercules: We were messing around on Google, and she has these earbuds in, right?

Hercules: And she types in a message. Something cute, like, "Hercules, you really need to shower after you go to the gym."

Hercules: And she plays the words in her ear off Google, like the voice-to-text thingy on your phone when it reads you messages.

Hercules: And then she opens her mouth and says it.

Tiresias: Whoa.

10:28 AM
Hercules: Breakthrough, right? Echo can say whatever she wants as long as she types it in first and hears it said back to her.

Hercules: It's not breaking her curse. But it's managing it. And I'm so happy for her.

Hercules: It's like Medusa's veil. This is Echo's veil.

Tiresias: That's great, buddy. Oh, Artemis is so happy to see you. You missed us, didn't you, girl? While we were out waging war?

Hercules: Pet, pet, pet, pet the puppy.

10:29 AM
Hercules: But you wanna know something else cool?

Hercules: Echo can communicate through song.

Hercules: Whenever she's panicked or can't type out how she's feeling, she'll pull up a song and sing about how she feels instead. To communicate emotions.

Hercules: She was crying when we figured this out after the battle yesterday. It was wild.

Tiresias: So you two are really hitting it off, eh?

Hercules: Yeah, real slow. Good things often take a lot of time.

10:30 AM
Tiresias: I have a feeling you didn't come over here just to give me donuts—ooh, is this a French cruller?

Hercules: Wanted to check in on you before the big date.

Hercules: I noticed you were not in fact kissing the face off Medusa yesterday after the battle, so I wanted to swing by.

Tiresias: I think we're taking things slowly in a different way, dude. Haha. It'll probably be months before we even reach the topic of … that sort of contact.

Hercules: Mind blown.

Hercules: Echo kisses nice.

10:31 AM
Tiresias: Mkay, didn't need to know that.

Tiresias: But I'm scared. She has so many reasons not to trust me, and I know with this bet looming over us we're some of the only contenders left.

Tiresias: And even though they put the app back up, most people are still recovering. And the Ancient Greek pantheon isn't exactly known for lasting relationships, and …

Hercules: Shhh, there, there.

Tiresias: Why are you patting my head?

Hercules: Because right now you don't have the words. And I don't think you have a singing voice like Echo, so you can't sing how you feel.

10:32 AM
Hercules: You know what the most important rule of workouts is, Tiresias?

> **Tiresias:** Always have a spotter and don't be a jerk by not cleaning off the equipment.

Hercules: No ... well yes, but ...

Hercules: Have plenty of recovery time.

Hercules: When you run a hard race, lift weights, whatever ... you take breaks. There's a reason why every day isn't leg day or arm day. You'll tear something.

Hercules: Not me, haha. I never tear anything. But, you know, mortals. It's a good rule for mortals. Your hair is so soft when I pat it.

> 10:33 AM
> **Tiresias:** And we're scooching further away from you on the couch.

Hercules: Point is, you and Medusa need some recovery time. You've both gone through a heavy workout, so it's okay if you go slow.

Hercules: Mr. and Mrs. Dead Guy will understand.

Hercules: Take things slow, and they will happen in time. I think that's how life is, Tiresias. It happens when you don't force it.

> **Tiresias:** You know, you have a tendency to be really profound, Hercules. Maybe you should enroll in a commu-

nity college, or something, to get the education you never quite got back in Ancient Greece.

10:34 AM
Hercules: Pet, pet, pet the puppy. What was that, Tiresias?

Tiresias: Nothing, Hercules. I'm sure we can readdress this.

Tiresias: In the meantime, before my nerves get to me, would you want to show me any more videos of Echo singing while you do workouts? I'd love to be a contributor to the views on Beats_and_Barbells.

Hercules: Oh boy, okay!

Hercules: Here's one she sang while I was on the elliptical. She calls it "A Vision in Steps."

Unknown Source: Everything is gonna be all right. He-e-ey.

Tiresias: That sounds perfect.

A Modest Proposal

September 9

1:34 PM
Arachne: Okay, squad, is everyone in position? Tiresias, I see you, no need to speak. We don't want to give anything away to Medusa, heehee.

> **Hercules:** Only turn on your recording when you start proposing. Achilles says he wants to listen to the replay.

Arachne: That's ... weird. But also do that so we know when Hercules should bring out ... the special item. ;)

> 1:35 PM
> **Hercules:** Okay, Hercules, remember Arachne just looks like a spider. She is not actually a spider. I know you scream every time you see her, but maybe today will be the day you do not do that.

Echo: Do NOT do that.

> **Arachne:** I'm in the same tree I was in the first time they

came to this graveyard. Was that really eight months ago? Ah, memories. A good call by Tiresias. Full circle.

1:36 PM
Hercules: Speaking of circles. I have the special item right here. But I hope I don't get tempted and eat it beforehand.

Echo: ... Eat it?

Hercules: Oh wait, here they come. Hide in the bushes with me, Echo!

Tiresias: So, Medusa, what did you think of the weird lunch place we were at today?

1:37 PM
Medusa: Well, I'm glad some of the monsters started their own restaurant, but I must say, their choices are ... interesting. Spider stew seems almost wrong considering some of our friends.

Hercules: Don't think about spiders. Don't think about spiders.

Tiresias: Oh for sure. It reminded me a lot of the Ancient Greek diet. Eating stingrays and such. Took me back to home.

Medusa: Speaking of old times ... this graveyard, huh? It's been a while. Is there a, uh, special reason we're here? Heehee.

1:38 PM
Tiresias: Whaaaaat? Let's sit down.

Tiresias: And no, not at all. We've been in this graveyard before? All graveyards look the same to me.

Medusa: Ha! This is why I love you.

Arachne: Aw, a kiss. Cute. Oh wait, don't look. Would stink to be turned to stone right now.

Hercules: No worries! I heard the word kiss and Echo and I are going for some of that right now.

1:39 PM
Tiresias: Wow, I will pretend I didn't hear that.

Medusa: Hear ... what?

Tiresias: Um, my heartbeat. Because it flutters so when you say you love me. Okay, anyway, it's been quite a few months since we've been here. So maybe we should recap everything?

1:40 PM
Medusa: Ah, a recap of all our adventures? Sure, let's take a stroll down memory lane.

Medusa: Well, remember our first date postwar? When Hercules burst in to let us know he was a chess champion? And we had to go to his celebration party?

Arachne: Oh yeah, I remember that. Herc beat the old man and then he and Echo were dancing in the street.

Tiresias: Yeah, the dude watched literally one season of *Queen's Gambit* and suddenly he's making treks all over the world with Echo for their channel and for him taking down some crying old men.

1:41 PM
Tiresias: Oh, and remember our first kiss? When we returned to the heraptorium.

Tiresias: Nothing says romance quite like kissing over the open cages of venomous snakes.

Medusa: It distracted Bobart and the others since they were so interested in their snakey relatives. I felt weird with them watching. It was a good call.

Unknown Source: *hsssss*

Medusa: Yes, Bobart, you've grown more comfortable with my love life, good job.

1:42 PM
Tiresias: Speaking of Bobart, remember that trek we made to Greece so he could learn more about his lineage?

Medusa: Our time in Greece was so much better than the first time around. And when we were at the Parthenon ... I think that's the first time we said "I love you."

Tiresias: Yeah, yeah it was.

Tiresias: You know, I was actually really scared to go back. Because Greece had so many bad memories, and it seemed like some sort of giant we had to face.

1:43 PM
Tiresias: But when we got there—when I was there with you. It felt so small. Like a mountain we'd already conquered.

Tiresias: And I don't think that feeling has ever gone away since.

Arachne: Awww, this is so cute. Hercules, he's reaching toward the bushes. Give him the ring!

Echo: Give him the ring!

1:44 PM
Medusa: Uh, did I just ... hear Echo?

> **Arachne:** Shhhhhhh, Echo, you get so loud when you're excited.

Tiresias: Um, no? This graveyard is just really echoey?

Tiresias: Guys, come on. Stick with the plan.

Tiresias: But you know what isn't echoey. This bush. And what? I think there's something inside it.

> 1:45 PM
> **Hercules:** I got you, bro. Here's the box with the special something.

Tiresias: Here is—um, why is this box so big?

Tiresias: Are these ... are these donuts?

> **Medusa:** Oh, yes, donuts. It's nice to have dessert after spider stew. Thanks, Ty.

Tiresias: Sure, haha.

Tiresias: Hercules, what the heck. We were talking about a certain OTHER special object yesterday.

1:46 PM
Hercules: Was I not supposed to get donuts? He was mentioning round things that could go around fingers. I don't know what he does with his pastries, but I— AAAAAAAH SPIDER! SPIDER SPIDER SPIDER!

Arachne: It's me, you idiot! Coming to strangle you, though! Because who thinks you propose WITH A DONUT?

Echo: Strangle? Strangle donut!

Tiresias: Maybe the graveyard is afraid of spiders and loves strangling things?

1:47 PM
Medusa: Uhhhh, there goes Hercules chased by Arachne. And ... Arachne chased by Echo? What is going on here?

Tiresias: So, um.

Tiresias: This was not supposed to be how this went.

Tiresias: Um, these donuts were supposed to be a different object that fit around your finger. And I probably should've asked literally anyone other than Hercules to be in charge of that. I guess the other special object is still on the kitchen counter at home.

1:48 PM
Medusa: Hahahaha! Oh my gods, I have tears in my eyes. Honestly, this is the most on-brand way this could've happened. But please, please continue. Heeheeheehee.

Tiresias: All right, well, um, I guess I'm gonna just take this glazed donut here and get on one knee.

Tiresias: So horrible ring aside ... Medusa, I know it's only been nine or so months, but I honestly can't imagine life without you, and—

Tiresias: I didn't think I'd get a second chance at life, let alone a second chance with such a wonderful person as you.

1:49 PM
Tiresias: So what do you think? A second chance with me each day, every day, for as long as we both shall live?

Medusa: Yes! Of course! Yes, yes, yes!

Arachne: Oh look, I think it worked. They're kissing. Hercules, I'M NOT DONE WITH YOU. GET BACK HERE!

Unknown Source: I'm turning off the voice chat now.

Echo: I'm turning off the voice chat now.

Wanna Commit Murder with Me, Babe?

September 10

3:27 PM

Persephone: HADES, of ALL the days to be missing from the Underworld, you choose today? Where are you? Don't make me send some sentient plants to transport you back here.

3:29 PM

Hades: Awww, babe, but you'll interrupt their choir practice. You know how much we love listening to the Venus Fly-Von-Trap Family Singers.

Persephone: Yes, yes, they're working on an Eric Whitacre piece right now, and I'd hate to ruin things, but also, WHERE DID YOU GO?

Hades: Sorry, Thanatos pulled me into his office to go over some things. He has some big visions for how the Underworld can be transformed. And let's just say, when you put a charcuterie board in front of the man, he won't stop yakking for hours.

3:30 PM
Hades: I'm waiting for a bullet train home, what's up?

Persephone: Demeter sent a note today.

Persephone: One year exactly from when we waged the bet.

Hades: ??!! And?

3:31 PM
Persephone: It was an envelope full of pomegranate seeds, with one note inside: "Scatter them."

Persephone: I did on the kitchen floor, and they magically rolled into the shape of letters.

Persephone: It spelled, "You won, and you have my blessing."

Hades: !!!

3:32 PM
Persephone: Well, some of the seeds got confused about shapes, so "won" was spelled like "wun," but I got the point.

Hades: Demeter finally approves?

Persephone: I wouldn't go that far, but we proved quirky love stories can be replicable. Even Zeus is having talks about how Aphrodite and Eros shouldn't be the only ones in charge of the love lives of those from Ancient Greece.

3:33 PM
Persephone: It seems the whole pantheon is reinvestigating

what roles look like. For the first time, maybe people can be someone they always wanted to be. And not goddess of the hunt or messenger god.

Hades: That's amazing!

3:34 PM
Persephone: Speaking of messenger god, Hermes delivered the wedding invitations this morning.

Hades: They sent them out already?

Persephone: Well, Iris and Hermes have been rooting for them the whole time, so they may have pressured the two to go ahead and use some free invitations Hermes had at the ready.

3:35 PM
Persephone: What do you think we should get them as a gift?

Persephone: Do you think this mansion I found in the middle of Pennsylvania is enough? It comes equipped with twenty dogs.

3:36 PM
Hades: Is that thing ten million?

Persephone: Pocket change, right?

Hades: Seph, it doesn't actually come with the dogs. Those are all dogs you pulled from adoption sites.

3:37 PM
Persephone: Okay, but they would love a mansion with twenty-something dogs. Sooooo.

Hades: How about a nice house between the theater and dog shelter where they work?

Hades sent a screenshot

3:38 PM
Hades: Like this one?

Hades: The train got delayed, so may be another twenty minutes.

Persephone: Yeah, I suppose that one works. :(

3:39 PM
Hades: And we can throw in a basket full of loose-leaf pomegranate tea, too.

Hades: And ONE more dog. Just one.

Persephone: Okay! That sounds good. :)

Persephone: I just want to make sure we get them something perfect.

3:40 PM
Persephone: I've heard rumors about the monsters making them a wedding quilt, and Echo giving them some cash from her record deal, and I just want to make sure they know we are so hyped for their wedding too.

Persephone: Since we didn't really get a dream wedding, you know?

3:41 PM
Persephone: No one from Olympus showed, and as much as I loved eloping with you, darling, I would've killed for a DJ.

Hades: There's an idea, then. A renewal of vows? Once we figure out what changes we want to bring to the Underworld?

Persephone: YES, yes!

3:42 PM
Persephone: And I'm glad you mentioned that, because I have IDEAS.

Persephone: First, let's figure out a way to reverse Asphodel sucking people's memories away. First of all, it makes teaching SO MUCH HARDER. But also, after seeing the lives of people being brought back, it's worth remembering.

3:43 PM
Persephone: Second, let's break down the barriers between Elysium and Asphodel. Some people we originally sent to Elysium—cough, cough Odysseus—don't even make any sense.

Persephone: Plus, from a lesson-planning standpoint, it would really bring down my commute time.

3:44 PM
Persephone: Third, let's quadruple the number of pome-granate ice cream stores.

Hades: Whoa, whoa, babe, slow down.

Persephone: Aw, come on, I only have forty-three more points.

3:45 PM
Persephone: Forty-four. I thought of another one.

Hades: Haha, this is why I love you.

Hades: And change will be good. I'm glad people are beginning to see myths in a different light now.

Persephone: Yeah?

3:46 PM
Hades: In the OGs, I was a villain. You had no agency. Medusa was some blood-lusting monster. Tiresias was this annoying guy who only popped onto the scene when someone massively screwed up.

Hades: But now we get to see the stories through a new lens.

3:47 PM
Hades: Like that I had little choice in the matter when I got put in charge of this dark Underworld. And fought major depression from having to spend lonely years down here, listening to the wails of suffering shades.

Hades: That you chose a new home. Chose me. And every day, continue to choose me.

3:48 PM
Hades: And that Medusa fell victim to the wrath of a goddess, not by any fault of her own. And that she was still able to find strength in the midst of a curse.

Hades: And Tiresias is so much more than his visions of his future. Comprised of his love and loyalty for people.

3:49 PM
Persephone: That's the thing about stories, love. It's incredibly important who tells them.

Hades: Agreed. So how would you tell ours?

3:50 PM
Persephone: I've got a few ideas.

THE END

Thank You!

Thank you for reading! If you enjoyed this book, please leave a review on Amazon, Goodreads, BookBub, The Story Graph, or anywhere else you like to track your recent reads. Alternatively, you could post online or tell a friend about it. This helps our authors more than you may know.

   - *The Team at Torchflame Books*

HOPE'S ACKNOWLEDGMENTS

I got very anxious to write this book before Alyssa had finished her deadline for another book. So here we are ... writing the acknowledgments early.

First and foremost, I want to thank my Lord and Savior Jesus Christ. Thankfully, unlike Greek deities and myths, you are perfect, holy. You have constituted an intricate plan for my life, instead of messing with the lives of mortals like so many deities in myths do. Thankfully, you are not a myth. You are real. And even if you don't have a perfect match waiting for me, I know that I can live a fulfilling life based on the wonderful plans you have set before me.

To my wonderful coauthor, Alyssa. Who has graciously dealt with the fact that I "accidentally wrote 5,000 words while I was waiting for you to finish *Castelon*" for this book. You and I have gone through a pretty intense stretch of two years where, combined, we wrote twelve books (all under deadline). Twelve books in two years. Girl. We need a vacation. We have stretched ourselves beyond what we thought we could do, and we did it together. Thank you.

To my wonderful friends and family who offer their unwavering support. I think specifically of Mom, Dad, Ian, Libby, Grace, Daniel, Carlee, James, Sonya, The Cyle Group, Nikki, Jess (who calls herself a 3000-year-old deity), and my wonderful grandparents.

To Michele who initially took on this undertaking of a series and a spinoff. We know we threw quite a quirky idea at you. But you loved it from the beginning and found a beautiful home for it. Thank you for carrying this story all the way through. To the wonderful team at L2L2 who has gone through this book, editing it, polishing it, dealing with my bizarre I-need-coffee-and-can't-think-straight humor (sadly am allergic to coffee btw). You made this into a beautiful book.

Thank you to Torchflame, who took on this book next, with so much enthusiasm. We were blessed to find you.

And to the readers. Those who share covers, those who write reviews, those who email us and tell us which lines made you laugh. Those who purchased this book in the first place. You encourage us to keep going. Because it's a tough industry, but you make us tougher. Thank you most of all.

Alyssa's Acknowledgments

I feel like it can't be normal to have so much fun while writing.

Like any kid, I adored Greek mythology, and I'm so glad to have had this chance to write about some of my favorite characters, especially with an awesome and hilarious coauthor like Hope. So, thank you to Hope. This is our sixth(!!) book we've written together. Seventh we'll release together, I believe. How does it feel? Thank you to my fifth and sixth grade teacher who provided me with so many books on Greek and Roman history. This teacher happens to be my mother, who also bought me the Percy Jackson books. Which leads me to thank my entire family—my parents, Steph, Nana and Papa, the Arkansas and New York family—who all are so very supportive and excited for my books.

To my ever-supportive friends, the PWRs in all the group chat iterations, the Indy friendos, the Skittles, the Cyle folks, Juli, and Nikki.

To Michele, who provided a new home for our books, and a home for this new book! We hope you got as much of a kick out of it as we did. We appreciate everything L2L2 did for us.

Torchflame, Jori, Teri, thank you for coming in to scoop up this book and this series and breathe new life into them. We're so excited to be working with you.

To a God who is a whole lot less fickle and chaotic than the Greek deities. I'm quite glad I feel secure and loved, part of a plan.

And to the readers, the reviewers, the fans who post about our books, share favorite lines, demand sequels, make fan art(!!). You're the ones who make this possible, and all of it means more than we can say.

HOPE BOLINGER

Hope Bolinger is the author of more than 25 books, including the award-winning Blaze trilogy, and has contributed to many more. She has worked for various publishing companies, magazines, newspapers, and literary agencies and has edited the work of 300+ authors. She has won awards for her essays, poetry, children's books, novels, and plays. She's a theater nerd and spends too much time hiking and petting her fat cats, Freya and Odin. She can be found online at hopebolinger.com and on social media @hopebolinger or @hopekbolinger.

facebook.com/hopebolinger

x.com/hopebolinger

instagram.com/hopekbolinger

bookbub.com/authors/hope-bolinger

goodreads.com/hopebolinger

tiktok.com/@hopebolinger

ALYSSA ROAT

Alyssa Roat lives in the cornfields of Indiana, but she hopes to soon discover a portal to a fantasy world where she will run a book-shop for magical creatures. For now, she is an award-winning multi-published author and has worked in a wide variety of roles within the publishing industry as an editor, agent, writer, and publicist. She and her partner have four black cats who allegedly have never been fed in their lives and occasionally help her write by walking across the keyboard. Her name is a pun, which means you can learn more about her at www.alyssawrote.com or on Instagram, Twitter, and Facebook as @alyssawrote.

f facebook.com/alyssawrote

O instagram.com/alyssawrote

BB bookbub.com/authors/alyssa-roat

♪ tiktok.com/@alyssawrote

Glossary of Characters

Since Greek mythology writers apparently liked to use a lot of characters, you'll notice myths don't always agree on these characters. Depending on who told the myths—and that person's particular views toward a group of people or a gender—you may get different versions of these people. Hence why pop culture has different "takes" on these beings.

Achilles: My goodness, what a drama queen. This guy didn't get to get with his favorite prisoner of war, so he decides not to fight in the Trojan War just to stick it to his war general. Then he finds out that his ... very good friend, Patroclus, fought in his armor and died. So he goes on a revenge fantasy until he murders a bunch of Trojans, and seals his fate in death.

Aglaope: One of the sirens. In Greek mythology, these are half-bird ladies, not the mermaid creatures you might be thinking of.

Alecto (Fury): A chaos agent, fury, known for her implacable anger. She can shape shift, instigate violence, and in DearHades, mess with the app. Not to be confused with a furry.

Ammit: Devourer of dead souls in Egyptian mythology. If your heart outweighed the feather of Ma'at (truth), you'd be her lunch.

Andromeda: The wife of Perseus, who is saved from being eaten by a sea monster by Perseus. Because Poseidon is always upset in mythology for some reason.

Antigone: One of the daughters of Oedipus who tragically dies when she cannot be united with her soon-to-be-husband Haemon. In our story, she comes back and is reunited with him. But the heroes use her as leverage for persuading Tiresias to kill Medusa.

Apollo: Back during Tiresias's first stay on earth, he served as a prophet for Apollo—one of the important Olympian gods. Apollo also drives a chariot that carries the sun across the world, bringing light to the people. Also a great getaway car after you attempt murder.

Arachne: Once human, but got cursed by Athena because she out-wove her. And I guess you don't out-weave a goddess. So now she looks like a spider.

Ares: One of the OG deities, and obsessed with war. So much that they made him the god of it. And not thumb wars, mind you.

Artemis: Goddess of the hunt, and the name of Tiresias's dog who failed to pass training to be his working dog. He decided to keep her anyway.

Asclepius: This guy—god and hero of medicine—in general is not important and doesn't really make an appearance in the book. But what he does with gorgon blood in mythological accounts, reviving the dead, plays an important role in this story.

Aphrodite: The goddess of love, and one of the OG deities from the time of the Titans. Born out of sea foam, she is beauty, she is grace, she will stab you in the face (if you think anyone is prettier than her). Unhappily married to Hephaestus, she finds herself in many liaisons apart from her marriage. One of the goddesses who started the Trojan War.

Athena: Sister of Ares, and apparently—even though she doesn't curse people as much as Zeus and Hera—she still gets a participation trophy or something.

Bellerophon: Don't let Disney trick you, this was actually the guy to tame Pegasus.

Briseis: A war captive. Don't let the Iliad fool you, Achilles really didn't love her. He saw her as a thing to be won.

Calypso: A daughter of a Titan and a nymph who found herself stuck on an island that Odysseus ends up on. Odysseus claims she came onto him, but he really doesn't seem insanely eager to get back to Penelope, considering he spends a full seven years on Calypso's island.

Cerberus: The three-headed dog who guards the gates of Hades. Heracles (Hercules) does capture Cerberus as one of the twelve labors he has to do for the love of his life. But we personally think he should've just given Cerberus a belly rub. Far more effective.

Charon: The ferryman of the dead, and apparently someone you don't pay according to some British song from the 80s. He's excited for a change of pace, to lead the dead through a jungle when Persephone's nervous plant habit gets out of hand.

Charybdis: Once a human, now a seventy-foot sea monster who swallows ships in a whirlpool. But she has a great personality.

Circe: A sorceress who did, in fact, turn Odysseus's men into pigs. Probably an apt metaphor. But despite what Odysseus claims, she most definitely did not come on to him.

Demeter: The goddess of the harvest, and one of the OG deities from the time of the Titans. Grain would've played a huge role in the Ancient Greek world, so we imagine the Ancient Greeks were not the happiest when Demeter would get mad at Persephone being in the Underworld and throw "winter" tantrums. In any version of the myth between Hades and Persephone, she's not the biggest fan of their union and will do whatever she can to prevent it.

Echidna: Called "the mother of all monsters." Half woman and half snake (or serpent, or dragon), she and her mate Typhon were the parents of all sorts of Greek monsters. Now that she's back from Hades, she's the mom figure to the monster squad.

Echo: In love with Narcissus, she gets cursed by Hera (surprise, surprise). She can only repeat what people say.

Eros (Cupid): The god of passionate love and fertility. Not surprisingly, the son of Aphrodite in most versions of his myths. You know him as the guy who flings arrows at people and makes them fall in love.

Eurydice: In her original myth, she's trapped in the Underworld. When her lover Orpheus comes to rescue her, she's given instructions to follow behind him on the way out of the Underworld. If Orpheus turns around, she dies. Well, Eurydice sneezes or something, IDK, and he turns around. So she dies. But in our story, they both get brought back.

Fates (also known as Moirai): These three beings determine someone's life by weaving a thread for them. They are referenced by the characters in terms of things being outside of their control and dictated by other beings with more power. A popular theme in the book, considering the gods can do whatever they want willy-nilly, and the characters take quite a few punches because of it.

Gaia: The Ancient Greek version of Mother Nature (or Mother Earth). She never makes an appearance in this book, but the characters frequently use her name to do an Ancient Greek version of cursing.

Gorgons (Stheno and Euryale): Other gorgons, apart from Medusa, existed in Greek myth, such as Stheno and Euryale. Unfortunately, during the time of our story, Medusa is the only gorgon to make it back to the land of the living.

Hades: The god of the Underworld and one of the OG gods involved in the war against the Titans. Important to note, he does not kill people. He just handles and organizes the dead people. In some myths, he kidnaps Persephone and makes her stay in the Underworld with him—not a great start to a relationship in our opinions. But in the more original versions of the myth, Persephone got annoyed with her overbearing mother and decided to chill in the land of the dead with Hades. You can take a wild guess at which version of the myth we went with.

Haemon: Antigone's soon-to-be husband. He dies in the play *Antigone*, but our story brings him back.

Hector: The person who killed Patroclus (who Achilles afterward killed, and dragged his body around for several days via chariots). It's interesting that they would've been in the same group chat—until Medusa un-alived Hector—considering how much they hated each other during the Trojan War. But they both had people they loved they wanted to bring back. So we can assume they had a temporary truce.

Hera: Like many deities, especially the OG deities from the time of the Titans, Hera doesn't like her marriage arrangement with Zeus. The goddess of a lot of things, queen of heaven, etc., hates the fact that her husband can't stay faithful to her for literally two seconds. This tends to make her embittered and not one to mess with. One of the goddesses who started the Trojan War.

Hercules (Heracles): Known better to us by his Roman name, rather than his Greek name—thanks to a certain Disney movie that has some bops and a sassy Hades—we also know him for his ability to complete several tasks for the woman he loves (twelve of them, to be specific). Unlike the Disney film, his union with Megara ends tragically when Hera, being Hera, turns Hercules mad and he kills Megara.

Hermes: Mainly the messenger of the gods—although he had a side job herding cattle. We translate his role into helping Hades and Persephone with the messaging capabilities of their app.

Hephaestus: The god of blacksmiths and fire, he is born with a disabled leg or foot. He marries Aphrodite, but Aphrodite isn't the biggest fan of the arrangement. He's also a craftsman and metalworker, and we've translated his role in the modern day as a master coder.

Hestia: Goddess of the hearth (aka the home). The home would've been an important concept in Ancient Greek culture, especially when it came to women making the home. Because Ancient Greece was all like, "Whaa? Women exist? This is terrible. We must hide them in houses." She plays a role in this book by providing housing to all the displaced mortals who returned from the dead. Although she's one of the nicer deities, we notice she chooses a place with cheap rent and not necessarily the nicest apartments. Gods had a tendency to bestow blessings rarely on humans in Greek culture, so this reflects their stinginess.

Hippolyta (Amazons): Queen of the Amazons. This group of female warriors made themselves adept in all areas of fighting. They show up in myths such as those featuring Hercules and Theseus. And briefly in *A Midsummer Night's Dream*, for some reason.

Io: One of the women Zeus goes after who gets transformed into a cow. Hera catches on and sends a gadfly (a bitey bitey bug) after her. She manages to reunite with the love of her life thanks to an app glitch.

Iris: Messenger goddess and goddess of the rainbow. She helps Hermes in developing the messenger capabilities of the DearHades app.

Jason: A famous Greek hero, most known for stealing some golden fleece. Because he's a hero, and heroes steal things.

Lamia: A beautiful woman with removable eyeballs. (Long story.) After Zeus got a little too interested in Lamia, Hera cursed her (surprise, surprise) and she went mad and began stealing and eating children. Depending on the myths, she may have moved on to seducing young men in order to devour them, able to shapeshift into a normal woman or a half-serpentine creature. Back from the dead, she's really excited about all the tasty young men in Hollywood.

Loki: A frost giant, from Norse mythology, who often makes Thor's life harder. Thor seeks to find him on the DearHades app, and suspects Medusa may be a disguise of Loki's, seeing that Loki sometimes had ties with snakes.

Manto: We don't know a ton about Tiresias's daughter. She makes cameos in certain myths, but we do know that she can prophesy. Like father, like daughter. As mentioned in the story, she was a war captive at an early age. Sadly, this wasn't an uncommon fate of many women back then.

Medea: A play, and a woman who killed her husband's new wife and her children after Jason (her husband) cheated on her.

Medusa: Once human, now a gorgon—a creature with snakes for her hair. How she becomes a gorgon depends on the myth. But she was most likely raped in Athena's temple by Poseidon. And Athena, seeing this go down, transforms Medusa. Some people reading the original myths say it's a punishment. Others say it's a blessing, to protect Medusa from men by turning them into stone. In either case, recently, many people have attempted to reclaim the myth, turning Medusa from a monster into a woman who, despite horrible circumstances, defends herself with her new powers.

Megara: Hercules's wife, who is tragically killed (along with her family) when Hera (wow, shocker) mind-controls Hercules and makes him murder them all.

Narcissus: You know him, probably hate him, have probably called someone his name as an insult. He is in love with himself. And in our story, keeps swiping right on himself with the multiple profiles he's set up.

Odysseus: Wow, this guy is the worst. He fights in the Trojan War and ends up taking twenty years to get back home. Killing all of his men due to his selfishness and sleeping with a bunch of women. And to make it worse, when he returns home, he goes in a disguise, to make sure his wife stayed faithful to him all this time. She did. But because some men have decided to hit on her—because, you know, Odysseus has been gone for two decades—Odysseus slaughters them all. Odysseus is known for his cleverness and tricking people into doing things they don't actually want to do.

Oracle at Delphi: Basically, priestesses at Delphi would inhale some noxious (and lethal) fumes and would spew out nonsense. And people were all like, "Wow. It's a prophecy. We must listen and travel from far lands to hear what she has to say." So when Odysseus says something is as understood as a Delphinian oracle, he really means that it *isn't* understood. He's a trickster, so, makes sense.

Orpheus: Eurydice's lover who also plays music. And is really bad at following instructions when leading people out of the Underworld.

Paris: The man who kidnapped Helen (the reason for the Trojan War). And who is the butt of the jokes throughout the *Iliad* for being more concerned with how he looks than his actual fighting skill. Medusa un-alives him during his second go in the mortal world.

Patroclus: The very good friend of Achilles who tragically died in the Trojan War. He's the whole reason Achilles goes on a rampage and kills a bunch of people in the *Iliad*.

Pegasus: A winged horse, who now apparently vibes with the Amazonians.

Penelope: The wife to Odysseus who has quite a few tricks up her sleeve. Odysseus is personally impressed with how she swindles the suitors who try to hit on her of all their wealth and possessions.

Persephone (Kore): Known as the goddess of spring, and the daughter of Demeter (and for three months out of the year "Queen of the Dead") Persephone has a very diversified resume. But overall, she—in the original myths—has a deep love for Hades. Enough to want to permanently stay in the Underworld with him. Of course the gods intervene and shorten that time period. In some myths, it is six months. In others three or four. For the purposes of this book, we went with three.

Perseus: Known for beheading Medusa before they all came back, he isn't super happy that she's returned along with the rest of them. Known as the "monster slayer," it would totally make sense why he'd join the Hero group chat in the first place, to make sure they rid the app of all monsters.

Plutus: The god of wealth in Greek culture, who kindly gives all of our mortals a yearly salary, so they can find their footing. Based on what Harper Lee's friends did for her. They paid her bills/expenses for a year, so she could go on to write *To Kill a Mockingbird.* So if you're ever wondering how to help your writing friends ...

Scylla: The bestie of Charybdis, Scylla lived on the opposite side of the narrow channel and ate some of Odysseus's men. You can't blame her, though, she does have, like, six dogs around her waist. They must get hungry.

Sirens: Greek sirens did drive men mad to the point of drowning. But unlike the modern depictions of sirens, the Ancient Greek ones had birdlike bodies.

Telegonus: Io's lover, and a king of Egypt.

Telemachus: Odysseus's "wimpy" son. Who allows suitors to flirt with his mom for years, for fear that if he stands up to them they will try to kill him. They still *do* try to kill him anyway.

Thanatos: The personification of death. He ACTUALLY deals in offing people. Unlike Hades, who often gets mistaken for doing that.

Thor: A Norse god of thunder. Many of us know a beloved iteration of him from Marvel movies.

Tiresias: A blind prophet from Thebes. He wasn't always blind. Accounts differ, but many point to him accidentally seeing Athena bathing—and Athena, not the biggest fan of that, strikes him blind. Tiresias has a history of being the bearer of bad news, especially to the family of Oedipus. He also has a briefly bizarre history where, when he stepped on two snakes doing the do, Hera transformed him into a woman for a few years. We don't get to find out much about his wife, but we do know he has a daughter named Manto. Also gifted with prophecy, she gets taken to Delphi as a prisoner of war.

Zeus: King of gods, and really not someone you want to model your dating life after. He has a history of trying to get with literally anything that has the slightest hint of femininity. His escapades have gotten him in trouble with Hera frequently. He also has a tendency to not do anything when gods or goddesses decide to start wars. Because he's kind of the worst.

Did you enjoy Dear Hades? Catch the rest of the Dear Series:

Dear Hero (#1)

Up-and-coming teen superhero Cortex is on top of the world—at least, until his villain dumps him. If he's going to save his reputation, he needs a new villain to fight, and fast. Meanwhile, the villainous Vortex has once again gotten a little overeager and taken out a hero prematurely. When the two meet on Meta-Match, a nemesis pairing site, it's hate at first text. As darkness from the past threatens them both, they may need each other for the fight to come—one with much higher stakes than their choreographed meet-ups on weekends.

Dear Henchman (#2)

Kevin and Himari didn't plan to be heroes. Henchmen and sidekicks are supposed to brew coffee, take pics of their hero or villain for social media, and stay in the background. But when a taxidermy-collecting villain robs Kevin's hero of his powers and leaves Himari's villain wounded, it's up to the sidekicks and henchmen to save the world regardless of whether they have superpowers or not.

Dear Hades (a Spinoff)

When Medusa and Tiresias rise from the Underworld as twenty-first-century teens and meet through Persephone and Hades' new dating app, it seems like a second chance. Not everyone is pleased with an app designed to kindle romance between mortal enemies, though, and soon distrust grows between the heroes, monsters, and gods making up the app's user base. With pressure building on both sides, Medusa and Tiresias accept their task: kill their date, no matter how much they bond over their love of dogs or their traumatic pasts at the hands of the gods.

More from Torchflame Books

The Obsidian Dagger, Celtic Mythos #1 by Brad A. Lamar

When a mad witch with a magical, powerful Obsidian Dagger threatens to obliterate humanity and overtake the magic clans of the Celtic Isles, destiny forces Brendan and Lizzie O'Neal to embark on an adventure to thwart the witch and save mankind. This action-packed fantasy adventure for fans of young adult fiction with a storytelling craft will appeal to adults and teens alike.

Darts and Flowers by Dean Backus

Zack Standish couldn't be happier that his best friend is back home, and although he's not sure how to respond to the fact that Josh is gay, there is one very clear silver lining: Missy, the girl of his dreams, is dating his best friend's crush. They hatch a plan to break them up, but when the plan spirals out of control, Zack and Josh must choose what matters most—their childhood friendship or the romance just within reach.

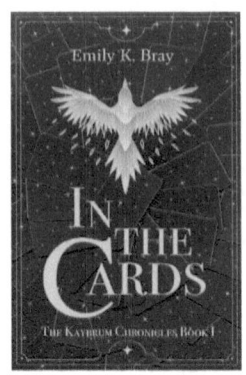

In the Cards, the Kaybrum Chronicles #1 by Emily K. Bray

In Kaybrum, magic isn't outlawed, but it's far from accepted. At seventeen years old, Korvo has spent his life learning all society will teach him and campaigning for the freedom of his fellow Magics. When a young fire magic arrives in the city, tensions rise among his adopted family. Change can't come fast enough, and soon Korvo is wrapped in a war eerily similar to the one that defined his childhood. But this time, he's determined to make the war end in his favor.

Find these books and more at torchflamebooks.com.